I0633403

Strictly by the Book

(Silverberry Seduction Seasoned Romance Series,
Book Four)

By Brenda Margriet

COPYRIGHT PAGE

STRICTLY BY THE BOOK
(Silverberry Seduction Seasoned Romance Series, Book Four)

First edition published April 2023
Copyright © 2022 Brenda Margriet Clotildes
Digital ISBN 978-1-990697-03-6
Print ISBN 978-1-990697-02-9

Cover Art by K. B. Barrett Designs

Natalie was dizzy from the turmoil of her emotions. Sure, gratitude was mixed up in it, but she knew that wasn't the true reason she'd launched herself at Rafe. The true reason was what she'd just confessed.

She wanted to *live*.

Rafe hadn't said a word. She held her breath, waiting, watching. Who knew what calculations were going on behind that proud forehead?

His hands on her hips, he pressed her away. Her heart sank. He didn't want her, not like she wanted him. He only felt sorry for her. That was why he'd kissed her back.

Without a word, he took her by the hand and led her out of the room. She had to trot to keep up with his long, sure strides. At the end of the hall, he drew her into what was obviously the master bedroom.

Her heart rebounded out of the depths of her stomach into her throat. He stopped at the foot of the massive king-sized bed with its charcoal cover, took her free hand, and placed both her palms on the bare skin of his chest. Her fingers spread, the crinkly hairs tickling between them. A dull, rapid thudding reverberated behind the wall of muscle.

Still without speaking, he tucked his hands under the waistband of her shorts and paused. He'd obviously discovered she was bare underneath. Sucking in a breath, he slipped them off until they puddled on the floor. She stepped out of them and flicked them away with her toes.

She lifted her gaze from her contemplation of his chest to his face.

Whatever he saw in hers seemed to please him. The faint lines of concern around his eyes softened and a tiny smile curled the corners of his mouth. "Is this what you want, Natalie?"

"Yes." She barely breathed the syllable. "This."

To the friends I've made in The Creative Academy for Writers. Your jazz hands keep me going. Thank you for your cheerful, unstinting support.

Chapter One

Swimsuit, sunscreen, sunglasses...check.

Bridesmaid's dress...check.

Empty savings account...check.

Natalie Minton bumped her wheeled carry-on down the stairs leading to her apartment building's front door. Through the glass entrance, wind whipped a billion flakes of snow around the parked vehicles already hidden under blankets of the chilly stuff. Her phone signalled a new email, and she fished it out of the purse slung over her shoulder, letting go of her suitcase. The hard plastic shell emblazoned with giant neon-yellow sunflowers promptly toppled over.

"Fine. Be like that." Using her heel, she dragged the extended handle closer as she thumbed her phone to life, scrolled to her inbox, and scowled at the latest irritating message from Raphael Talbot.

Ms. Minton:

It is unfortunate you cannot meet with me sooner than next week. If that is your first availability, then it will have to suffice. Below is my address. I will expect you at 7 pm, Monday, February 20.

Raphael Talbot

"Stuffy, arrogant jerk." She swept back to his first

equally terse email, which she'd received less than an hour ago, and re-read the text sandwiched between the same salutation and signature.

I understand my brother Otto Talbot approached you about writing a biography of our mother Eugenia Smythe Talbot Messing. I have reservations about the project that I wish to discuss with you. Thursday evening would be convenient for me.

Suppressing the urge to mimic his snobby style, she'd replied in her usual breezy and friendly way, explaining she wouldn't be available as she would be out of town attending a friend's wedding. Her attempt at appealing to his romantic side had failed, as he'd ignored her sentimental reason for delaying and simply set a second appointment, again without asking for her input.

If she hadn't been desperate for this job, she would have sent her own curt message of rejection. Working for Mr. Raphael Talbot would be painful and irritating.

But beggars couldn't be choosers. And if she didn't find an income stream soon, a beggar she would be.

Stifling her annoyance, she confirmed the appointment in as few words as possible, dropped her phone back in her purse, and peered outside. Still no sign of Terrance Renfrew, whose husband Bennett was delivering them to the airport. Aubrey Windt and Phillip Church were getting re-married in two days on a Mexican beach, and most of the Silverberry Book Club members were attending. As a bridesmaid, Natalie hadn't felt able to refuse, even though her credit card had shrieked at the expense. Aubrey would have paid her way if she'd known the state of her finances, but her pride had taken enough blows lately. It was too shaky to accept further charity.

A woman swaddled in a dark parka appeared from behind the apartment block opposite. Arms crossed and hands tucked under her shoulders, the figure approached in a scurrying shuffle, the fur-lined hood shrouding her face. Once inside the relative shelter of the doorway, she shrugged off the covering and pressed buttons on the intercom's keypad.

Natalie stared through the glass as the phone in her hand chimed to indicate someone had buzzed her apartment. As if hearing the high-pitched peal, the woman outside turned her head and met her shocked gaze, eyes widening.

Moving slowly, like she'd been dipped in molasses, she reached for the handle and pulled the door open. Freezing air swirled in. "Shyla?"

"Thank god you're here." Her sister—the younger sister she hadn't seen or spoken to in more than a year—stepped through the door. It clanged shut behind her. "I need two thousand dollars."

The desperate frenzy of the airport waiting room made Rafe Talbot's skin itch. Cabin-fevered Canadians eager to escape winter's bite made for a manic crowd. A gaggle of giggling women arrived through security, adding to the heightened atmosphere. One of them rolled her gaudy, sunflower-patterned carry-on over his toes without a backward glance. Overflowing with irritating vitality, they lay claim to a circle of seats and were joined by several indulgently smiling men ranging in age from mid-twenties to Methuselah.

Damn Elizabeth for deciding on a destination wedding. He wasn't the Mexican resort type. Not only was he far too old to enjoy unlimited alcohol and noisy pool games, he was far too...boring? Grumpy? Tetchy? But he would put up with a lot for his stepsister, and it was only three days. He'd be back to his quiet, solitary existence by Wednesday evening.

Otto flopped onto the seat beside him. "Skittle?" He held out the crinkly bag he'd just purchased from a vending machine.

Rafe waved it off and dove back into the conversation they'd been having before his older brother had reverted to childhood and needed a nuclear-coloured sugar fix. "I'm not saying Mom doesn't deserve to have her biography written. But maybe now isn't the right time."

"You were gung-ho when I mentioned it in December. What changed?"

Nothing. And everything. He remained silent.

"Anyway, it has to be now." Otto tilted his head back and tossed another hard-shelled candy into his mouth, his blond hair flashing in the waiting room's bright lights. "It will take several months to get it written and published, but we could have it out by the anniversary of her death next year if we push it."

Rafe had grown up in Otto's golden shadow. With his almost black hair and olive skin, he was the dark to his brother's light. And it wasn't only their contrasting looks. Everyone liked outgoing and friendly Otto, and success came easy and often to him. As for himself...well, not so much.

"Aren't you planning to announce your candidacy for the election then?" Rafe hated politics, but Otto had embraced the family's long-standing tradition. While he hadn't yet attempted to run for provincial office, he was heavily involved in his party and one of their most successful fundraisers.

"I need to get the nomination first." His tone held affectionate condescension at Rafe's ignorance. "Since the opposition took the seat in the election last year, there will be competition from within the party for who will replace Aubrey Windt. I'll need all the support I can drum up in order to be chosen. If you think I'm riding on Mom's coattails, getting some buzz for myself by promoting her biography, you're right. She'd be the first to encourage me to use every advantage I have."

That was the truth. Their mother had had a take-no-prisoners approach to politics. The trouble was, Rafe had recently discovered exactly how far she had gone to secure her own political career...and if the world found out, Otto's dreams would be shattered.

Which was why he couldn't let the biography be published, let alone written. If he put up enough roadblocks, maybe his brother would forget all about it. "Where did you find this writer, anyway? What are her credentials for a project like this?" He didn't mention Natalie Minton's unprofessional reply to his request for a meeting. She'd come across like a scatterbrained teenager, not the sober, serious person who could be trusted to write a sober, serious biography.

"Actually, Aubrey recommended her. Natalie ran both her campaigns and was in charge of her constituency office. She has several degrees, including one in Library Science and another in Political Science, and has been in between jobs since the last election."

A librarian? And a politically astute one at that? Rafe frowned. That didn't sound like the woman who had written that first email.

A burst of laughter startled him, and he shot a glare at the eclectic group he'd noticed before. The woman with the sunflower carry-on had her head back, wide mouth curled with laughter, dark eyes behind heavy frames flashing with delight.

A pang of—desire? jealousy?—flared in his chest. When was the last time he'd laughed with such abandon? And why did he suddenly feel his life was missing something important?

Shrugging off the unusual and unwanted sensation, he turned back to Otto. "I'll reserve judgment until I meet her next week. But I seriously wish you'd reconsider the whole thing."

"You always expect the worst. Don't worry. Everything will be fine." Otto winked, blue eyes gleaming. His charm worked on constituents, colleagues, and competitors, but Rafe no longer hero-worshipped his older brother. More than forty years of it had made him immune.

Natalie's seat was next to the window in the same row as Helen Mansfield and her husband, Nathan Spieth, the founders of the Silverberry Book Club. The other members, along with Aubrey and Phillip's family, were scattered about the plane.

The only Silverberry not attending the wedding was Lynn Kolmyn. She was seven months pregnant, and her husband Benjamin had put his foot down, backed up by her doctor. Not that she'd fought the decree. Lynn was nothing if not practical, and at forty-two years old knew her pregnancy was at risk for increased complications. She would never take unnecessary chances.

Natalie had joined the Silverberry Book Club after her divorce a few years ago and didn't know what she would have done without the friends she'd made there. She had known Helen before then, and quickly did the math as she buckled her seatbelt. It was sixteen years since they'd first met, and fourteen since Natalie had lived with Helen and her first husband during her final semester of university. She'd never forget the older woman's stable, comforting presence during that tumultuous time.

Shyla's sudden appearance that morning had thrown her off her stride. In the waiting room, she'd done her best to exhibit the same excitement as the other Silverberries, laughing when it seemed appropriate, smiling constantly. But if she were honest, she couldn't remember what anyone had said.

Once the plane was in the air droning its way south, she tried to focus on her e-reader, and then a game on her phone, and then by flipping through the in-flight magazine. Nothing distracted her from the dread hovering like an icy cloud over her shoulder. Finally, she turned to Helen. She was the only Silverberry who knew about Shyla's issues. Not even Aubrey knew the whole story. If she didn't discuss it with someone, her brain was going to vibrate out of her skull.

She nudged Helen's arm. The older woman looked up from her book. "Do you mind if we talk a minute?" She spoke just loudly enough to be heard over the hum of the plane.

Helen immediately closed her paperback. "I've been waiting for you to say something. You've been fidgety the whole flight."

"I know. Sorry." Natalie scratched her fingernail on the metal armrest between them, picking at a flaking, discoloured patch. "Shyla showed up at my apartment. Just before Terrance and Bennett picked me up."

"Oh." Helen's eyes searched her face, her head with its short cap of silver hair tilted. "Have you seen her recently?"

"Not for a year. More, actually. Two Christmases ago." And hadn't that been a disaster. Their parents had been so happy to have both their daughters home. The peace lasted for two hours, until Shyla re-appeared after a trip to the bathroom stoned out of her mind, lethargic and yet combative.

"What did she want?" Natalie raised her eyebrows and Helen shook her head. "Of course she wanted something. I'm guessing money, as that seems to be her pattern."

"Two thousand dollars. She says it's to reserve a place in a rehab program." Natalie didn't have two thousand dollars lying around. She'd received a decent pay cheque as the executive administrator of Aubrey's constituency office, but that job had ended last May, and it was now February. Temporary work at the local university and government employment insurance had supported her since then, though neither were generous enough to allow her to stockpile funds.

"She's done rehab before." Helen's tone was neutral.

"Yes. But before it was me or Mom and Dad pushing her to go." Except on one other occasion, one that haunted her to this day. She shied away from the memory. The possibility she might have the chance to rectify that mistake made her dizzy with hope and nauseous with remorse.

"What did you tell her?"

As much as she'd wanted to give her sister what she'd asked for right away, it hadn't been possible. "That she'd have to wait until I got back from Mexico." *That* hadn't gone over well. Shyla had accused her of purposely spending the rehab money on a tropical vacation, which was illogical given Natalie had had no clue she was in town, let alone going to show up on her doorstep. Not that Shyla was ever logical, especially when in the grip of her current drug of choice.

Helen patted her hand. "That gives you time to decide what to do. I hope it doesn't ruin your holiday."

It would. It already had. Shyla's addictive habits had ruined many things in her life, from family celebrations to Natalie's marriage. It was a sickness, and if Shyla had cancer Natalie would pay anything to cure her. Years of being taken advantage of, though, had chipped away at her faith and patience. Still, she couldn't give up on her sister. She'd done that once with tragic, near-fatal consequences.

She smiled at Helen. "Thanks for listening. I'll let you get back to reading."

She felt a little guilty not telling the other woman everything, but knew her friend's answer would be the same, no matter what the amount. Shyla hadn't asked for only two thousand dollars. She'd asked for fifteen thousand more to pay for the first thirty days of the program.

Otto Talbot had offered her twenty thousand dollars to write his mother's biography. She'd looked on it as a delightful windfall on which to rest while searching for a more permanent position. Now it would be just enough to give her a tiny buffer after paying for Shyla's treatment.

And she still had to convince Raphael Talbot she was the perfect person for the project. A project she now needed to secure more desperately than ever.

Chapter Two

Rafe hadn't given up on talking Otto out of the biography but had no time to continue his campaign after they arrived at the resort. Their stepsister Elizabeth—the only child of their mother's second husband Randall Messing—had planned every minute of their days, including a whale-watching tour, tequila tasting, and the bachelor party for her fiancé Jude Goldman the night before the wedding ceremony.

Elizabeth had been six years old, quiet, shy, and still grieving her mother's death, when he first met her. Rafe had been nineteen, also grieving his father, and stunned by his mother's rapid remarriage. Otto had been twenty-one and at school in Toronto, but Rafe had elected to go to the local university and was living at home. Seeing a reflection of himself in his precocious stepsister, they'd forged a strong sibling bond despite their age difference. Their connection had waxed and waned as life went on, but the foundation was there, and he was deeply satisfied to see her fall in love with a good, steady man like Jude.

Rafe might not deserve happiness, but Elizabeth definitely did.

She'd elected to have photos done before the evening formalities so they could catch the dramatic Pacific Ocean sunset. All the guests had been instructed to attend, and Rafe posed and smiled as directed. When the sun drew close to the distant curve of the earth, the bridal couple headed off with the photographer, set to return in an hour for the torchlight beach ceremony.

"Time for a drink?" Otto said to the group in general, which included their stepfather Randall, several of Elizabeth's girlfriends and their assorted partners, as well as Jude's parents and various other Goldman family and friends.

Rafe trekked behind as they returned to the resort, sand gritting inside the deck shoes Elizabeth had decreed he must wear with bare feet. His attention was drawn to a small gathering just ahead. He'd seen various members of the laughing group from the airport waiting room since arriving at the hotel, including the dark-haired owner of the sunflower suitcase. It appeared two of them were celebrating their own wedding ceremony tonight, as well.

Otto led everyone along a paved path that wound through palm trees and various flowering shrubs to one of the poolside bars. As Rafe waited for his drink, the ceremony on the beach finished with guests offering hugs and kisses to the newly joined couple. The group then scattered, moving slowly away as the bride and groom headed to the long, narrow pier jutting out in front of the resort with their own photographer.

Sunflower Woman set off alone. She pulled a phone out of a small, glittering purse and thumbed it with an irritated frown, a small floral bouquet trailing shimmery ribbons dangling from her free hand. Her strapless dress barely reached from her breasts to her knees, clinging to curves that even a curmudgeon like himself couldn't help but appreciate. She drew near, dodging deck chairs and other resort guests without looking up from the screen, threading a route between the loungers and the pool.

Rafe saw the imminent disaster too late to stop it.

A toddler escaped from her parents, giggling and shrieking and paying no attention to where she was going. Sunflower Woman looked up, startled, an instant before the child stumbled into her at knee level.

He stretched out a hand in a useless reflex and shouted. Sunflower Woman teetered on her high slim heels...and tumbled ass first into the deep end of the pool.

One moment Natalie was reading yet another frantic, demanding text from Shyla, and the next she was floundering in six feet of chlorinated water. It surged up her nose and burned behind her eyes. As she kicked reflexively, one shoe fell off and the long ribbons on her bouquet tangled around her legs.

A heavy object landed in the water beside her. She broke the surface, coughing and sputtering. A hand gripped her bicep, and she was towed, willy-nilly, toward the shallow end.

"The baby." Too deep to find a footing, she had no leverage to pull away from her unnecessary rescuer. "Save the baby."

"She's fine. She didn't fall in." The tugging continued, keeping her off balance and making it difficult to float.

"Let me go." Her toes touched bottom, and she got enough traction to yank out of his grasp. She wiped water out of her face with the back of her wrist. "I can swim, for Pete's sake."

The blond man grinning at her wore a now ruined linen blazer, the white shirt under it transparent and clinging to his chest. "I've always wanted to rescue a damsel in distress."

"I'm not in distress." Humiliated, maybe. She clutched the bodice of her strapless dress, not wanting to add to her embarrassment by flashing her boobs, too. She struggled to the stairs, her dramatic flounce sorely hampered by the waist deep water and her single remaining shoe.

The pool was lined with gawking guests. None of

the Silverberries were there, thank goodness. It would be bad enough explaining why she was no longer wearing her bridesmaid's dress at the reception without having them witness the debacle. The thin, drenched fabric adhered to her body like plastic wrap. A brisk breeze swept up from the beach and she shivered as she limped up the steps leading out of the water.

Something warm and dry embraced her shoulders and she gripped its protection thankfully.

"Are you all right?"

The deep, serious voice sent a different kind of shiver through her flesh. She turned and was confronted by yet another wide chest in a white shirt, this one crisp and dry. A linen blazer just like the one the man in the pool wore hung on straight, set shoulders. She looked up—way up—and was greeted by an intense, dark gaze, a lock of black hair curling like a question mark on a high forehead.

It was the man from the airport lounge. The one she'd seen glaring at the Silverberries as if laughter was verboten. She'd seen him around the resort a couple of times, too. He was tall, well over six feet, but it wasn't only his height that made him stand out. His grim expression was at odds to his casual vacation wear, and she'd wondered what a spoilsport like him was doing here at all.

"Miss? Are you all right?" A vee creased the skin between his heavy eyebrows.

"No. I mean, yes. I'm fine." She fumbled with the edges of the towel he'd draped over her, her bouquet in one hand and her cell in the other. "Unlike my phone, which must be ruined."

"Ask at the front desk for a bag of rice. I'm sure it's not the first time they've had to rescue an electronic device." His matter-of-fact suggestion eased some of her tension. At least *he* wasn't treating her like an incompetent.

Over his shoulder she saw the blond man encircled by spectators, accepting their congratulations for his quick thinking. She scowled.

The man in front of her followed her gaze and shrugged. "He meant well."

"Sure. Just a white knight doing his job." Still, the needless rescue irritated her. Searching for her usual good humour, she quirked a small grin. "Although I imagine it was a fairly spectacular splash."

He stared down at her impassively. Something in his intensity warned that the emotions flickering behind his mask might burn if he released them. She took a wary step back.

"We are so sorry!" A light, breathless voice jerked her out of her trance. "Amanda wasn't looking where she was going."

With a sharp nod, the man turned away. As Natalie assured the young mother that no real harm was done, he lifted a long-handled net off a hook near the towel cabana. With a few deft moves, he fished her shoe out of the depths of the pool. Catching her eye, he held it up, and then placed it on a nearby table. By the time Amanda's mother was done apologizing, he was gone.

Elizabeth scolded Otto, clucking like a mother hen. "What were you thinking? Was it really necessary to jump in after her?"

No, it wasn't. Rafe remembered Sunflower Woman's annoyance with an oddly warm feeling. He was used to Otto getting the lion's share of attention. He was the cheerful one, the charming one, unlike Rafe's sedate, staid persona. It was gratifying that, for once, Otto's exuberance hadn't been appreciated.

"Thank goodness we took the formal photos already." Elizabeth smoothed her palms on Otto's crumpled lapels, tugged at the hem of his dripping blazer. "It will serve you right if I tell the photographer to avoid you in the ceremony shots."

Otto's grin was unrepentant. "You know no one will be looking at me anyway. They'll all be staring at the beautiful bride."

Elizabeth blushed and tucked back a tendril of hair the breeze had tugged across her face. "Are you ready?" She included Rafe in her question.

He nodded. He and Otto went to stand next to Jude, waiting under the flower-covered arch with his best man. Elizabeth vanished behind a huge hibiscus bush and the resort event organizer started the entrance music. Three of Elizabeth's girlfriends made the slow trek toward the arch one after the other, and then his sister reappeared on her father's arm, with eyes for no one but Jude.

As the short ceremony proceeded, Rafe was continually distracted by thoughts of Sunflower Woman. She might as well have been naked when she'd climbed out of the pool, her nipples pinpoints under the thin material of her dress, the skirt clinging to her thighs and buttocks. She hadn't been wearing her glasses, and the snap in her eyes as she glared at Otto had made him want to laugh. He'd held it back, worried she would think he was making fun of her predicament, not enjoying her annoyed reaction to his brother's heroics.

Up until an hour ago, he'd been counting the minutes until he could board the plane tomorrow and head back to Prince George. He had to gather his weapons in order to defeat Otto's intentions regarding their mother's biography, all without letting anyone know the real reason such a biography would be a disaster. Now he found himself wishing he was staying longer at the resort so he might have a chance to see Sunflower Woman again.

He shook off the thought. He didn't have time for a vacation flirtation. Besides, he wasn't the kind of guy women wanted to have a fling with. Just because he was attracted to the brown-haired stranger didn't mean she felt the same way toward him.

All in all, it was a good thing he was going home tomorrow. It really was.

Chapter Three

After two days in a bag of rice, Natalie's cell phone lurched back to life. It was glitchy and unreliable, but she couldn't afford to buy a new one so would have to baby it for now.

She'd messaged her parents from Helen's phone to warn them she was out of service. Only her parents. She hadn't wanted Shyla to have the means to hound her friend the way she'd been hounding Natalie. When her phone reactivated, it was to a barrage of text notifications from her sister that almost made her wish it had died for good. She replied to one, placating and pleading for patience, and then ignored the rest, but they itched like a bad rash at the back of her neck.

The rest of the week sauntered along with no further dramatics. Natalie kept an eye open for the dark stranger but didn't see him or her blond would-be rescuer again. On Sunday, she and the rest of the wedding guests left Aubrey and Phillip to enjoy a few days at the resort alone. Six hours after boarding, she stepped onto the Prince George airport tarmac and into freezing temperatures. It was a shock to her system after the balminess of Mexico, a chilly and stark reminder she had returned to real life. Her first order of business would be to secure the biography contract. She was looking forward with grim determination to her meeting with Raphael Talbot. He wasn't going to wiggle his way out of his brother's job offer. She wouldn't let him.

Couldn't let him.

Her resolve suffered a small blow the next evening

when she pulled up in front of the black wood and shiny glass monstrosity at the address he'd given her. The person who chose to live in such an imposing, austere home might be difficult to persuade.

She pressed her lips together, the conversation she'd had with Shyla earlier in the day echoing in her head.

"You have to help me. I can't go to Mom and Dad, not again. Besides, you owe me. You know you do."

"I will help you. You're my sister, and I love you, no matter what you might think. I'll get the money. Just give me a few days."

Clutching the black folder with her tablet and a copy of her CV inside, she strode the concrete path to the over-height front door. Snow mounded on either side but the surface itself was clear of ice in a manner that suggested the owner was compulsively diligent in his shovelling. Or in paying someone to shovel.

She pressed the button to the right of the matte-black panel with its heavy crossbeams and long iron hinges. A dungeon door, she thought, her imagination conjuring up a stone passageway lit with torches and dripping with moisture. Grinning at her flight of fancy, she was unprepared for the suddenness with which the door swung open. She squeaked.

And then stared. Because standing inside was the dark-haired man from Mexico.

Rafe was irritated with Natalie Minton well before the doorbell rang signalling her arrival. Because of her, he'd had to leave before he'd finished a fascinating examination of a tumour that had been excised from a seventy-two-year-old man. His conclusions would determine future treatment, and he hated leaving his study undone. Once he assured himself Ms. Minton was unsuitable to write his mother's biography and had secured enough ammunition to defeat Otto's intentions, he'd head back to his laboratory in the hospital. It was important he wrap up his experiments so the attending physician could read his recommendations first thing in the morning.

When the chime echoed down the entry hall, his first thought was *at least she's prompt*.

Upon opening the door, his second thought was *what the hell is Sunflower Woman doing here?*

"You?" Her eyes opened almost as wide as her heavy-framed glasses. "*You're* Raphael Talbot?"

The gears in his brain double-clutched, the sensation physical. "Natalie Minton?"

"Yup." She huffed out a breath, a white cloud puffing from her pink lips, mist forming on her lenses. "Well, this is interesting."

His fingers clenched the handle so hard his knuckles ached. He hadn't forgotten Sunflower Woman, despite his best efforts. She'd made more than one appearance in his dreams since his return from Mexico, but he'd hoped her affect would wear off soon.

Now here she was. In the flesh. Much less flesh than she'd revealed the last time he'd seen her. He stopped himself from mentally stripping her out of her puffy parka.

"Can I come in?"

Her question snapped him out of his fugue. "Of course." He stepped back and she brushed passed, bringing with her the fresh scent of icy air and a contrasting whiff of summery citrus.

He shut the door and leaned against it briefly, reorganizing his defences. This didn't change anything. He still couldn't let the biography be written. It was just going to be a bit more awkward, that was all.

Sunflower Woman—Natalie—had politely toed off her damp boots and then moved into the middle of the hall. Staring upward, she craned her neck at the ceiling stretching two storeys above. A railed mezzanine gave glimpses of the doors on the second level.

"This is quite the place." She spun in a slow circle, taking it in. Her mittened hands clutched a black leather folder, and a multi-coloured toque with an outrageously large pompom covered her chin-length brown hair.

"Thank you." He wasn't one hundred percent sure she meant it as a compliment. "Let me take your coat."

She tucked her toque and mittens into pockets, unzipped her parka, and handed it to him. Her nose wrinkled. "Do I smell chlorine?"

"I have a pool." He hung her coat in the closet. Its bright red glowed among his sober blacks and browns.

Her eyebrows rose. "Really? That's cool."

He definitely heard approval that time. Not that it mattered what she thought. It was his house, and he liked it well enough. The pool was a convenience, not a luxury, as swimming was his exercise of choice.

"I'll do my best not to fall into this one." Her mouth curved in a self-deprecating smile.

His heart thumped uncomfortably. He'd just managed to scrub the tantalizing vision of her, drenched and irritated, from his thoughts. Now she'd brought it up again. *Up* was an unfortunate choice of words, given his body's reaction to her presence. "Not your fault. The first time." His voice sounded hoarse. He cleared his throat.

"No toddlers here to trip me?" Her tone was teasing, but it struck a tender chord deep in his gut.

"No. And no brother to needlessly rescue you. No one but me." She flinched, but he marched past without comment. His brusqueness was one reason he didn't directly practice medicine on patients with a pulse anymore. "The living room's through here."

After a pause her footsteps sounded behind him.

"That was your brother? Otto?"

"Yes." He led her to the back of the house, where soaring windows overlooked his backyard, currently a smooth expanse of unbroken white, as well as the rear of the houses on the next street. Most of those yards held the snow-covered paraphernalia of children—swing sets and playhouses and trampolines. When he'd moved in several years ago, those spaces had been as bare as his own. Then one had sprouted toys, followed by another and another, and now he was the lone bachelor surrounded by young families.

He shoved away the ache of loneliness. This was his life. It was a good life. As good as he could expect.

"Let me be blunt." He turned his back on his barren yard and squared off to Natalie. She regarded him warily. "I don't want this biography written. Not by you, not by anyone. I'll give you a thousand dollars for your time and inconvenience if you leave now."

Natalie's world had tilted off axis the moment the door opened. She'd babbled meaningless comments about the house and the pool as she'd tried desperately to regain her balance. She'd almost had it when Raphael Talbot's mention of his brother had knocked her sideways again. Reconciling the grinning blond who had dragged her from the pool to the man who'd offered her a very business-like proposal via email would take some doing.

And now she'd been offered a thousand bucks to do nothing. To walk away. She drew in a breath, hoping to restore her equilibrium.

Walking away wasn't an option, and not only because of Shyla. Preliminary research on Elizabeth Smythe Talbot Messing had intrigued her. She might need the job because of her sister, but she *wanted* the job because of what she'd discovered.

"Why?" She lifted her chin in challenge. And so

she could meet his eyes. Why did he have to be so tall? "Why don't you want this written?"

His brows drew together as if having his wishes ignored was a new and unsettling experience. "That's a family matter. I don't have to explain my reasons to you."

"Otto is your brother, right? He's family. And he wants it written."

"Otto has his own reasons. I have mine."

"And yours supersede his? Again, I ask why?"

His lips pinched together, drawing attention to his sharp features. He was a man of angles...lean and wiry, with wide shoulders and slim hips, a tight slash of a mouth and hard cheekbones. His almost-black hair with silver threads at the temples was brushed sleekly back, just as it had been in Mexico.

Since he appeared at a loss for words, she continued her attack. "Your mother was a huge political force in the eighties and nineties. She lobbied for the rights of women and children, was devoted to the improvement of British Columbia both financially and socially, and was the first female Deputy Premier of the province. She deserves to be recognized for her achievements."

"I am well aware of all that."

She pulled her CV from her folder and held it out. He took it but didn't look at it. She bulled on. "I am ideally suited to write the biography. I did a double major in History and Political Science and have a Master's in Library Sciences. I know how to research, how to be non-biased and fair. I've been involved behind the scenes politically since high school. I was aware of your mother's career well before your brother contacted me, and everything I've learned since has only made me more determined to do this project."

"You can't do it without my support." The pages of her resume crinkled as he gripped them.

"Why not?" Desperation gave her courage. "Otto

wants me to. I'll work with him."

"Otto doesn't have my mother's archives."

Her curiosity spiked. "Archives?"

"Diaries. Journals. Files." Raphael pointed to the ceiling. "All stored here. Otto might want you to write the book, but if I don't give you access to those, you'll be doing nothing but rehashing what's already common knowledge."

Her fingers itched to dig into those documents. It was a researcher's dream...not just primary sources but personal documentation. "The biography would honour your mother. It's not an exposé, if that's what you're worried about."

His gaze flickered away. Her senses tingled. He seemed an intensely private man and she'd thought he was only being obstructive because he wasn't interested in the publicity the book might generate. Was it possible there was more behind his reluctance? Could he be hiding something?

Chapter Four

A chill chased down Rafe's spine. Natalie was edging a little too close to the truth. If he continued to fight her, she might circumvent him and do the book anyway. Even though they'd had limited interaction, he hadn't missed the signs of stubborn independence. Who knew what she might dig up from other sources? Maybe it would be best to keep her close.

The warm glow that lit behind his breastbone had nothing to do with that. It was a *warning* glow, urging him to be cautious. He couldn't give into an itch he'd been trying to scratch since Mexico.

He sighed and resigned himself to his fate. "Fine." Delight blazed across her features, and he held up a repressive hand. "I'll go through the archives first and give them to you as needed. And I get final say on everything you want to include."

"Of course." She agreed so readily he was instantly suspicious. Her expression was guileless and open, but something fluttered behind those warm brown eyes that he didn't quite trust.

"I mean it, Natalie. If I don't approve it, it doesn't get printed."

Her reply didn't exactly bolster his confidence. "We'll see how it goes. Do we have a deal, Raphael?" She held out a hand.

He hesitated before accepting it, a sense of inevitability tickling under his skin. "Call me Rafe." Her small fingers gripped his firmly, releasing him after one short, sharp shake. The brief touch left his nerves tingling.

"Can you show me now?" She stepped briskly toward the wooden open riser stairs leading to the second floor and tossed an eager look over her shoulder.

"No." He needed time to reconcile himself to the development and the intrusion she would be in his home. "Tomorrow."

"In the morning?" Her tone was hopeful.

"No. The evening. Same time." He motioned to the front door. She looked as if she was going to argue, but then trudged toward it, shoulders slumped. "I'll have Otto send you the contract. You'll want to review it before you start. If you have any questions, you can ask me tomorrow. See you then."

He closed the door behind her and watched her drive away in a small, grey SUV, totally at odds to her bright, colourful presence. The electricity she'd brought to his home faded, the atmosphere dwindling to its usual dull lifelessness.

If he wasn't careful, he might begin to enjoy having her around. And that would be nothing but trouble.

An electronic contract appeared in Natalie's inbox around two the following afternoon. She read it carefully. Well, she skimmed all the legalese mumbo-jumbo, but paid strict attention to the payments, the schedule, and the final approval requirements.

She had no problem with Rafe and Otto having a say in what ended up in the book. It was about their mother, after all, and they would want to protect her memory. Plenty of the drama in Eugenia Smythe Talbot Messing's political life was already public knowledge. There would be no reason to avoid including those events and many reasons to share her side of the story. Eugenia deserved a fitting tribute and Natalie wanted to give her one.

Payment details matched what she'd arranged

verbally with Otto that morning. Two thousand upon signing—the amount of the advance chosen solely for Shyla's benefit—and the remaining eighteen thousand paid half on completion of the first draft and half on delivery of the final approved manuscript. Otto was taking care of the publishing end of things, so once the writing was done Natalie's commitment would be fulfilled.

The timeline was tight, and she might need to forgo sleep to achieve it, but the rush would help her meet Shyla's demands, too.

Not that she appreciated that fact. She slouched on Natalie's couch, scowling. "What do you mean you don't have it yet?"

Despite her angry glare, Shyla looked cleaner and healthier than the last time Natalie had seen her. If she was clinging to sobriety, Natalie could understand how she might disguise fear with fury. She held back the first sharp, short retort that sprang to mind. "I've got the deposit. You told me it might be a couple months before they have space for you, right? By then I'll have the rest of the money."

"I guess." Shyla bit her thumbnail. Her hands were dry and chapped, but there was no grime around her nails or in the creases of her knuckles. "You'll e-transfer it to me, so I can pay them?"

Natalie shifted uneasily in her customary seat, a padded rocker that was a hand-me-down from their grandmother. "Why don't I send it to White Spruce Wellness for you? Save you the trouble." She'd looked up the clinic online. It was well respected, with a long history of successfully treating substance abuse disorders. At least it wasn't the fly-by-night, alternative, woo-woo set-up she'd expected Shyla to choose.

"You don't trust me, do you?" She sprang up and paced restlessly to the sliding glass doors leading to the tiny deck of the equally tiny apartment. She fidgeted with the cord of the vertical blinds. Her back to Natalie, she spoke quietly. "I'm clean, and I want to stay that way. I promise."

She had heard that before. So had their parents. She'd spoken to them on her return from Mexico and discovered that Shyla had approached them while she had been gone. Which meant her sister had told a fib when she'd declared she was too ashamed to ask them for the money.

In the grand scheme of things, it was one of the smaller lies Shyla had told. And challenging her honesty usually led to tears and recriminations and, on Natalie's part, a crushing guilt that her own life was so much better than her sister's. Also, she had to prove to her sister that she *did* trust her, especially after her failure to answer her plea in the past.

Still, she hesitated. "I want you to stay that way, too. And I want to trust you. But it's a lot of money. Things have been a little tight lately. I want to make sure it's put to good use."

"Keeping your sister out of the gutter isn't good use?"

Her bitter tone gnawed away the rest of Natalie's resistance. She sighed. "I'll send it to you later today, once it's in my account."

"Thank you!" In one of her mercurial changes of mood, Shyla flew toward her, dropping to her knees to hug her tight. Her arms were thin but strong, and she smelled faintly of dirty linen and harsh soap. "You won't regret it. I promise."

Many of her promises had already led to many regrets, but Natalie hugged her back, wishing she could heal her sister by osmosis, by the strength of wishing.

Maybe this time, she told herself with faint belief. Maybe this time.

That evening, Rafe was prepared when he opened the door to Natalie. His heart still did an odd little pump and his senses tingled, but he put that down to nerves. He'd spent much of the night before going through several boxes of his mother's documents and removing anything that might lead to the scandal he was determined to hide. But he didn't underestimate Natalie's intelligence or instincts, and just having her in the room with his mother's files was cause for concern.

But Otto had forwarded the contract signed by both himself and Natalie and he'd affixed his own digital signature to it. He was committed now.

"Come in." He stepped back and she moved forward eagerly, unfastening her coat and shedding her boots.

"This is so exciting." Her eyes gleamed through the lenses of her glasses. The frames were dark and bold and should have overwhelmed her delicate features, yet somehow only enhanced them. "I love starting new projects."

"Follow me." He knew he sounded gruff and unfriendly, but it didn't seem to bother her. As he climbed the stairs to the second floor, she was so close on his heels his spine prickled. He opened the door to the spare room where he'd stored his mother's effects and heard a gasp.

"When you said you had your mother's files, I didn't imagine anything like this." Natalie stepped past him into the room.

He stopped himself from leaning in and sniffing her summery scent as she went by. "She always had a home office. When she died, I packed it all up, brought it here, and was going through it as I had time. Then Otto came up with the idea for the biography." He'd started going through it faster after that—and faster yet once he'd discovered his mother's misdeeds, hunting for more skeletons in the closet.

One wall was hidden behind stacks of banker's boxes. Behind the partially open closet doors, yet more boxes were visible. A large trestle table under the window held an ancient computer with a cube-shaped monitor and several smaller cartons filled with floppy disks in various sizes.

He pointed at a second table piled with still more banker's boxes. "Files I have previewed and which you can study are on that table. All others, including the digital files, are out of bounds. I'll let you know when I have more ready for you." He indicated the empty end of the table with the computer. "I left room for you to work."

She quirked an eyebrow as she lifted the strap of the satchel over her head and shrugged out of her coat. "I wasn't expecting to set up here. I figured I'd take what I need home."

He shook his head. "I'd prefer everything remain where it is. And, as you can see, transporting it might be a bigger job than you anticipated."

She grinned. "No kidding." She spun slowly on her heel, taking in the space. "If you want me to get this done in two months, I'm going to need to spend a lot of time here. Not just a few hours in the evening."

He'd known this was coming and steeled himself. If he was trusting Natalie with his mother's reputation, he could trust her with his house. "I'll give you the lock and security codes. I'm usually gone between seven and five. You won't be disturbed if you come during that time."

"You'll let me do that?" An odd tone echoed in her voice, but he couldn't figure out the emotion behind it.

"Of course. Otto had you vetted."

She nodded, as if such an investigation into her life was routine. Apparently, she had no secrets to hide.

Unlike him.

She stroked the lid of one of the pre-approved boxes with reverence. "I'd love to get started tonight. I won't stay too late."

He opened his mouth to tell her she could stay as long as she liked, but snapped it shut. That would give the wrong impression. He'd been manipulated into a corner and forced to agree to this project, but he didn't have to welcome it.

"Fine. I'll be in my office. It's just down the hall. Let me know when you leave." He exited the room, conscious of her gaze on his nape, and escaped to his tidy, well-organized sanctum. Sinking into the leather chair near the low window, he stared out into the darkness. His own reflection stared back.

An unfamiliar sensation filled his chest. It took him several minutes to figure out what it was. Or rather, what it *wasn't*.

At this moment, he wasn't *lonely*. Though he couldn't see Natalie, he could feel her presence.

He'd allow himself to savour it tonight. But he wouldn't get used to it. She was only here for a couple of months. Once the book was done, she'd be gone from his life, and things would get back to normal.

He was starting to hate normal.

Chapter Five

Natalie arrived the next morning at seven thirty, eager to start the day. Rafe had assured her he would be gone by then, but just in case, she rang the bell at the front door and waited a couple of minutes. When there was no response, she followed the path along the side of the garage as he'd directed, where she used the code he'd given her on the keypad by the back door and stepped inside. She disabled the alarm, pressing the buttons with precision to avoid making a mistake. Her shoulders relaxed when the all-clear notice appeared.

The urge to snoop was strong, her natural curiosity heightened by Rafe's taciturn demeanor, but she was determined to do nothing that would damage the trust he'd placed—albeit reluctantly—in her. Averting her gaze from any open doors, she went straight upstairs and settled in among the boxes with her travel mug of coffee, laptop, notebook, and pens.

Hours later, she surfaced long enough to have the sandwich and apple she'd brought for her lunch, and then used the bathroom he'd pointed out to her last night. She refilled her water bottle awkwardly from the low faucet, not comfortable enough to make use of the kitchen below, and buried herself back in the spare room.

At four o'clock the alarm on her phone startled her out of a perusal of the appointment diary from Eugenia's first year in office. Knowing her habit of getting lost in research, she'd set it to ensure she had plenty of time to be out of the house before Rafe returned from work. Whatever that work was. She had meant to ask him what he did for a living but had been too enthralled by the treasures waiting to be uncovered and forgotten.

Her fingers itched to take the next box with her so she could continue at home, but didn't dare. In a week or so, once she'd proven herself trustworthy and eased his suspicions, she'd ask him to change that decree.

It felt wrong to leave without providing some sort of an update. Tearing a sheet from her notebook, she scribbled a quick message and left it on the table, tucked under a mug she'd brought to keep her pens, highlighters, and other writing paraphernalia, and then crept down the stairs, reset the alarm, and escaped outside.

Rafe left work on Friday evening with unexpected eagerness. His career as a pathologist at the University Hospital of Northern British Columbia was fulfilling and consuming, and it wasn't unusual for him to spend twelve or fourteen hours in his lab. But he'd arrived home on Wednesday and Thursday to breezy, cheerful notes from Natalie detailing her discoveries, and today he'd found himself watching the clock instead of losing all track of time while buried in his analyses.

He parked in the garage and stepped through the door connecting it to the main floor. He knew it was his imagination, but the atmosphere in his home seemed to have *softened* during the last few days. It was as if Natalie exuded molecules of joy and contentment while she worked, and those molecules drifted in the air long after she left. He drew in a deep, steadying breath and felt some of that contentment ease the pressure behind his temples.

Hurrying upstairs, he entered the spare room and for the third straight day found her note tucked under the bright yellow mug with its sunflower-shaped handle. He tugged it out, repressing the ridiculous urge to lift the paper to his nose to try and catch a whiff of her scent.

Hi, Rafe!

Another good day. I'm almost done with the boxes you set out for me. If you're adamant I don't look at any before you, you'd better get a move on. :)

I'll be working on the book this weekend. Hope that's okay with you.

Have a great evening!

Natalie

It was brisk and business-like enough—other than the smiley face she'd sketched—with absolutely nothing to warrant the heat spreading through his chest. He read it again, and then walked slowly down the hall to his office and placed it in the drawer with her earlier notes. Saving the meaningless pieces of paper was absurd, but he couldn't bring himself to toss them in recycling.

Shaking his head at his foolishness, he headed back to the lower level to prepare his solitary dinner with an unusual lightness in his step. A lightness tempered by disappointment, as he wouldn't receive another note until Monday, but a lightness, nonetheless.

Natalie had debated whether or not she should go to Rafe's on Saturday. She assumed whatever job he had didn't involve working weekends, which meant he'd probably be home while she was there. The thought of being in such close proximity to his dark, brooding presence ruffled her nerves. Not that they'd be in the same room, and the house was plenty big enough for both of them. Still...

The thing was, she needed more data before she could begin even a sketchy draft, and with the timeline so tight she couldn't afford to lose two days. In the end, wariness of Rafe lost out to that urgency. She'd given him fair warning in her note. If he had an issue with it, he knew how to get a hold of her.

In deference to the weekend, she delayed arriving until nine. She hustled through a blustery, frigid breeze and huddled into herself as she rang the front doorbell. Shifting from foot to foot in a futile attempt to keep warm, she waited less than thirty seconds before ringing it again. When there was still no response, she hurried around the garage and through the rear door as usual. His vehicle was there—a sleek black Mercedes that sparked envy in her chest.

"Rafe?" She stepped tentatively from the back entrance into the living space, unwinding her scarf and brushing flecks of snow from her shoulders. The scent of fresh coffee hung in the air and on the kitchen island at the far side of the open concept main floor the remnants of breakfast—a small plate, a mug, and a pile of orange peels—were visible. "Rafe? Are you here?"

Nothing.

She had intended to go straight to her room, but it didn't feel right, not when she suspected he was somewhere about. Hovering, undecided, in the quiet room, she became aware of music playing in the distance.

Leaving her satchel on the sofa, she followed the drumbeats and soaring guitars of a rock classic down a hall leading behind the kitchen. The scent of chlorine, which had become so familiar over the last few days she'd forgotten about it, tickled her nostrils. A single door at the far end was the only break in the long length of barren hall. She pushed it open and stepped into warmth and humidity. The lenses of her glasses fogged up and she used the end of her scarf to clear them, the room blurry and indistinct until she replaced them on her nose.

The pool took up most of the floor space. A sleek form cut through the pale blue water, long arms stroking up and down smoothly, strong legs kicking under the surface, revealed in a flurry of bubbles. At the far end, a dark head popped up briefly before he executed a neat forward roll.

A roll that revealed one very disturbing fact.

Raphael Talbot swam in the nude.

Swimming put Rafe into a meditative state. He simply *was* as he swam from end to end, the motion hypnotic, the pattern of breaths and strokes so deeply ingrained he didn't have to think.

He switched from freestyle to breaststroke, gliding with the force of his kicks, lifting his head out of the water as his arms and shoulders pulled him forward. He turned at the end of the pool and started back.

Someone was standing at the door.

He came to an abrupt stop, liquid surging up his nose. Coughing and choking, he tread water and stared at the intruder.

Natalie stared back, mouth parted in a shocked O, brown eyes wide behind her glasses.

"What the hell are you doing here?" In the instant he made his demand, he remembered he was naked. It was his house. He lived alone. He always swam naked.

It didn't mean he was comfortable being found in the buff by a relative stranger.

Instead of heading for the shallow end—the end

nearest Natalie—he stroked to the side, turned his hips to the wall, crossed his elbows on the edge, and glared. "Well? Why are you here?"

She still wore her heavy winter coat, a scarf draped over her shoulders. Her cheeks were flushed. "I came to work. I wanted to let you know I was here. I followed the music." Her eyes darted about the room, unable to meet his.

Great. She knew he was naked. Goddamn perfect. "It's Saturday." He gritted the words out between clenched teeth. "Take off your coat before you faint from the heat."

She did as instructed, keeping her face averted. "I don't have a lot of time if you want me to meet the deadline. I can't afford to waste any days. I told you I'd be here. In my note yesterday."

I'll be working on the book this weekend. He'd read the words but thought—if he'd thought of it at all—that she meant she'd be working at her own place. That's what he got for mooning over her messages instead of paying proper attention. "I haven't had a chance to go through any more boxes. Go upstairs. I'll join you in a few minutes." He planted his palms flat on the pool deck, elbows bent in preparation to lift him out of the water.

She didn't move.

"If you don't mind." He lifted an eyebrow with as much arrogance as he could muster, considering he was nude and at eye level with her knees.

"Oh." Her breath huffed out. "Of course."

She vanished.

Natalie stumbled up the stairs, her sock feet silent on the shiny wooden treads, and arrived in her room gasping for breath. Resisting the urge to shut the door and barricade herself in, she draped her coat neatly on the back of her chair and unloaded her satchel with precise, careful movements.

And thought of nothing but Rafe as she'd last seen him.

Rivulets of water beading on his broad shoulders. Black hair slicked to his scalp. Dark eyes hot and angry.

Though she'd caught only a brief flash of taut buttocks, her imagination had no trouble filling in the rest.

Strong thighs and slim hips and what swung between them.

She popped the lid of her water bottle and gulped down cold liquid. Rafe had assumed her flushed face was due to the heat of the pool room, but if he saw her still red and rosy, he'd know it was because of him.

Because of what she'd seen and not seen.

Enough. She had to stop thinking about it. About *him*. She wasn't even sure she *liked* him. It was just her hormones talking. Since her divorce a few years ago, she'd gone on a few dates, but no relationship had lasted long enough for her to consider having sex.

Steps sounded on the stairs, and she squeezed her eyes shut to block out the image of a naked Rafe mounting them. Moments later the chunk of a door closing indicated he was in his own room, and she opened her eyes, breathing a sigh of relief.

By the time he appeared in her office, she was seated at the table with a folder open, concentrating fiercely on the pages before her without absorbing a single detail. She flicked him a glance while keeping her head down. "I'm sorry for disturbing you. I thought you knew I was coming today."

"I misunderstood your note." His voice was low and gravelly.

Anger seemed to be missing from his tone, so she risked a second glance. His hair was damp, and he was now discreetly clad in a white T-shirt and jeans. Her mouth watered anyway, and she swallowed and looked away quickly.

He stepped farther into the room. "You're here now. We might as well get started."

"We?" The word came out as a squeak and her gaze flew to him again. He had to leave. There was no way she'd get an iota of work done with him in the room.

Chapter Six

Natalie sat at the table with the computer, still flushed and unable to meet his eye, which wasn't a surprise. No one wanted to find their temporary boss in the nude. She couldn't have gotten much of a show, but that was beside the point.

"Yes, we." His own discomfort made him sharp and abrupt. "I told you I haven't had a chance to go through any more boxes. If you insist on working today, you can finish off the first batch while I get started on the next." He turned his back on her, pulled a random carton from the stack against the wall, and marched to the other table. It now held only one box, its lid propped against it, revealing the contents. Other boxes were piled beneath the table—the ones Natalie had already completed, as he knew from one of her first notes.

He pulled off the lid of the carton he'd picked from the stack and discovered several bulging file folders, as expected. Keeping his focus on the documents, he pulled out the first folder, laid it on top, and flipped it open.

They worked in silence for several minutes, the only sound the soft susurrus of pages turning. A small scuffing noise warned him Natalie was approaching. His skin prickled as she stopped beside him and pulled a folder from the other box.

He was just starting to relax when he came across a letter from his mother written toward the end of her second term in office. A name blazed out at him as if written in fire.

Dennis Parrish.

He slid a glance toward Natalie. She appeared engrossed in the folder she'd chosen, and even as he watched, she drifted back to the computer table, lowered to the only chair in the room, and absently woke her laptop without taking her eyes from the pages she held.

He refocused on the hot coal in his hand. On the surface, the letter seemed innocuous. His mother was asking Parrish to provide details regarding several infrastructure projects that his company was bidding on. She had been Minister of Transportation at the time, and the British Columbia government had designed an enormous stimulus package that involved building and upgrading highways throughout the province. Taken on its own, the letter meant nothing.

But given the other documents he'd already found—the ones hinting his mother had known about a scheme to divert funds from those projects to the party's campaign chest—it was as dangerous as a lit fuse.

Natalie must never see it.

He closed the file with hands that were surprisingly steady considering the pounding of his heart. "Want some coffee?"

She looked up from her laptop with a distracted expression. "Sorry?"

"I could use some coffee. Going through this stuff puts me to sleep."

"Really? I find it fascinating. Sure, I could drink a cup."

"I'll just take this with me, keep going through it while I wait."

Her brows drew together. "Whatever you like."

Damn it. He should have just left with the folder in hand. Why had he felt the urge to explain? Before he could send any other suspicious signals, he strode out of the room and down to the main level.

He started the coffeemaker and quickly scanned the rest of the documents in the folder. He saw nothing else incriminating, so removed the memo, opened a drawer, and tucked it under the silverware tray. He'd put it in his safe later, where the other documents he'd already found lurked, ticking like time bombs.

When he'd discovered the first evidence of his mother's perfidy, he'd almost thrown up. She had been an icon, a towering symbol of political savvy and blazing intelligence. His love for her might have felt more like duty, but no one could help but respect and admire her, least of all him. To discover that reputation had been built on clay had shattered his life-long perspective with nausea-inducing suddenness.

She'd never been a warm and cozy mom. Otto, her first born, had been her golden boy, the son who never disappointed. Rafe had spent his youth trying to match his brother's prowess and at the same time stay out of range of his mother's laser gaze. He'd chosen medicine instead of following Otto into law due to an overwhelming urge to forge his own path, find acclaim for his own skills and talent. He'd only partially succeeded.

The coffee machine burbled and gasped to its finale. He rarely had coffee in the middle of the day, but after making the offer, it might look odd if he didn't bring one for himself. Filling two mugs, he tucked the now defused folder under his elbow and returned upstairs. Natalie thanked him with a vague nod. He placed his own mug down, returned the pages to their box, and plucked out the next set.

Finding the memo had dashed any hope there was no further evidence of his mother's crimes. He would have to review everything with a fine-tooth comb if he wanted to protect her legacy.

If only he believed she deserved his protection. He

hated lying, even when he was the only one that knew of the deception. But he couldn't let Otto's life be ruined by their mother's scandalous actions. Concealing them was his only option.

The hours Natalie spent with Rafe on Saturday and Sunday had been fraught with unspoken tension, at least from her perspective. After his initial irritation, he had seemed unruffled by her presence, and he'd worked methodically through several boxes while she'd struggled to focus.

It wasn't just the memory of her glimpse of his naked body that distracted her. It was his single-mindedness, his icy intellect, his very *existence* that pulled her from her work.

When she arrived at his place on Monday morning, knowing he wouldn't be there, she should have been relieved. Instead, the house felt empty and abandoned and an odd sense of loss settled over her.

Not that it looked any different. It was always neat and tidy—the breakfast dishes left on the counter Saturday were the only signs of occupancy she'd ever seen—but that morning it seemed colourless and sterile. Shrugging off her disquieting emotions, she opened a new box and began work.

The documents in this one were from the mid-1990s and appeared to be mostly newspaper clippings and memorabilia. There were pictures of Eugenia with the premier, with the prime minister, even with Queen Elizabeth at the opening of the Prince George campus of the University of Northern British Columbia. Natalie had only been six at the time, but her family had driven from Fraser Lake, the small community about an hour and half west of Prince George where she'd grown up, and joined the thousands that had lined the streets to wave at the royal cavalcade as it went by.

Turning over one of the yellowed pages carefully, she came upon an eight by ten photo. In it the queen stood, regal and dignified, surrounded by a small cluster of people. It was obviously taken at a formal meet and greet where guests were shuffled in and out as quickly as possible.

Eugenia was immediately recognizable, tall and stately with the large nose, deep set eyes, and dark hair she'd bequeathed her younger son. The man beside her must be Bartholomew Talbot, and the youth next to him, Otto. Bartholomew was not quite as tall as his wife, and Otto had inherited his blond, blue-eyed looks. She gave only a passing glance to the teenager who would someday drag her from a Mexican pool without regard to her wishes or competence. Instead, her attention fastened on Rafe.

She calculated he was only thirteen or fourteen. His hair was cropped short at the nape and sides with long strands hanging over his eyes and ears. It had been a fashionable style at the time, but combined with his serious gaze and flat mouth, it gave him a sullen look.

Most telling of all was his position. He stood slightly detached from the rest of the group, his body angled away from the camera, as if he couldn't wait to escape its focus. He was a raven in a cuckoo's nest, longing for flight.

Her heart did an odd little tumble. Though he stood scant inches from his mother, compared to the close coziness of the other three members of his family it might as well have been the Grand Canyon. Was it possible he was still seeking her acceptance, even though he was an adult and she'd been gone almost a year? Was this why he was so protective of her reputation?

Feeling foolish and sentimental but unable to resist the impulse, she pinned the photo to the bulletin board she'd brought that morning. It hadn't been worth making holes in the wall for the short time she'd be there, so she'd propped it on the table, leaned it into the corner, and anchored it in place with Scotch tape.

Apparently, she hadn't done a good enough job. The tape gave way as she pressed the tack into the cork and the board slid down, shoving one of the shoeboxes stacked next to the ancient computer onto the floor. Floppy discs and cassettes cascaded across the carpet. Muttering curses, she cleaned up the mess and then headed downstairs.

Saturday, when Rafe had realized she was bringing her own food and drink, he had grumpily told her to help herself to his coffee, tea, and water. She didn't intend to take him up on his grudging offer, but she figured it gave her permission to search for better tape. Everyone had a junk drawer in the kitchen, right?

Exploring several spaces, she found only neatly slotted silverware, aggressively organized storage containers, and alphabetized spices. She thought she'd exhausted her options, and then spied one more drawer tucked into an awkward corner.

It rattled loudly when she pulled it open. Her breath caught in her throat, and she stared at the dozen or so pill bottles she'd revealed. Prescription and over the counter labels, opaque and clear containers, white tablets and blue capsules. Two syringes, still sealed in their protective wrappings.

Her hand hovered over the drawer as if a forcefield prevented her from touching the medications. Her mind skipped and raced, searching for an explanation.

Rafe appeared fit and healthy, but what did she really know about him? Addicts were experts at hiding both their highs and their lows, as she knew from bitter personal experience.

She peered closer. A part of her recognized this was a horrible invasion of privacy, but if Rafe was concerned about others knowing about the pills, surely he wouldn't have left them in such a public place.

Unlike his other tidy cupboards, the containers in this one lay higgledy-piggledy, many of the labels partially hidden from view. But she saw *Messing* on one and *Eugenia* on another, and enough of several others to decide most if not all of the medications had been prescribed to her.

The knowledge did nothing to ease her anxiety. In fact, it only added to her concern. Eugenia had died from cancer almost a year ago. Why would Rafe still have all her pills?

Chapter Seven

Now it was March, the days had noticeably lengthened. The light was just starting to fade when Rafe returned home on Monday evening, but even if it had been black as midnight, he couldn't have failed to see Natalie's car parked in front of his house.

His pulse picked up at the same time his stomach sank. His body's tug of war was a familiar sensation after the past weekend. Part of him had quietly yet intensely enjoyed the time they'd spent together, even though they had interacted only as necessary, and only in the most professional of manners. The other part of him had yearned for something more. More intimate, more personal...just *more.*

Eagerness pressurized his chest like helium in a balloon as he swung around the newel post and hurried up the stairs. Just outside the room he was beginning to think of as Natalie's, he paused. It wouldn't do to rush in like a randy groom panting to bed his bride.

Now what had brought that analogy to mind?

"Rafe?" Natalie appeared in the doorway. "I thought I heard you on the stairs. What are you doing?"

"Nothing." He cleared his throat and made himself walk sedately toward her. "Why are you still here?"

He winced. He hadn't meant to sound so adversarial.

Her smile faltered. "I hope you don't mind. I wanted to talk to you."

Oh, god. I missed something. She found it. He laid

a hand on the door frame for balance, his legs unsteady. "What?"

"I'm sure you have friends of your own. I mean, who doesn't, right? But if you ever needed, you know, help, I want you to know you can trust me."

That didn't sound like she'd discovered his mother was a criminal. She would be offering condemnation, not support, if that were the case. He drew a breath in through his nose, relieved yet confused. "I don't know what you're talking about."

Her shoulders sagged as if he had disappointed her. He was familiar with the gesture. It had been one of his mother's favourites. "Nothing in particular. It's just, I know I'm only doing a job for you, but that doesn't mean we can't be friends, too."

"Friends." The word felt awkward on his lips. Natalie was the type of person who had friends— outgoing and cheerful and attractive. He, on the other hand, had acquaintances and colleagues.

"Yes." As if suddenly realizing they were still standing in the doorway, she tilted her head—was she really inviting him into a room in his own house?— and went to sit in the swivelling office chair he'd provided her.

At some point during the weekend, he'd carried up a spare dining room chair for himself. He took that seat, noting vaguely a bulletin board was now propped on the table she used as a desk. She hadn't been in the room a week and she'd already put her stamp on it, what with the sunflower mug and the pair of slippers she'd begun leaving under the table and her scent, which seemed to permeate the air.

"How was work?" She asked the question as if she really wanted to know, meeting his eyes with an open and inquiring expression.

Her attention made the tips of his ears burn. He couldn't remember the last time someone had asked about his day. Loneliness struck him a fierce blow. He usually avoided thoughts of his solitary state, but since Natalie had come into his life, they were continually bubbling to the surface.

She waited for his response, her slim fingers toying with the hem of her cable knit sweater.

He became grossly aware of his own hands, large and ungainly and awkward. "Good. It was good." He crossed his arms, and then unfolded them when he realized it might make him appear defensive.

"I'm glad." Her grin was mischievous. "Of course, it would help if I knew what you did for a living."

"You don't know?" He frowned. "I assumed you'd researched me before you agreed to take the job."

She shook her head. "I try not to invade people's privacy more than necessary." A faint flush coloured her cheekbones. "What you do for a living had no bearing on what you hired me for."

Strangers had one of two reactions when he told them he was a pathologist. Either they blanched and turned the subject immediately, or they called him Quincy and asked if he'd ever autopsied a murder victim.

He wasn't sure which reaction he hated the most. What would Natalie's be?

Natalie already knew Rafe wasn't exactly chatty, but apparently asking him what he did for a living made him clam up tighter than a...well...a clam.

"If you tell me, will you have to kill me?" Her teasing question only made him blink his long thick lashes. Her stomach fluttered.

"I'm a pathologist." He bit out the words as if he resented them.

"That's a doctor, right?" Why would he be so leery of telling her that?

"Yes. With a focus on studying diseases. I mostly work in a lab." He watched her narrowly.

She nodded, turning the information over in her head, aware of his scrutiny. "It suits you. You're detailed, analytical, careful. And you care about people. I can see you wanting a career in the health field."

His eyes widened as if shocked at her analysis.

"What?" Did he really think so little of her that he was surprised she might have such insight? "I haven't known you long, but it doesn't take a genius to figure that out."

"It's just that..." He shook his head. "Never mind."

Confused by his response, she determined to draw him out. "How does one go about becoming a pathologist?"

"Med school first. Then a specialized residency." His shoulders relaxed and the tense lines around his mouth eased.

"Cool. That's a lot of education."

"Not much more than you." He wrinkled his nose with a boyishly apologetic air. "I did read your CV after you gave it to me that night. I also looked you up online later."

"I'd expect nothing less. You were hiring me to work on a project that's important to you." Doing her best to be inconspicuous, she studied him. Try as she might, she could find no signs he was abusing any of the substances she'd found in the kitchen drawer. She was wrong. She had to be. He just hadn't gotten rid of his mother's drugs yet. He'd probably forgotten all about them.

Still, he was a solitary man. During the hours they'd spent together, he'd received no texts, no phone calls, and he'd given no indication he had anyone other than his brother in his life. She knew there was a stepsister, too, but he'd said nothing about her. While he seemed perfectly content, she couldn't imagine a life without the plethora of friends and family she enjoyed. Well, mostly enjoyed.

She also couldn't stand the thought of Rafe seeking solace in drugs or alcohol to ease his lonely hours.

"My book club is going rock climbing this weekend." The words blurted out before she could reconsider them. "Would you like to come along?"

Several things in Natalie's pronouncement confounded Rafe. He frowned.

Book club?

Rock climbing?

She wanted him to join her?

"I don't understand." That seemed to cover everything.

"I belong to the Silverberry Book Club. We never changed the name, even though it's not really a book club anymore. Instead, we get together once a month or so and do different activities. The point is to try something new, be adventurous. This weekend we're going rock climbing at The Crag."

He'd heard of the indoor climbing facility, though he'd never had the urge to visit. Her answer cleared up two of his questions though it left the most important one dangling. "You're inviting me?"

She tilted her head, and the light reflected off her lenses, shielding the expression in her eyes. "Yes. We're always looking for new members."

Oh. Something fragile in his chest crumbled. She had invited him to join the club, not join *her*. The distinction was important in a way he didn't want to define. "I don't think it's my sort of thing."

"That's the point, to step outside your comfort zone. I assure you, it's perfectly safe. That's a club rule. Nothing illegal, and if it could be considered dangerous, it has to be done under the guidance of a professional. That's why we're climbing indoors. I wanted to do some *real* climbing this summer, but I got vetoed at our annual planning meeting last year."

He let *illegal* slide past him to focus on Natalie's other jaw-dropping revelation. "Real climbing? Like on a mountain?" He swayed dizzily thinking about it. He hated heights and preferred not to risk his very existence for so-called fun.

She nodded eagerly. "I love it. There's nothing like clinging to a cliff by your fingernails to make you feel alive."

He didn't doubt it, but it was a type of alive he could do without.

"Indoors isn't the adrenalin rush outdoors can be, but it's a good start for novices like you."

He didn't think she had meant it as a dare, but it echoed in his head like one.

Nothing about her screamed daredevil. She waited for his answer, prim and neat in her cozy sweater and slim black pants, dark hair sweeping her jaw in a smooth wing, heavy glasses perched on her small nose. He was taller than her, stronger than her, older than her...and apparently a bigger coward than her.

"When and where?" he growled.

Chapter Eight

"So, what's it like, having a hot librarian in your house doing your bidding?"

Otto's question stabbed Rafe's brain like chewing tinfoil on a filling. He knew his older brother was teasing, knew he didn't really see Natalie only as a sexy bimbo, but it was still wrong to joke about it.

It would be dangerous to reprimand him. Otto might learn more about Rafe's feelings than he needed to. Not that Rafe had feelings for Natalie. Not at all.

He tried to make his disapproval known by just the tone of his voice as he answered the question Otto *should* have asked. "Natalie is bright, intelligent, and industrious. She tells me she's already working on a draft." He glared at Otto's image on his phone for added emphasis.

It was Thursday evening. Otto, who was currently in Victoria doing whatever it was he did for his political party, had video-called just as Rafe was pouring a finger of Scotch, preparing for another solitary evening reading the newest release by Yann Martel with the background accompaniment of his favourite composition from Jennifer Higdon.

He hadn't seen Natalie since Monday. She had texted the information on the rock-climbing-disaster-waiting-to-happen but nothing since, so he assumed that was still on for Saturday afternoon. In preparation, he'd spent several hours online researching techniques and equipment and had gone so far as to call The Crag to book a private lesson. They said they had no openings for weeks—he had trouble believing there were *that* many people eager to risk their lives for entertainment—so he'd have to trust he had enough natural athleticism not to make a total fool of himself.

It was bad enough he'd come in second to his brother all his life. The thought of looking like a dunce in front of members of a *book club* when he failed to scramble up a fake rock face made his nerves crawl.

"That's fantastic." Otto gave him a thumbs up, beaming excitement. He was charismatic and charming even in two dimensions. Natalie had the same magnetism. She was bright and bubbly, character traits that should have irritated Rafe no end but didn't for some inexplicable reason.

He placed his phone on the low glass coffee table, propping it against a heavy stack of his favourite art books, and slouched onto the black leather sofa. "Yes. She's not wasting any time." He'd wanted to ask her if she'd be coming to work the morning before the impending misadventure, but didn't want her to think it was expected. While she seemed perfectly happy working seven days a week, he would never enforce such a schedule.

It wasn't that he missed her. How could you miss someone you rarely saw? But while their paths hadn't crossed recently, she continued to leave him jaunty, cheery notes, which he collected and stored with absurd solemnity. How Otto would laugh if he knew that.

His brother was grinning now, even without knowing this humiliating secret. "I knew you'd come around. She's great, isn't she?"

A burning sensation lit under Rafe's sternum, and he rubbed his chest. "I didn't think you knew her."

Otto shrugged. "Never met her. But we had a fairly long email conversation before I asked her to do the biography. You can tell a lot about a person by the way they write."

It occurred to Rafe that Otto didn't know Natalie was the woman he'd "saved" from the pool in Mexico. He opened his mouth to tell him, and then shut it again.

He remembered mentioning the connection to Natalie the day they met and wondered if she had thought of it since. Otto's jocular "hot librarian" comment skated across the surface of his mind. If he knew Natalie was the woman from the pool, wouldn't that complicate things? He could protect her from that, at least.

Even if he couldn't protect himself from a wild attraction that grew every day.

When Rafe walked into The Crag's reception area, a coil of tension in Natalie's belly eased.

She'd half-expected him to cry off. Oh, he would have had a good excuse—something important to do at work, perhaps—but the horror that had flitted across his face at her invitation had been an unmistakable indication of his true feelings.

Not that it mattered whether he came or not. She'd had time to think, and no longer worried he was a secret addict. She'd checked the drawer every day, ignoring the tickling sensation that warned her she was unforgivably breaching his privacy each time she did so. As far as she could tell—and she'd taken several close looks—none of the bottles had been touched, and the syringes hadn't shifted.

His gaze swept over Helen and Nathan and other assorted Silverberries and then settled on her. The focused power in his eyes tightened the coil that had just relaxed. As he stalked forward, her weight shifted to the balls of her feet, her body straining toward him like iron to a magnet. Which made no sense at all. He was totally not her type.

By which she meant he was *exactly* what she was

usually drawn to—tall, dark, and intense. Just like her ex-husband Ricky.

He stopped just outside her personal space. Her feet shifted of their own accord, shuffling closer to his heat, his scent.

He didn't seem to notice. "You didn't come to the house this morning." Straight to the chase. That was Rafe to a T.

"I did some writing at home." She clasped her fingers behind her back, subduing the urge to brush away the lock of hair that had fallen on his forehead.

His lashes flickered and nostrils flared. "I wasn't checking up on you. I just thought you might stop by."

"Oh." Her breath escaped on a soft whoosh. Last weekend he'd been irritated at her appearance. This weekend he'd been waiting for her? "I could come by tomorrow." It was more of a question than a statement.

"It's fine. Whatever you like."

Coming on the heels of his seeming encouragement, his ambivalence stung. "Okay then. I'll see what happens." She pressed her lips together. He was here at her invitation, so she couldn't cold-shoulder him now. She waved a hand at the group scattered around them. "Let me introduce you to everyone."

"I recognize some of them." He nodded toward Aubrey and Phillip, standing shoulder to shoulder while talking with Penta and Stephanie. "That's Aubrey Windt, right? The politician and your previous boss? I didn't realize it was her at the time, but I saw her in Mexico. She was married on the beach, just before my stepsister was."

"To Phillip Church, the man next to her. Your stepsister is Elizabeth, right?" Given his silence on his sibling before now, she was pleased to know he had some sort of relationship with her.

"Yes. Her father is Randall Messing. My mother

married him when I was nineteen. Elizabeth was six."

His expression was the softest she'd seen, and her irritation vanished at this further evidence of affection. He was so reserved, so stoic. She didn't imagine he opened his heart to just anyone. It would take someone truly special to earn his love.

"I wondered why you were in Mexico." She grinned when his mouth quirked self-deprecatingly. "Yes, you looked a little out of place. But now it makes sense."

"I could only make it for a couple nights, and Elizabeth kept us busy." His brows drew together, and she almost giggled at his aggrieved look. She longed to tease him out of his grumpiness but wasn't sure they were in that place in their relationship yet.

If they ever would be.

The door opened and Lynn walked in, followed by Benjamin. She knew her heavily pregnant friend would leave scaling the walls to her husband, but when Rafe's mouth dropped open at the sight, she couldn't resist the urge to have some fun at his expense.

"Come on." Surrendering to the need to touch him, she took his hand and tugged him along. His palm was smooth and warm. "Time to meet the Silverberries."

Rafe took a deep breath and craned his neck. Three storeys above, Natalie clung to the wall, toes perched on narrow knobs, fingers gripping brightly coloured bulges.

She called down to him. "Take the green route. I'll wait here for you."

His harness clanked as he moved into position. It snugged him between the legs, bunching the fabric of his loose shorts uncomfortably, and was attached to a long rope looped through a pulley in the ceiling high above. Standing next to him and clasping the other end of the rope was Benjamin Whitestone, the husband of the very pregnant woman Natalie had tried to make him believe was there to participate, not just watch. He wasn't that gullible, thank goodness.

Mind you, he was gullible enough to sign a waiver that listed an alarming number of scenarios, from bruises to brain damage. His pride often got him into trouble, but he had never allowed a woman to goad him into risking life and limb. Before now.

It was disconcerting to realize that Natalie might be able to goad him into almost anything.

"You've got this." Benjamin tapped him encouragingly on the shoulder. "Just like the instructor showed you."

The hour-long introductory session had eased the worst of Rafe's worries. Watching Natalie swarm up the wall like a Lycra-clad gecko, though, had brought back his insecurities. He never tried anything new until he was one hundred percent certain he'd be good at it.

He didn't have that luxury at the moment. It was either climb or flee.

After wiping sweaty fingers on his thighs, he gripped a green knob an arm's length above his head. Placing the opposing foot into a tiny notch, he pushed up, leaving the safety and security of the floor behind.

He focused solely on the next hold for his fingers and toes—and the next and the next—resolutely refusing to calculate how high he was climbing. His intellect knew he wasn't in real danger, that Benjamin would stop him if he fell, that despite the risks involved, this was a safe activity performed by children. His gut told him he was insane to do this just to impress a woman.

He gritted his teeth and kept on going, afraid if he stopped for an instant he would never get started again.

"Well, hello there."

Blinking sweat out of his eyes, he realized his nose was level with a slim ankle protruding from a pair of worn climbing shoes. Lifting his chin, his gaze trailed up a smooth calf, along a strong thigh encased in form-fitting bicycle shorts, past a fuchsia athletic top snuggling rounded breasts, and ended on a pair of glittering, amused brown eyes unprotected by their usual glasses.

"Hello there." His voice was hoarse with a mixture of exertion and fear.

"You might as well come all the way, since you made it this far."

He worked his way up the last few feet until his face was the same level as Natalie's. Chest heaving, he laid his forehead against the concrete wall and closed his eyes.

"Well done." The sincerity in her tone was a surprise. She was so much better than he was. Having her compliment him meant something. "You did excellently. I knew you would, though, given your muscle tone."

He opened his eyes. The memory of exactly how she knew about his muscle tone was no longer as disconcerting as it had been, possibly trumped by the fact he was stuck to a wall like a petrified spider. "Thanks."

"How do you feel?"

She asked as if she really cared, so he did her the courtesy of a thorough self-examination before answering.

And was surprised to find a sense of exhilaration overpowering any lingering anxiety.

"Good. Great, actually. I don't know if I'm ready for the Matterhorn, but I'd try this again."

Her lips curved, teeth flashing. Her left lateral incisor slightly overlapped its neighbour in an asymmetrically charming fashion. "I'm glad. That's what being a Silverberry is all about."

He wasn't sure he qualified for Silverberry status yet but was pleased she thought he'd earned the title. His pulse, which had started to settle, kicked up again when she licked her upper lip. The shouts and laughter of other climbers echoed in the cavernous space, but at this moment he and Natalie were in their own private aerie.

Her gaze dropped to his mouth. Her tongue flicked out again, wetting her lips. His cock tightened against the restrictions of the harness and athletic shorts. He shifted slightly on his toes, leaning toward her...

...and slipped off his precarious perch.

Chapter Nine

Rafe let out a startled bellow as his feet shot out from underneath him.

Natalie stretched out a hand to steady him. "It's all good. Benjamin's got you. Just get another hold. You can do it." She kept her voice low and soothing.

He scrambled for purchase, kicking and swinging. His fingertips, gripping a protrusion right at her eye level, were bloodless with tension. It was only seconds before he was secure again, but she knew exactly how terrifying it felt to free fall even a few inches when you weren't expecting it.

Almost as terrifying as knowing he'd been about to kiss her only moments before. Her heart still pounded in her throat.

His shoulder was granite under her fingertips, rock-hard with fear. She patted it and then drew her hand away. "Okay now? That can be scary." He stared at her, speechless, the whites of his eyes showing around the almost black irises. "Do you want Benjamin to belay you?"

"No." His reply was sharp and definite. He sucked in a breath, held it, and then let it out slowly. "I made it up under my own power. And I'll make it down, too. See you at the bottom."

She gave him a head start, and then followed using a slightly different route. She took her time, not wanting to rush him, and reached the bottom a few moments after.

It took her a little while to recognize the starburst shining in her chest. Pride. She could see how much the climb had taxed him, knew how much willpower it had taken to risk this new adventure. Yet, he hadn't let it conquer him.

She flung her arms around him. He staggered back against the wall, his hands clamping on her waist. "Well done. Congratulations!" She lifted on tiptoe and pressed a quick kiss on his sweaty cheek, tasting salt, his short whiskers tickling her lips.

His embrace tightened as he stared down at her. He was so much taller that the top of her head barely reached his chin. She had the sudden urge to press her nose into the hollow at the base of his throat and bask in his essence.

Mouth dry, she hurriedly released him. As soon as her arms dropped, his hold slackened, and she stepped to a safer distance.

"There's a pub next door. We're all going for dinner and drinks. You should come." She was babbling, his continued silence only increasing her nervousness. "Or not. Whatever you like. I'm going to go shower now."

She escaped.

In the end, neither went to the pub.

Natalie had just finished getting dressed and was packing up her climbing gear when her phone rang.

Shyla. *This won't be good* was her first ungracious thought. She smothered it.

"You go on." She waved to Helen, Stephanie, and Penta. "I'll catch up in a minute. If Rafe is waiting, will you take him along?" It was very possible he had already gone home, but on the off chance he'd decided to come to the pub, this would give her even more time to recover from the disconcerting feelings that had assaulted her at the end of their climb.

She connected the call as soon as the door clanged shut. "Hello?"

"Took you long enough. Thought I'd get your voicemail."

Natalie stiffened, disappointment a dagger in her throat. Shyla's voice was slow and slurred. She hadn't heard from her sister in more than a week and had allowed herself to hope yet again that *this time*... More fool her.

"Are you high or drunk?" It was only four in the afternoon. Shyla had started early—or, more than likely, had never quit.

"None of your business." Despite the blurred edges of the words, she managed to sound pissed off. "I need a ride."

"Where are you?" The question she wanted to ask was what had happened to the deposit money, but didn't bother for two reasons. One, she was pretty sure she knew the answer. Two, she'd never get the truth while Shyla was in this state.

Her reply was both unexpected and unwelcome. "Quesnel."

The small town was just over an hour south of Prince George. "What are you doing there?"

"A friend brought me to a party last night. Stupid bitch left without me."

Natalie's gut churned. *A friend* could be anyone from a random stranger to a dealer to one of Shyla's seedier acquaintances. "I have plans for tonight. Are you sure you can't get another ride?"

"Of course I'm sure." *Idiot* was implied in her tone. "It's too fucking cold to hitch."

"Don't hitch." Shyla wouldn't care it was illegal as well as dangerous, but she was right about the weather. It might be spring in other parts of the world, but in northern British Columbia early March was still winter. The temperatures were well below freezing and when Natalie had arrived hours ago at the climbing gym, hard pellets of snow were being flung around by an angry wind. "I'll be there as soon as I can, but it will be almost two hours. Where should I meet you?"

"Don't know. Maybe here, maybe somewheres else. Call when you get to town. Don't take too long." She hung up.

Fear for Shyla's safety warred with irritation. What kind of adult lived with such casual uncertainty?

The locker room door swung open, and three women strode in, chattering and laughing. Shoving her phone in the pocket of her coat and slinging her duffel bag over her shoulder, she stalked out. A new group of climbers filled the reception area, and she threaded her way through, half-blind with annoyance and worry.

"Natalie? Wait up."

She froze, her hand on the door's push bar. What was Rafe still doing here?

Rafe had fought off the invitation from the other Silverberries as politely as he could. If he went to the pub—and there was still doubt about that—it would be with Natalie. These people weren't his friends. He was here because of her, no one else.

He tucked himself into a corner as a crowd filled the reception area. He'd barely begun to wonder what was keeping her when she appeared from the change room. Intent on the exit, she didn't spare him a glance, and he called out to get her attention.

She stared, one hand on the door. "What are you still doing here?"

"Waiting for you." He thought that was pretty obvious. He examined her. "Are you okay?"

Worry lines carved between her eyebrows and her mouth pinched tight. "Yes. I can't go to the pub, though. You still should." She shoved through the door and into the bitter late afternoon.

He followed, hunching his shoulders against the

wind. "What happened? Why aren't you going?"

"I have to get my sister." She muttered the words without looking at him. Stopping beside her vehicle, she popped the locks and threw her bag in the backseat. "Really, you go ahead."

"Is she okay?" He never bullied his way into other people's personal business. But something in her defeated posture roused his protective instincts.

"As fine as she ever is." Anger laced the words, along with a thin thread of pain. "Don't worry about it. You go on. If not to the pub, then home."

No way could he follow that command. This went deeper than irritation at picking up an annoying sister. He probed gently. "You have to go get her? From where?"

Natalie leaned into her car, pulled out a long-handled brush, and slammed the rear door shut with more force than necessary. Snow shivered off the window and drifted to the ground. "Quesnel."

Heavy flakes had been falling all afternoon and lay in a thick layer everywhere. "Don't tell me you're driving all that way in weather like this."

"It's just a skiff. I'll be fine." She swept the accumulation off her windshield with fierce, brisk strokes.

His nose burned from the chilly wind as he bit back further protests while watching her clear her vehicle. She was a grown woman and obviously intended to make the trip no matter what he said. But that didn't mean she had to go alone.

"I can come along if you like." He took a step back as she made an especially vigorous movement, and a wing of snow flew in his direction.

"No, thank you." She didn't even look at him.

Her polite but terse rejection slid like a shard of glass under his skin. He knew they weren't friends, even though she'd invited him today. And he doubted she shared the attraction he was having more and more trouble ignoring. But she was upset, and he'd thought she might want company, even if it was his.

Apparently not.

"All right." He dug his keys out of his jacket pocket, determined to leave her be, but his feet refused to move. Despite the fierceness of her tone and gestures, he couldn't shake the feeling she was hurting inside. And no one should be alone when they were hurting. Other than himself, that was. There was an exception to every rule.

Natalie knew she was taking her anger and frustration out on Rafe. It wasn't fair, but since he insisted on sticking around, he'd have to lump it.

She finished cleaning off the snow, aware of his silent presence by the rear bumper. She'd thought her last rude response would chase him away, yet there he remained.

The reality was, she really did want his company. The thought of the silent, solitary drive to Quesnel, followed by an acrimonious, tension-filled trip home with no buffer between her and Shyla made bile rise in her throat.

"Fine." She opened the rear door, threw in the snow brush, and slammed it shut again. "You can come along."

His answer betrayed no second thoughts on his part. "Let me get rid of my bag." He hurried to his Mercedes and returned, the security system beeping behind him.

She climbed in behind the wheel as he folded himself into the front of her practical, boxy SUV. Though he slid the seat back as far as it would go, his knees bent at a sharp angle. He made no complaint and remained quiet while she navigated onto the highway heading south and left the city behind.

The flurries gave up about fifteen minutes later.

Despite the recent snowfall, the asphalt was clear and dry, and she increased her speed slightly. The sooner she got to Quesnel, the sooner this would all be over.

Her nerves twitched with restless energy. She tapped her fingers on the steering wheel, wishing she'd turned on the radio before leaving town. If she switched it on now it might reveal how uncomfortable she was with the silence stretching tautly between her and her taciturn companion.

When he cleared his throat, she just about jumped out of her seat.

"You don't have to tell me if you don't want to." He spoke with wary caution, as if she were a bomb that might detonate at any time. "But I get the impression there's conflict between you and your sister. If so, it might be best if you give me some of the background, so I don't make things worse by accident."

Stalling for time, she unwound the scarf she'd tossed around her neck before leaving The Crag and threw it in the backseat. Shame flushed her chest at the thought of explaining her relationship with Shyla, but she'd known it would be unavoidable from the moment she'd accepted his offer to come along.

"You'll find out for yourself as soon as you meet her. Shyla needs a ride because she is drunk. Or high. Possibly both." She slid him a sideways glance but saw only his profile as he kept his gaze straight ahead. Her fingers tightened on the wheel as she waited for that laser-sharp brain to connect the dots.

His first question was mild enough. "Does she live in Quesnel?"

"No. She went there for a party and got stranded by whoever brought her there."

"I take it this isn't the first time you've had to retrieve her."

He made Shyla sound like lost luggage. It was an analogy that was depressingly close to the truth. "No."

"Younger or older?"

"Younger. There's just Shyla and me."

"And you feel responsible."

"Yes." And no. But that was too complicated to go into right now.

Chapter Ten

Rafe could sympathize with the crushing weight of duty he sensed in Natalie's reply. He felt the same for Otto and Elizabeth, though neither of them led lives that were as high risk as Shyla's appeared to be. His interference had led to several acrimonious disputes, especially with a teenaged Elizabeth. She had now resigned herself with irritated grace to what she referred to as his meddling.

His inability to disassociate from those he considered in his care had caused issues during his medical residency, as well. It was one of the reasons he'd chosen pathology. Making life and death decisions while a patient or their family gazed at him with hope and fear in their eyes had been too much to bear. In the cool silence of his lab, he was a step removed from the burden of humanity. Even when he knew the samples he studied were from living people, people anxiously awaiting his findings to determine their futures, he was able to dismiss that knowledge. All he did was provide facts and data. It was up to someone else to explain what the results meant to the patient and implement treatment.

It seemed that Natalie had joined the ranks of people he couldn't bear to see suffer. He twisted slightly in his seat to see her better. Tension was an almost visible aura surrounding her. The only way he knew to ease it was to be blunt. "Shyla has a substance abuse disorder."

Natalie drew in a breath and let it out slowly. "Yes." The simple syllable held a world of meaning.

"And you're going to rescue her."

She bristled, though he hadn't meant to sound accusing. "She's my sister. I can't leave her stranded."

"I didn't say you should." He searched for the words that would show he was concerned for Natalie, not denouncing Shyla. "I'm trying to imagine how tough it must be for you."

"I'm not the one living on a knife's edge. I'm fine. It's Shyla who's in danger."

That might be true, but it didn't mean Natalie wasn't experiencing her own trauma. He assumed she wouldn't appreciate him saying so, however. "How long have you been dealing with it?"

She hesitated so long he began to wonder if she would ever answer. Dusk had fallen, staining the snow lining the edge of the highway a dull grayish blue. Taillights blinked scarlet ahead of them as a loaded transport truck put on its four-way flashers and crawled up a steep incline. Natalie swept past.

When she finally did reply, the syllables were clipped and frozen. "High school. I was in Grade Twelve, she was two years behind me. She came home drunk from a party and begged me to cover with Mom and Dad. I did, of course. All teenagers experiment with alcohol, right?"

He grunted a soft acknowledgment. He hadn't. But then, he'd been older than his years from the day he was born.

"At first it was just once in a while, and then it was every weekend. I still didn't worry, not then. Shyla and I had never been especially close. I liked that she needed me, wanted my help to keep her out of trouble." Her voice trembled. "I still feel guilty about that. I should have recognized she was in over her head and done something about it. Instead, I basically encouraged her so I could feel good about myself."

He couldn't let that go. "I'm sure that wasn't the case. You were young, too. Too young to fully understand the situation. No one can foresee the future, and you were only trying to protect your sister the best way you knew how."

She shrugged that off. "When I left for university, it was a relief. No more lying to my parents. By then, they knew some of it, of course. It had been impossible to hide everything."

"And it just got worse over the years."

"She can be sober for weeks, even months, but it never lasts. My parents have paid for all sorts of treatment programs. Nothing works."

"Shyla has to want it."

"I know. That's why I was so excited this time." Her profile was taut with strain as she stared out the windshield.

"This time?"

Her breath trembled on a sigh. "Just before Mexico, she came to me. Said she'd been accepted into a program and needed two thousand dollars to reserve her place."

Given what had precipitated this mission, it wasn't difficult to guess what had happened. "You gave her the money. And she bought drugs with it."

She slapped her palm against the steering wheel. "Damn it! I wanted to believe her. I *needed* to believe her. She's only initiated her own treatment once before." Her lips pressed tight, and her swallow was audible over the hum of the engine. "That didn't end well. I'm determined to make it different this time."

In the glare of oncoming headlights, he saw the sheen of tears in her eyes. "Pull over." She ignored him and he sharpened his voice. "Pull over, Natalie. I don't want you driving while you're upset."

"Afraid I'll cause an accident?" She spoke with a lighthearted bravado that couldn't hide the truth.

"Yes. Now pull over."

She did so with exaggerated care. That was fine. She could be as pissy as she wanted. He didn't really believe she'd cause a collision, but he had to do something to ease her turmoil. Letting her relax—if that was even possible in her present state—while he drove was the best thing he could think of.

Natalie jerked the gear shift into park and swung open her door. The knot of her heart was so tight it hurt to breathe, and her eyes burned with unshed tears.

She should be thanking Rafe for insisting they change seats. Despite her earlier bluster, it was probably for the best.

When they crossed in front of the hood, she kept her eyes averted, not wanting to see pity on his face.

They climbed back in. He adjusted his seat and mirrors and shoulder-checked for long seconds before pulling back onto the highway. As the shush of tires filled the interior, she punched the seat-warmer to high, hoping the heat would ease the tension in her aching lower back.

She felt a perverted kind of relief now that Rafe knew about Shyla. Not the whole story, of course. She hadn't been able to bring herself to share how her own actions had led to one of Shyla's most critical breakdowns. But he knew enough for tonight.

In fact, he'd been remarkably open and accepting. For a man who did everything strictly by the book, he'd barely blinked at her sordid revelations. She'd thought he might withdraw into his frozen shell once he knew exactly what he'd barged into. Instead, he'd been supportive and comforting—in his own blunt, forthright way, of course.

"Sorry you insisted on coming along? I don't imagine you were expecting all this." She waved her hand, encompassing herself, her sister, the whole screwed up world in one gesture.

"No." He flashed her a wry look. "To both. Are you sorry you let me?"

"Did I have a choice?" She had been going for flippant and was chagrined to see him flinch. "Sorry again. Bad joke. You didn't force your way in. I accepted your very kind offer and have been repaying by burying you in family drama."

"All families have drama. Some is just more public than others." His tone was grim.

She didn't think he wasn't talking about Shyla anymore. More than willing to leave the subject of her sister behind, she said, "You must have had your own issues, growing up with a mother so much in the spotlight." The photo she'd pinned to the bulletin board was etched in her memory—a reluctant Rafe surrounded by others much more comfortable with scrutiny. It wouldn't have been the only time he'd been forced into a similar situation.

"I flew under the radar, mostly." One corner of his mouth curled up in a rueful smile. "My parents and Otto never minded the attention. I hated it."

Just this afternoon she had compared Rafe to her ex-husband Ricky, but she was coming to realize that hadn't been fair. While they might be similar on the surface, Rafe was frank, outspoken, and brutally honest, with himself and with others, in a way Ricky had never been. She might not like what he said, but at least she knew where she stood.

She shifted restlessly, wondering if she should tell him Shyla was the reason Natalie had pushed to write his mother's biography. With guilty relief, she decided to keep quiet. *Why* she needed the job wouldn't affect *how* she did it, so the point was moot.

Exhausted, both from the strenuous activity of the afternoon and the emotional turmoil of the last hour, she let herself be lulled into a daze by the endless centre line and Rafe's smooth handling of her vehicle. She would have missed the distance marker if not for the shine of its reflective paint. They were less than fifteen minutes from Quesnel.

"I have to call Shyla. I don't know exactly where we're meeting her." She didn't lift her phone.

He laid his large palm on her hand, lying limp in her lap, rubbed it briefly, and then gripped the wheel again. "It's going to be okay. Go ahead and call her. We'll figure it out together."

They were the most comforting words she had heard in a long time.

An irritated sounding Shyla gave an address on the west side of Quesnel. She wasn't slurring her words as badly, but Shyla coming down from a high was a feral creature that needed to be handled with kid gloves. Natalie's fingers ached from clenching them together as Rafe followed the directions intoned by the navigation system.

She was waiting for them outside a ramshackle mobile home on a large lot. Hulks of discarded vehicles loomed in the darkness, rotten snow piled on rusted bumpers and heaped against empty axles. The glow of a bare bulb lit the crooked wooden porch where she stood and revealed stuffing escaping from a slash on the sleeve of her parka. It hadn't been there when she'd come to Natalie's apartment before Mexico.

She yanked open the passenger door and her brows clenched when she saw Natalie. Bending over, she stared inside. "Who's that?"

She winced at her sister's ungracious tone. "This is my friend, Rafe. He offered to keep me company on the drive." She reached for her seatbelt. "I can sit in the back if you want the front."

"I don't give a fuck." Shyla slammed the door in her face and climbed in behind, shutting that door with the same force. "What took you so long?"

Rafe's shoulders twitched, but he didn't say anything. Natalie hurried to stem the tide of fury. "We came as fast as we could. You weren't waiting outside the whole time, were you?"

"Of course I was. Fucking freezing, too. Asshole wouldn't let me in. Said I broke his stupid TV."

Without a word, Rafe reversed onto the road and headed back the way they had come.

"I'm starving." Shyla poked her head between the front seats. Natalie caught the funky scents of unwashed hair, beer, and cannabis. "Stop at the A&W, will ya? I need onion rings."

It was dinner time, but Natalie had no appetite. Without asking, Rafe ordered her a burger and fries, as well as a burger for himself and Shyla's onion rings. When she tried to pay, he ignored her and dug out his own wallet. On the road again, she partially unwrapped his burger and handed it to him to eat while he drove. He gave her an imperturbable nod.

Around mouthfuls, Shyla continued her complaints, blaming everyone except herself for the troubles of the last few days. Her sister's list of grievances made Natalie vaguely nauseous. She left her burger untouched and only nibbled at her fries.

Rafe kept his attention on the road while taking bites of his own meal. Other than in the drive-through, he hadn't spoken a word since they'd retrieved Shyla. He was retreating into his shell, and she didn't know how to stop him. It had been a mistake letting him come. The closeness she'd hoped was growing between them wouldn't survive the drive home. And who could blame him? If she wasn't related to Shyla, she wouldn't—

She cut off her thoughts. She *loved* her sister. Any troubles Natalie had paled in comparison to her issues. If she had to put her own life on hold so that Shyla could be healed, she would.

The ranting devolved to mutters and finally

silence. She risked a look over her shoulder to find her draped over the climbing bag, eyes closed, mouth hanging open.

"She's asleep." She leaned back in her own seat and let her shoulders sag.

Rafe grunted but made no further comment. Natalie slumped lower and tried to stifle her resentment...at her sister, at Rafe, at the world.

No one spoke for the remainder of the trip.

Chapter Eleven

Rafe wasn't worried when Natalie didn't show up at his house on Sunday. As they'd stood next to her SUV in The Crag's parking lot, she'd warned him she probably wouldn't.

With a weary expression, she'd regarded Shyla, still passed out in the back seat. "I'll take her to my place tonight. I can't leave her until she's sobered up."

"I understand." Though the drive to Quesnel and back had taken just over three hours, it wasn't yet eight o'clock. The climbing gym was still open, the lot full of vehicles. His own had a healthy layer of snow and he used the remote to start the engine. "You'll call if you need anything?"

Natalie's mouth widened in a smile that didn't reach her eyes. "Don't worry. We'll be fine." She had slipped into the driver's seat and driven away.

Monday morning, she had sent a text saying she'd be working from home, with no mention of her sister. He'd wanted to ask how things were going, but hadn't wanted to pry, so simply sent back a one-word acknowledgment.

He'd received no other messages and left his house Tuesday morning with the hope he might come home to one of her chatty, breezy notes. When he drove up the street on his return from the lab, however, her grey SUV was still parked out front.

A voice inside him whispered *yes*.

Half-ashamed of his reaction, he exited his car and raced inside. Her boots rested on the mat by the garage door, and he relaxed a fraction more at this additional evidence of her presence. Slowing his steps, he paced deliberately up the flight to the second floor and down the hall to her room.

He paused in the doorway. She sat at the table that held his mother's ancient computer, frowning at her laptop, an age-battered folder open next to it. Her mug was within arm's reach, and he caught the whiff of herbal tea. One dark wing of hair was tucked behind her ear, revealing a white earbud. He wondered what she was listening to.

Since she hadn't yet seen him, he took a moment to scrutinize her. Was she paler than normal? Were there circles under her eyes from sleepless nights? His fingers itched to turn her chin toward him so he could ascertain for himself that the worry and sorrow etched on her face Saturday had disappeared.

She reached for her phone and woke the screen. "Damn it." Pushing her chair back from the table, she plucked the earbuds out and tossed them on the desk.

He didn't want her to leave. "Stay for dinner."

With a shriek she launched out of her seat, spinning around and clutching her chest. "Rafe! How long have you been there?"

"Not long. Honest." Great, now she thought he was a stalker. "I didn't mean to startle you."

Her palm pressed flat between her breasts as if holding her heart in place. "My alarm went off, but I wanted to finish one thing. I guess I got caught up."

Why had she set an alarm? It wasn't like she was being paid by the hour, so there was no set time for her to clock out.

His mind made the leap. She wanted to ensure she'd be gone before he got home. He swallowed down the hurt. "Don't leave on my account. I'll stay out of your way." He took a step back.

"Wait." She lifted a hand, and then dropped it heavily, like a stone.

His heart rate sped up. She worried her lower lip

with her teeth and his attention was drawn to the plushness of her mouth. A tingle in his fingertips presaged the desire that flared in his belly.

"I never thanked you. For Saturday." She shifted her weight from one foot to the other, her fingers flexing at her sides.

"It was nothing."

She shook her head. "Don't. Don't brush it off. Shyla was rude and demanding and ungrateful. I don't want you to think the same of me."

Her large brown eyes stared soberly from behind her dark frames. He wanted to put the smile back on her face. She didn't look like his Natalie when she looked this way. He missed her sparkle, her cheerful charm.

Three quick strides put him in front of her. She lifted her chin as he cupped her jaw in his palms. Her soft inhalation checked him, but only for a moment. "I didn't do it for Shyla. I did it for you. And I would never think you ungrateful. You ask for so little."

Her hands came up to rest on his forearms, her touch warm through the fabric of his shirt. "I don't like to be a bother."

He wanted to tell her she could bother him any time, day or night, but something stayed the declaration. "You look tired."

She huffed a breath that tickled under his chin. "Just what I wanted to hear."

His thumbs traced small circles on her cheeks. She didn't seem to mind. Was it his imagination or was she letting her head rest in his hands? "Is Shyla still with you?"

Tiny muscles flexed as the corners of her mouth turned down. "No. She left Sunday."

"Where did she go?"

Her fingers clenched his wrists then relaxed. "I don't know. I took a shower and when I came out, she was gone. Along with—" She cut herself off. "She hasn't called since."

He didn't press her on her unfinished comment. He could guess what she'd been going to say. Shyla had probably helped herself to easily sellable items or handily available cash. "You haven't answered my question."

A wrinkle creased between her brows. "Which question?"

"About dinner."

"That wasn't a question. That was a statement." This time, her smile was reflected in her eyes, but it faded quickly. "Are you sure, though? Do you really want me to stay? I don't want to disrupt your plans."

Natalie searched Rafe's face for the pity she was certain she'd see. He had asked her for dinner because he felt sorry for her. What other reason could there be?

All she saw was welcome—and a glimmer of something deep in his eyes she wasn't ready to examine.

"Yes. I'm sure." His tone was firm. "I wouldn't have asked otherwise."

That she believed. He would never do anything he didn't want to. It should have been reassuring, but instead it made her feel weak and indecisive. Her relationship with Shyla had always been a tug-of-war between what she knew she should do and what she ended up doing. Standing firm while watching her sister destroy herself was impossible, especially since the single instance she'd tried tough love, she'd only caused pain for her whole family.

"Well—" The thought of her empty apartment was suddenly too much to bear. "If you mean it, then, yes, I will."

Pleasure softened his harsh features. "Great." His gaze dipped from her eyes to his hands, still cupping her face. Heat scorched her cheeks when she realized she was leaning into his caress in a display of embarrassing fragility. She stiffened her neck, drawing back.

He immediately let go and tucked his hands in his pockets. "So, are you done here? Or do you need to finish up?"

"I'm done."

"Come with me, then."

She followed him down the stairs, wondering if she'd made a mistake agreeing to dinner. She hated baring her vulnerabilities, especially to someone as self-sufficient as Rafe. But after the last two days, she needed the comfort of rational adult companionship, even if it was offered from such an unexpected quarter.

She'd spoken nothing but the truth when she'd told him Shyla had left while she was in the shower, but she hadn't made a complete confession. Shyla had definitely vanished—along with what little cash Natalie had in her purse and two of her credit cards.

And her laptop.

Lightheaded at the thought of all the work she might have lost if she wasn't compulsive about backing everything up on the cloud, Natalie gripped the stair rail for support, pausing briefly before continuing her descent.

She had suffered a twinge of guilt when she cancelled the cards. If only she trusted Shyla would use them to buy nutritious food or safe shelter. But she couldn't risk the possibility her sister would sell them on to someone even more unscrupulous. The rest of the day had been taken up with purchasing another computer—on the credit card she kept hidden in the freezer for emergencies—and setting everything up again so she could get back to work. It was an expense in money and time she could little afford.

When she'd discovered the theft, she'd been so

furiously distraught she'd considered giving up on the whole project. Shyla obviously wasn't committed to the treatment program, so Natalie's most pressing reason for the job was moot. In the end, it wasn't only her reluctance to break her contract with Otto and Rafe or her own need for income that prevented her from backing out. It was her growing fascination with Eugenia herself. Every day she learned something new, and she wanted to write her story now more than ever.

That determination had prodded her back to Rafe's that morning. She had fully intended to be long gone by the time he arrived home. Not only did it keep true to the schedule she'd set the first day, but it had the added bonus of preventing her from having to face his rejection.

Now he knew about Shyla, he would treat her differently. How could he not?

Her subconscious had played against her, however. She'd been following a fascinating thread about Eugenia's involvement in the several multimillion-dollar infrastructure programs that had been enacted during her time in office, and her alarm hadn't been strong enough to pull her away.

Instead of the cold shoulder she'd been expecting, though, Rafe was now escorting her to the kitchen and gesturing to one of the chrome and leather barstools tucked under the high ledge of the island. "Wine? Sparkling water? Something else?"

"Red wine if you have it." She used the brace encircling the stool's legs a few inches from the floor as a step and hitched herself up onto the high seat. Wriggling to get settled, she folded her arms on the white and grey quartz counter. Other than the sounds of Rafe selecting a bottle of wine from the rack and retrieving a corkscrew, the house was hushed, the air heavy with awkwardness. She racked her brain for something innocuous to talk about and settled on the safest subject she could think of. His mother.

"I was reading about Eugenia in her role as Transport Minister. That's what kept me here late."

Rafe was glad his back was to Natalie. It made it easier to hide his shock at her words.

His pleasure at her decision to stay for dinner drained away. She'd be furious with him if she knew he was keeping secrets. Despite the deep well of forgiveness she offered Shyla, he didn't expect her to extend it to him.

He finished pouring the rich red wine into two large goblets and placed the bottle on the counter with precise motions while his brain cycled frantically. He had to know what she'd learned. Picking up the glasses, he took a moment to compose his face before turning to her. "What was so fascinating?"

"It was an era of huge change in the province." Her expression rapt, she accepted the glass he held out, clasping the stem with her thumb and forefingers. "Infrastructure that had been thrown up quickly during the booming sixties was no longer enough for the growing population. Your mother was at the forefront of that change, making decisions that would affect us for decades."

You have no idea. He grunted noncommittally and then sought refuge from her enthusiasm by opening the refrigerator. Luckily, he had taken four chicken breasts from the freezer that morning, intending to use the extra in future meals.

A thought struck him. He closed the door and turned back to Natalie. "You didn't eat your burger on Saturday. I never even asked before I ordered for you. That was very presumptuous. I'm sorry. Do you have any dietary restrictions or preferences?"

She made a moue. "I wasn't hungry on Saturday. I'm sorry I wasted the meal. I try to keep my carb intake low, but I'm not fanatical about it. Other than that, I'm good."

"Grilled chicken breasts, rice, and a green salad okay?"

"Perfect. What can I do to help?"

Chapter Twelve

Rafe had had Elizabeth and Jude over for dinner shortly after they'd announced their engagement last year, and Otto showed up at his door at random intervals, so it wasn't like he never hosted guests.

The last time he'd had someone unrelated seated across from him, though?

He had no idea.

His dining table was set in a loosely defined area between the regular height ceiling kitchen and the vaulted living room. The empty chamber soared two storeys above the glossy wooden surface, yet Natalie filled it with effortless effervescence. Thankfully, she hadn't mentioned his mother again while they'd prepared the meal, instead chattering on about inconsequential subjects. He should have been bored and irritated by her stories about people he didn't know and on topics in which he had no interest. But she didn't seem to require his input, and he found himself relaxing under the constant, undemanding flow.

They finished their meals, and he was about to suggest coffee when his cell phone rang. Since he had it connected to a smart screen propped on the kitchen counter, Natalie could see as well as he could that Otto was requesting a video call.

"Go ahead and take that." She rose from her seat and reached for his plate. "I'll start cleaning up."

He had no problem ignoring his brother when it suited. Natalie, on the other hand, rushed to her sister's aid even when it disrupted her entire life. What would she think if she knew he treated his brother so cavalierly? He connected the call.

"Hey, there." Otto beamed his characteristic smile from the small screen. "Did I interrupt anything?" Before Rafe could reply, he barked a boisterous laugh and answered his own question. "Of course not. It's a weeknight. You're home alone like a good boy."

His jaw locked. Irritation, humiliation, and desperation warred to keep him from speaking.

A soft cheek brushed his bicep as Natalie leaned so she could be seen on camera. He stared down at her. She smiled, though the pinched corners of her eyes belied her cheerful air. "He might be home, but he's not alone."

She sounded...angry? Why would she be angry? He added confused to the list of emotions he was trying to process.

"Oh. Oh!" Otto's shock was both insulting and rewarding. "I'm sorry. I *am* interrupting, I guess."

Rafe finally found his voice. "You're not. We just finished dinner." He'd automatically wrapped his arm around Natalie's waist when she'd tucked herself against his side. Realizing that would give Otto the wrong impression, he hastily released her.

"I'm Otto, Rafe's brother." He waggled his fingers at the screen. "And you are..."

"Natalie Minton. Your mother's biographer." For the first time, she sounded like the fusty librarian he'd hoped she'd be. He pressed his lips together to prevent a grin. "We've met, by the way."

Since the start of the call, Otto's expression had cycled from teasing to speculative to surprised to astonished. "We have? I'm sure I would remember that."

"In Mexico." Natalie didn't appear impressed by the implied flattery. "You were needlessly heroic when I was knocked into a pool."

"That was you? And what do you mean, needlessly

heroic?" Otto's eyebrows shot up. "I was trying to help."

Rafe couldn't remember the last time he'd seen his brother discombobulated. He was too used to being right all the time, to being deferred to and respected without having to exert himself. Having a pint-sized brunette upbraid him would be a good experience.

"I'm a good swimmer. Maybe not as good as Rafe"—here she shot him a glance and pink tinged her cheeks—"but I certainly didn't need to be rescued."

"Well." Otto swallowed. "I apologize then."

"Thank you." Natalie's nod was regal. A laughing bubble of appreciation welled in Rafe's chest. Not just at her easy handling of Otto's officiousness, but at her confidence and composure in what could have been an awkward scene.

"Did you need something?" As much as he was enjoying the conversation, he would rather have Natalie to himself. A thought that should have disturbed him but didn't. His arm muscles still echoed with the sensation of her soft hips and curvy warmth, like the phantom pain of a missing limb.

"No, not really. I was just checking in."

"I'm fine."

"Okay then. I'll let you go." Otto looked like he wanted to say more, but in a rare show of forbearance simply disconnected with a swift goodbye.

Natalie twisted so she was between him and the counter and showered him with a brilliant smile. "Maybe I shouldn't have tweaked him about his so-called rescue. But I didn't like him making fun of you being alone. What business is it of his?"

It was an ingrained habit to defend his brother, whether he needed it or not. "On any other night, he would have been right. This is the first time I've had anyone over for dinner in a long time."

"Then I am honoured you asked me." She patted his chest, rose up on tiptoe, and brushed a soft kiss on his lips.

He froze, a lightning bolt of desire fusing him to the floor.

She drew away, her eyes searching his, wide with wonder.

Then she leaned up again and pressed her mouth to his.

Again. Kiss him again.

Natalie obeyed her soul's demand. She sipped from Rafe's lips like a connoisseur with a fine wine. He stood stock still, and she would have retreated if his mouth hadn't clung to hers when she pulled a hair's breadth away, his head dipping to keep their connection.

Her hands slid from his chest to the back of his neck, bringing their bodies closer. Standing on tiptoe, she thanked yoga for the strength in her ankles. She'd never be able to reach his mouth otherwise.

His dark chocolate, deliciously bitter mouth.

Hesitant pressure on her hips presaged the warmth of his palms. She licked the seam of his lips in wordless encouragement, purring low in her throat. This time she'd make sure he knew she approved his touch. Wanted it. *Craved* it. If he pulled away again, as he had when he held her face before dinner or when his arm had snaked around her waist for an instant while they'd talked to Otto, she might scream.

His grip on her hips tightened and suddenly she was sitting on the counter.

"Is that better?" He whispered the words against her mouth, and then trailed a heated path to the skin behind her ear.

In answer, she wrapped her legs around his waist, locking them at the small of his back and tugging him tight to her centre. The hard bulge of his erection pressed her core. She gasped, letting her head fall back. "Much better."

Dizzy from the sensations sparked by his lips and teeth on her neck, she dug her fingers into his shoulders and simply held on. He made his way from one collarbone to the other, nuzzling the fabric of her blouse out of his way, his crisp, silky hair caressing the underside of her chin. His scent filled her nostrils, woodsy and clean and fresh. Heat coiled low in her belly. She clenched her thighs on his hips, desperate to get closer.

His mouth found hers again as he leaned over, pressing her back to the solid surface. The quartz counter was cool under her, Rafe's chest hot and firm above. Her breasts swelled and tingled, squashed delightfully by his weight. His tongue demanded entrance, and she opened willingly. If it was possible to get drunk by kissing someone, she never wanted to be sober.

The thought dashed cold water on her blazing libido.

Drunk. Sober. Shyla.

Shyla had been the catalyst that imploded her marriage to Ricky, and Natalie had learned her lesson. Until her sister's situation was resolved, she needed to stay away from relationships.

Reluctantly she cupped his jaw, the bristles of his whiskers soft yet prickly under her palms. At the pressure of her hands, he immediately broke the kiss. She realized her eyes were closed and opened them, the pendant light dangling from the ceiling creating a halo around his head. His gaze was dark and intense, half-hidden behind heavy lids.

She couldn't keep herself from touching him. But she couldn't keep kissing him, either. She'd never felt this combustible before, as if his mere presence set her alight. It frightened and delighted her.

It made her yearn.

Rafe's heart thundered in his chest, and he struggled to control his breathing. Natalie's hair spread out on the shiny white and grey counter, a sable fan around her flushed face. Her fingers trembled and he turned his head to brush his lips against her palm.

The refrigerator motor kicked in, the hum loud in the silence fizzing between them. Though she'd indicated a halt to the proceedings by her pressure on his jaw, she had given no other hint she wanted him to move. Instead, her hands swept down his neck, over his shoulders to his biceps and back again, and her heels remained tucked into the hollows of his knees.

He braced his forearms on the counter, holding himself above her, and toyed with the strands of her hair framing her head. "Well." It was the best his lust-fogged brain could come up with.

Her eyelids flickered and a small grin tugged the corners of her rose-pink mouth. "Well, indeed." Her thumb traced his lower lip. His tongue darted out to taste it. She sucked in a breath. "I don't do this with everyone I work for."

He froze. Good god. He'd forgotten. He shoved off the counter and stepped backward so fast he almost stumbled. "I am so sorry."

She winced. "Now it's my turn to apologize. That's not what I meant. I'm not accusing you of anything." She wriggled to a sitting position and smoothed the fabric of her blouse. "I was trying to explain *my* actions. I'm the one who kissed *you*, remember?"

She appeared sincere, but that was no comfort. "I should know better."

"We're both intelligent adults." Her exasperated tone suggested she wasn't certain whether to include him in that description or not. "Surely we can handle a little thing like a kiss without calling in the cavalry."

Little thing like a kiss. It hadn't been a *little thing*

to him. Desire had engulfed him like wildfire, fierce, demanding, possessive. But if she considered it nothing more than flirtation, he would never push the issue. "Right. Of course." He circled around her, taking a wide path between the island and the wall of cabinets, and opened the dishwasher, half-blind with arousal, shame, and disappointment.

A soft thump signalled she'd slid off the counter. "Rafe. Look at me."

Reluctantly, he raised his gaze from the dirty silverware in his hand. She regarded him with her head tilted to one side. "I liked kissing you. *Really* liked it. But we don't know each other that well, and we're working on a project that neither of us wants to screw up."

She was right. Though he felt he knew her in his soul, she didn't know *him*. She didn't know he was keeping secrets from her, secrets that affected her ability to do her job properly. If he continued to hide his mother's corrupt practices, and she wrote the book, and then someone *else* discovered what had happened, she would look like a fool.

He didn't want Natalie to look like a fool.

He couldn't reveal his mother wasn't the paragon everyone believed her to be.

"I understand. There can't be anything between us." It had been a mistake to give in and kiss her. And his mistakes were never small or insignificant. His mistakes meant people suffered.

Even died.

Chapter Thirteen

Natalie fell asleep that night trying not to think of
the way Rafe's kisses had touched every nerve in her
body and set them dancing.

She woke to a searing, choking sensation burning
her chest and the shriek of an alarm shattering her
skull. Bolting upright, she stared wildly about her
bedroom, disoriented and terrified. Her gasp of shock
drew heated air into her lungs and set off a racking
cough. She rolled off the bed and flattened onto the
floor.

Fire.

A menacing roar rumbled through the wall
separating her room from the neighbour's apartment.
Keeping her head low, she swung an arm up and
scrabbled on her nightstand. Her wild motions
knocked her phone down and it disappeared behind
the bed, but she managed to grab her glasses. Shoving
them onto her nose, she stared in disbelief.

The paint on the wall was *bubbling.*

The skin on her scalp prickled and primal instincts
screamed *run!* Abandoning her phone, she scuttled
backwards on hands and knees. In the living room,
cooler air swept up her thighs and under her over-
sized T-shirt and she risked rising into a crouch. She
snatched up the coat she'd tossed onto the back of her
couch the night before and her brand-new laptop from
the coffee table, raced to the door leading to the hall—

—and came to a screeching halt.

Caution warred with panic. A long-lost memory
from a safety course she'd taken as a teenager surfaced

and she pressed her palm to the door.

Hot.

Were the flames already licking at the other side?

She fled back down the short hall to the living room and the sliding glass doors opening onto her tiny balcony. Freezing night air bit her exposed skin, raising goosebumps. With her coat draped over her arm and laptop tucked under the same elbow, she leaned over the metal railing. Thank god she lived on the first floor, which meant the ground was only about two metres away.

Glass shattered and the roar of the fire rose in volume. Smoke billowed from behind the solid wooden barrier separating her deck from her neighbour's. Taking a deep breath, she gripped the top rail with her free hand, tucked her bare foot onto the bottom support of the railing, and swung her other leg over. Icy metal gnawed into her sole and palm and other tender bits as she straddled the rail. Hurriedly, she shifted her weight until she was clinging to the outer edge.

Sirens wailed, growing louder and louder, and red lights flashed on the glass of her patio doors. Perched precariously on her toes, she didn't wait to be rescued. She pushed off from the deck.

A winter's accumulation of snow softened her landing, though a crust of ice scraped her shins and calves when she broke through. She fell backward onto her ass and squeaked at the arctic dampness. Struggling rapidly to her feet, she floundered through the chilly drifts, across two lanes thankfully empty of traffic, and onto a snow-covered boulevard.

Only then did she turn to look at the building. Greedy orange flames licked around the now glassless door and window frames of her neighbour's apartment. An odd glow danced behind the curtains of her own bedroom window. She stared, transfixed.

"Miss? Ma'am? Are you okay?"

Dazed, she turned her head with aching slowness. After the flurry of her escape, her body was shutting down, every muscle locking tight, making movement near impossible. "What?" It took extreme effort to unhinge her jaw enough for the single syllable to sneak through.

A hulking man loomed next to her. He wore a black knit cap, and his face was hidden behind a huge beard. "It's cold out here. You should get in my truck."

Her thought processes were sluggish, fogged with fear. It took her several moments to realize that not all of the rumbling and roaring assaulting her ears was coming from the blazing building. A huge diesel pickup was parked, engine running, on the other side of the two lanes farthest from her apartment. In fact, several vehicles lined the street, though it was a no parking zone and it was as dark as midnight. People stood on the sidewalk, gawking and taking videos.

She couldn't feel her feet and the thin fabric of her T-shirt did nothing to protect her from the wind. "What time is it?"

"Just after five. Please, ma'am. Get in my truck. You're freezing." He touched her elbow gently. "Let's put your coat on, too."

Silently, she let him help her into her coat, climbed into his monster truck, and placed her laptop on the seat beside her. Shuddering with relief at the heat pouring from the vents, she tucked her knees inside her coat and pulled the puffy fabric over her toes. The pain as they thawed wasn't nearly strong enough to distract her from the inferno raging outside her window.

Rafe climbed the steps out of the pool after his early morning swim. Since Natalie had discovered him in the nude, his morning workout had become both amusing and arousing. After last night, it *definitely* leaned more toward the latter.

Snagging a towel off the neat stack he kept on a wooden shelf, he gave himself a quick rub down, stepped into his black rubber slides, and headed down the hall to the main part of the house, passing the kitchen counter on his way.

The kitchen counter on which, less than twelve hours ago, he'd kissed Natalie. Where Natalie had kissed him.

Kissed. What a weak word for the sensations that had flooded him.

He'd had a small panic attack when she'd reminded him of their professional relationship, but she'd calmed those fears. He trusted himself not to take advantage of the situation and it was good to know she didn't feel pressured in any way.

Not that it mattered. It wasn't the possible impropriety that might prevent a repeat of those actions. It would be her concerns that they didn't know each other well and that his mother's biography had to be a priority.

As he made his way up the stairs to the second floor, he pondered those two issues. The solution to getting to know each other was easy—all they needed was time. And the book would be done in less than two months if Natalie met Otto's deadline—which he had no doubts she would.

Which left the question—what did *he* want? While he hadn't been a monk since reaching adulthood, he'd conducted his relationships at arm's length. Maybe once he'd dreamed of a wife and family, but for a long time now he'd believed that wasn't in his future. He hated being unprepared, being uncertain. And what could be more uncertain than trusting another human being with his heart?

In his bedroom, he tossed the towel to the floor. Exactly as scheduled, his smart screen beeped into life. Six am. His routine was so set that NASA could use it to schedule their launches.

"Local news headlines." The eerily natural voice followed him into the ensuite. "An apartment fire on Ospika Avenue causes evacuation of all tenants." His hand froze on the shower faucet.

Natalie lived in an apartment building on Ospika Avenue.

The address was on the contract she'd signed. He might have driven by once or twice in the past week for no particular reason.

"Emergency services responded to an early morning fire at Tiffany Place Apartments. Bystanders reported seeing at least one tenant jumping from a first story balcony to escape the flames. Drivers are being asked to avoid the area while fire crews work to contain the blaze."

Natalie lived in Tiffany Place Apartments.

He abandoned his shower. Snatching up his phone, he searched for her number, hit connect and speaker, and tossed it on the bed. As the first ring trilled out, he grabbed yesterday's shirt. The material clung to his still damp skin, and he cursed as he struggled to push his arms into the sleeves.

The call rang...and rang and rang and rang. His pants caused yet more trouble and he staggered, almost falling, as it went to voicemail. Her cheerful, carefree message was *not* reassuring. He disconnected.

He flew down the stairs, risking life and limb on the open riser wooden treads. Once in his car, he tried calling again as he waited for the garage door to rise. Every second he was delayed ratcheted his anxiety up another notch.

Voicemail again.

By the time he slammed to a stop a couple blocks away from her apartment, he was in a frenzy. His heart beat so high in his throat he saw stars. Or maybe that was the flashing emergency lights. Police vehicles, various-sized fire trucks, and ambulances blocked two lanes of the wide divided street. A pumper truck poured water from four-storeys high and people in heavy fire protection gear moved with purposeful intent.

Leaving his car illegally parked for the first time in his life, he jogged toward the chaotic scene. Smoke billowed in huge clouds and the scent of burning wood and plastic stung his nose. Despite the early morning, crowds lined the barricades that had been placed a safe distance away.

He scanned the onlookers, searching for a familiar cap of dark-brown hair, the bright red of her coat, the multi-coloured bobble on her toque.

Nothing.

The apartment was on an intersection. He strode to the corner, snow melted from the press of many feet seeping through his shoes, and made his way up the cross street.

This also had two lanes heading in each direction, with a boulevard in between. Emergency vehicles clogged the lanes nearest the building, but several cars and trucks were parked on the far side of the wide divider.

He was beginning to despair of ever finding her in the chaos when a gruff voice claimed his attention. "Hey! Mister!"

He turned to see a man his own height but twice as broad standing near a jacked up black pickup. "Are you talking to me?"

"Yeah." The man jerked a thumb over his burly shoulder. "There's a lady in my truck says she knows you. Natalie, her name is."

When Natalie spied Rafe through the windshield of Tank's truck, she thought he was a figment of her imagination.

Tank. Even her rescuer's name added to the otherworldliness feeling she was swimming in. She'd been praying for more than an hour that the whole morning was something her brain had conjured up and that she'd wake from the nightmare soon. But seeing Rafe striding with ferocious intent through the slushy snow of the boulevard brought that wishful thinking crashing down around her.

"That's a friend of mine. The tall man with the dark hair in the black jacket." Her limbs were leaden, and she couldn't even raise the energy to point. "Would you get him for me?"

"You bet." Tank opened the driver's door, stepped out, and closed it. She heard his shout through muffled ears.

He had done his best to comfort her and given no indication he had anywhere else to be, but she couldn't impose on him any longer. He'd explained he was on his way home from graveyard shift at one of the nearby pulp mills when he'd seen her jump from her balcony and had already stifled several yawns.

Her door opened with a suddenness that made her flinch and she was enveloped by strong arms. The tears she'd been holding at bay welled and overflowed.

"Natalie. My god. Why didn't you answer your phone?"

"It's in my apartment." She stuttered the words through choking sobs as she pressed her cheek against Rafe's chest. The arm of her glasses dug into her temple. She didn't care. He smelled strongly of chlorine and his bark was savage, yet she'd never felt so safe. "Tank let me use his. The only number I could remember was my parents' old landline. I called them and told them not to worry." They'd asked if she wanted them to come, but the village where they lived was ninety minutes away and there was nothing they could do. She'd told them to stay put and she'd phone again when she had more news.

"What happened?"

"I don't know." She sniffed noisily. "I woke up and there was smoke and heat. The paint was boiling on the walls. The *paint*, Rafe."

Chapter Fourteen

He squeezed her tighter and she burrowed in, shoulders heaving as she tried to control her sobs. The composure she'd been clinging to shattered as the memories of those terrifying minutes hurricaned through her.

"It's okay. I've got you now." His hand cupped the back of her head in a protective gesture. She had the oddest sensation her lungs had filled with smoke again.

This time, it was a sweet, tender smoke that soothed and warmed her. Slowly her breathing eased and trembling subsided. In a distant corner of her mind, she wondered what exactly had brought him to her at this moment, but she didn't have the energy to ask. She was just happy he was here.

"Have the medics checked you?"

She shook her head without moving out of his embrace. "I'm fine. I didn't get burned. I got out in time." Her shudders threatened to return at the thought of what could have happened, but she willed them away.

"She jumped off a balcony." Tank's bass tones rumbled from behind. "I saw her walk away, so I don't think she hurt anything."

"I told you, I'm fine." With great reluctance she lifted her head from the shelter of Rafe's chest. Avoiding his piercing gaze, she reached around and patted her laptop. "At least I saved this. I can keep working on the biography."

"For Christ's sake. I don't care about that." Red fury sparked embers in his dark eyes. She knew it wasn't directed at her, and in a perverse way his rage made her feel even more protected, as if he had the power to douse the flames tearing through her home with sheer willpower. "And I don't care what you say. I'm a doctor, and you're getting checked out. Now."

He scooped her off the seat. Her protest was automatic. "I can walk."

"You don't have any shoes. You're not walking."

"My computer!" She squirmed and his hold tightened. With a grumble so deep she could feel it vibrating his chest, he twisted so she was facing the cab of the truck.

"Here." Tank leaned across the seat, the laptop looking small in his meaty hand. She reached for it, but he didn't let go. "Are you okay going with this guy? I can stick around if you want."

She glanced at Rafe's face and sighed. He looked his fiercest and most forbidding, with narrowed eyelids and clenched jaw. "He's much nicer than he looks. Really. Thanks for everything."

"No worries. I'm sorry about your apartment."

Rafe stepped back and she swung the door shut. Tank waved through the window and pulled away from the curb. Grief swept through her, as if her best friend was heading off to war. God, she was a mess if a random stranger—no matter how friendly and kind—could make her feel like that.

"What am I going to do?" She couldn't help the quaver in her voice. "I've lost everything."

"You don't know that." He set off toward the nearest ambulance. The only indication he was aware of her weight in his arms was the tightness of tendons in his neck. "Try not to worry until you get an official report. Right now, you're going to the paramedics."

Much to Rafe's relief, Natalie's self-assessment was confirmed by the medics. During medical school and residency, he'd seen terrible trauma caused by house fires and it held a special horror for him.

The medic treated the abrasions the icy snow had scraped on her legs. "Don't be surprised if you have a tendency to cough from the smoke inhalation during the next few days," she warned as she pulled off her rubber gloves, "and if it gets worse than it is now, please seek further medical attention."

"I will." Natalie shifted on the collapsed cot inside the ambulance and stood up. He was waiting at the wide-open rear doors, and she shuffled toward him. The medic had given her blue disposable booties for her bare feet, but they would be no better than tissue paper in the snow.

He handed her the laptop, which he'd been in charge of during her examination. She took it and then scowled when he held out his arms. "You're not carrying me again."

"I carry you or you stay here." He planted his feet, his arms extended and steady. Behind her, the medic shook her head and rolled her eyes, whether at his Neanderthal tone or Natalie's stubbornness, he wasn't sure.

He also didn't care what she thought. He was carrying Natalie and that was that.

"Good grief." She glared down at him, hands on her hips. The movement revealed the threadbare T-shirt she wore under her coat and her naked legs pebbled with gooseflesh.

He glared back. "Stop being pig-headed and let me take you home."

Her bottom lip wobbled, desolation sweeping across her features. "I don't have a home."

"Come home with me, Natalie." He patted her foot, her toes icy through the feeble paper covering. "You'll stay with me. Until you figure things out."

Mouth pressed in a thin line, she gave a jerky nod, crouched, and slid into his arms. His heart rate slowed and his pulse settled, simply by having her near, protected. Safe.

After thanking the medic, he threaded his way outside the barricade, down the street, and to his car. He'd started it by the app on his phone before leaving the ambulance and she moaned as he lowered her to the heated seat. "That feels so good."

The drive home took only a few minutes. In the garage, she pushed open her door before he had the gearshift in park. He followed her inside. She peeled off the booties, crumpled them up, and shoved them in her pocket.

And then stood in the middle of his living room, shoulders slumped, her back to him.

He circled around so he could see her face. Shock and sorrow had etched deep lines around her mouth and dark pouches under her eyes.

"Now what?" She lifted her palms and let them drop to her side in a helpless motion that made him want to fold her into his arms and never let her go. "What do I do now?"

"Is there anyone you should let know you're safe? You said you called your parents, but what about Shyla? Or the Silverberries?"

Her eyes widened. "The Silverberries. Oh my god, they'll be frantic."

He pulled out his phone. "Use mine."

She didn't take it, just stared with frustration. "I don't remember any numbers. Who memorizes phone numbers these days?"

"What about social media?" He hated it himself but figured she would be the type to use it. "Or where they work? We can Google business numbers."

"Yes." She pressed her fingers to her eyes. "I'm not thinking clearly. Helen will be at her tattoo parlor today. I can call her there and she'll tell everyone else.

What time is it?"

Tattoo parlor? The grey-haired woman he'd met at the rock-climbing gym didn't fit his image of a tattoo parlor owner. He shrugged that away for now. "Not yet eight o'clock."

"God. This day has lasted forever already." She scrubbed her hands in her hair and the scent of smoke intensified. She sniffed. "Is that me?"

"You'll want a shower. I'll find some clothes. They won't fit, but they'll do until we can get you something else."

"You keep saying *we*." Her gaze was luminous, eyes huge behind her glasses, pupils still blown in lingering shock.

"I'm not leaving you to deal with this on your own, Natalie."

She bit her lip, but not before he saw it tremble. Then she frowned. "Wait a minute. Did you say eight? You should be at work."

"I'll let them know I'm not coming in today." He was never sick and always booked his mandated vacation well in advance. His lab partners would think he was dying.

"No. You should go. I'll have that shower and appreciate the offer of clothes." She clutched the fabric of her coat in grimy hands.

He would have offered to take it, but was pretty sure she didn't want to stand before him in nothing but a ratty T-shirt that barely skimmed her thighs. "You shouldn't be alone."

She straightened her shoulders. "I'll be fine. I need to find out what I have to do, for insurance and...stuff." She waggled her fingers. "Maybe it's not as bad as I think, and I'll only have to be out of the apartment for a few days."

Given her description of bubbling paint, he didn't think that was the case, but he wasn't cruel enough to say so. She was looking more like herself, and he didn't want to kill the light in her eyes.

Still... "Are you sure?"

"I'm sure." Her stomach rumbled and she giggled with a faint edge of hysteria. "And I'll order myself some breakfast, I guess. Once I'm presentable and get my laptop up and running."

"You will not." Her eyebrows lifted at his growl. He softened his tone. "You'll help yourself to what's in my kitchen. There's cereal, yogurt, eggs—everything you need."

"Really, Rafe, there's no need—"

"There is a need. *My* need." He used his thumb to brush a trace of soot off her cheek. "I didn't know I could be as terrified as I was this morning. Make yourself at home, Natalie. I mean it."

She blinked and he was relieved to see her dazed, shocked look receding. "What made you come, Rafe? How did you know?"

"I heard it on the news." He couldn't help it. He needed to feel her safe in his arms again. He folded her into his embrace, ducking his head and shoulders to shelter her. "I remembered your address from the contract. I couldn't *not* go to you."

For a moment she held on like she'd held on in Tank's truck—like he was her rock, her anchor. Then she gave a small wriggle, and he released her.

She tucked her hair behind her ears and shot him a shy glance. "I stink. And the saying 'nothing but the clothes on my back' has never had a more personal meaning. But I'm going to be okay, Rafe. Thank you. Now go to work."

It took several minutes of nagging, but Natalie finally convinced Rafe to leave. Before he did, he brought her upstairs, led her past the room where she usually worked to another spare room, this one with a bed and dresser and nothing else, brought her a pile of clothes, and kissed her.

Gently. Sweetly. Heartbreakingly.

If she wasn't careful, she'd fall in love with him. And that would never do.

As she showered away the stench clinging to her skin and hair, she distracted herself from her own woes by thinking of Shyla.

It seemed much longer, but it had only been a few days since they'd brought her home from Quesnel. The cash and laptop she'd stolen wouldn't support her for long. Waiting for her to get in touch was like waiting to be mowed down by an avalanche. She knew it was coming. She just didn't know when. It could be two years or two hours. Relief intertwined with guilt when she pondered the possibility she may never reach out again.

Despite the crushing disappointment of Shyla squandering Natalie's hard-earned money and compounding the crime with theft, she couldn't give up on her.

Even after multiple applications of shampoo, her hair still smelled of smoke. Giving it up as a bad job, she left the warm, humid comfort of the shower, wrapped a towel around her torso, and scurried quickly to the bedroom. As she dried herself, she regarded the selection of clothes Rafe had left her. She didn't exactly have a stick figure, so the waists might not be too big, but he was so tall she would be swimming in them, nonetheless. Yet what choice did she have? She resolutely refused to think of her wardrobe, if not in ashes, then ruined by the very water needed to douse the flames.

In the end she chose a pair of athletic shorts that hung so far below her knees they were almost capris, along with a short-sleeved T-shirt. She had to roll the sleeves of the fleece hoodie she layered over top several times to stop them from falling over her hands. In the kitchen, she found a couple safety pins and cinched the waist of the shorts. At least she wouldn't have to worry about them falling off any second.

Feeling slightly more human, she planned her day. Breakfast first, followed by calls to Helen, her apartment manager, and her insurance company.

After that, she'd take it one step at a time.

Chapter Fifteen

As a pathologist, Rafe was detailed and meticulous. He scrutinized his results, avoided assumptions, and distrusted coincidences. And he never made mistakes.

The day of the fire, he did his work with even more painstaking attention, refusing to be distracted by thoughts of Natalie. Yet, she took over his mind to the exclusion of all else far too often. It was dangerous—not just to his own peace but the health of the patients whose lives hung on the accuracy of his analyses.

This was why he couldn't afford a relationship. His focus had to be on his job, or the results could be fatal. Literally.

As if sensing he was grimmer than usual, his lab mates left him alone. Not that they were ever a chatty bunch—they were as socially awkward as he was, which made for a soothingly quiet atmosphere.

After one especially delicate analysis, he took a short break. Not wanting to be overheard, he found refuge at the bottom of a stairwell, took out his phone, and dialled Elizabeth's number.

"Rafe! How are you?" His stepsister's greeting was bright and bubbly and his heart immediately lightened.

"I'm fine. Jude treating you well?"

"Like a princess. Which you'd know already if you'd called when we got home, like Otto did."

He winced. He hadn't spoken with Elizabeth or Jude since their Mexican wedding, though they'd been back in town for more than a week. It wasn't that he didn't want to see them. It was more that he didn't want to be the grumpy third wheel. Hoping this call wasn't a mistake, he plowed on. "I have a favour to ask."

"You?" Shock rang through the speaker. "You never ask for favours."

He gritted his teeth. "I am now."

"What do you need? Of course I'll do it." She sounded positively *thrilled* at the idea.

He couldn't understand her pleasure, but he'd go with it. "I need you to buy some women's clothes."

Silence. "Um...what?"

This was excruciating. "Did you hear about the apartment building fire this morning?" Elizabeth made an assenting sound that managed to combine compassion and curiosity. "A friend of mine lived there. Right next door to where the fire started from the looks of it. She needs to replace her clothes."

"A friend. A *female* friend."

"Yes." His palm was sweating, and he switched the phone to his other hand. "Can you buy her a few things? I'll pay you back, but you'll know what she needs. I'll come by your place after work to pick them up." He couldn't have her discovering that the female friend she was so shocked to hear about was actually *living* with him, no matter how temporary the arrangement.

"I can do that." Elizabeth was a freelance graphic designer. Her flexible schedule was one reason he had thought of her.

That and the fact he was pretty sure Natalie would be far more comfortable knowing Elizabeth had bought her underwear and bras than knowing he had.

Natalie knew it was pointless to expect Rafe home any time before five at the very earliest, but that didn't stop her from watching the clock.

She'd spent the day mired in frustration and

futility. She had attempted to set up her laptop as a phone but had mostly relied on email and chat functions. The apartment manager had no idea when she might be able to return to see if anything was salvageable, and the insurance company wanted an itemized list of everything she owned down to the spices in her cupboard. She was put off and pushed around and patronized more times than she could count.

She needed to *do* something—*any*thing—to try and get back to normal, yet was stymied at every turn. If only she had her car...but she'd abandoned her keys in her frantic escape.

Feeling trapped and anxious, she couldn't focus. Working on Eugenia's biography would have given her a sorely needed sense of accomplishment, but it had seemed almost...disrespectful...to use her as a distraction from the morning's disaster.

She also rejected going for a swim. She knew Rafe had been sincere when he'd told her to make herself at home, but she didn't want to overstep any unspoken boundaries.

Besides, *he* might be comfortable swimming in the nude, but *she* wasn't.

By the time his car pulled into the driveway just before six o'clock, she was fizzing with pent-up energy. She'd been pacing in the entryway, peering out the glass side panels that framed the heavy door on every pass. Hurrying to the garage, she entered before he'd even finished parking, and then shifted her weight from foot to foot until he climbed out of the driver's seat and nodded over the car's roof.

"I'm so glad you're back. I'm going crazy on my own."

Her effusive welcome seemed to disconcert him. A faint flush coloured his hard cheekbones. "Rough day?" He frowned. "What a stupid thing to say. Of course it was."

"I don't want to talk about it. Or think about it." Though the fire and its ramifications had consumed her for hours, she realized she'd used the busy work to stop herself from accepting what had happened, from fully acknowledging the truth.

Her home was gone.

Her skin prickled and she closed her eyes tightly to hold back tears. After a moment, she opened them to find Rafe still in position on the other side of the car, watching her intently.

"I'm sorry." What had possessed her to greet him in the garage? It was like she was a sentry preventing entry. "This is weird, isn't it? I'll get out of your way."

He rolled his shoulders in an odd sort of shrug. "Since you're here, you can help me bring some things in."

"Of course." Thankful for a task, any task, she crossed the concrete floor, icy under her bare feet, opened the rear door—

—and stared.

If she'd expected anything, it would have been groceries or household supplies. Instead, she saw a pile of shopping bags emblazoned with the names of women's clothing stores. A dozen or more, in a rainbow of colours.

On the far side, Rafe bent down and hooked his fingers in the loops of several bags. "Can you get the rest?"

Speechless, she nodded and gathered up what was left. He held the interior door open with his foot and let her pass.

"We might as well bring them to your room." His tone was matter of fact as he headed for the stairs. Still trying to process what was going on, she followed.

In the second spare room—*her* room as he'd called it—he plunked his burdens on the bed and stepped back. "I hope this is enough to get by for a few days. If something doesn't fit, I have all the receipts. I had to guess at your size."

She couldn't catch her breath. When she put the bags she carried next to his, most of the bed was covered. "You bought me clothes?"

He made that odd rolling shrug again, as if his shirt was itchy. "Not me. My sister Elizabeth. I figured she'd do a better job. There's shampoo and hand cream and stuff, too."

The tears that had been so close to the surface all day boiled at the back of her nose. She'd never felt so cared for. This was something she'd expect from the Silverberries—in fact, Helen had offered to take her shopping as soon as she felt up to it—but not Rafe.

What was she going to do with him?

Natalie's stare swept from the bed full of bags to him and back again. She should have looked ridiculous in his far too big clothing—the shorts hanging to her shins, the huge, baggy sweatshirt hiding her curves. Instead, he felt a curl of possessiveness that made his fingers itch to touch her.

She remained silent and he began to worry, his skin stretched taut. Had he made a mistake, presenting her with these gifts? He'd only been trying to help.

He opened his mouth to apologize. Before a syllable could escape, she flew into his arms, the force of her embrace staggering him back into the wall.

"Thank you." The words were whispered against his chest. "I'll pay you back, I promise."

"No, you won't." He buried his nose in her hair. Despite the faint underlay of smoke that still lingered, she smelled of his own shampoo and soap and his body tightened.

She smelled like *his*.

"I will. It's the least I can do."

He straightened and tipped her chin up with two

fingers on the silky underside of her jaw. Her warm brown eyes sheened with tears and a single drop tracked down her cheek. He wiped it with his thumb, bumping her glasses with his knuckle. "They are a gift, Natalie. Thanks is enough."

"No, it's not. Just saying it is not enough at all."

Her kiss started sweet and gentle, closed lips brushing back and forth on his. A groan rumbled in his throat and his hands swept down her body to her hips. She rose on tiptoe, her breasts sliding up his chest in soft, pillowy temptation, her leg hooking behind his knee, opening her centre.

The thin, slippery fabric of the athletic shorts did little to hide the heat she pressed against his thigh. His hands found the loose hem of the sweatshirt and slid underneath seeking skin, only to be thwarted by another layer of clothing.

All the while her mouth was busy on his, her tongue tangling, her lips caressing. Her fingers unfastened the buttons of his shirt and spread the edges wide. She licked a trail from his jaw to his pecs, rubbing her nose in the wiry hairs there.

Through the haze of lust, a warning voice whispered that she was only doing this out of gratitude. Pressing his thumbs gently on her jaw, he pushed her away. "You don't have to do this."

Her eyelids drooped over almost black irises, her lips plump and rosy, her cheeks flushed. "What?"

"You don't have to thank me like this."

She stiffened, lowering her raised leg, and her sleepy, satisfied look evaporated. "You think this is because you bought me clothes?"

Her anger seemed unwarranted. He was trying to be a gentleman. "You said *saying* thanks wasn't enough." His spine was to the wall so he couldn't step back. Despite the snap in her eyes, she hadn't moved away. It was sweet torture to have her pressed warmly against him from groin to knee while she glared.

"The clothes were just the tipping point. You opened your home to me. Searched me out to make sure I was safe. I have so *much* to thank you for. But I would never, *never* use sex to pay off a debt."

"Then why? Why the kisses? Why *this*?" He pressed his hips forward, his erection unmistakable and challenging.

The fire faded from her face, leaving her bleak and vulnerable. "I don't want to say it." The whispered words tore at his heart.

"You can tell me, Natalie." He crouched and rubbed his nose against hers in a tender caress. "You can tell me anything."

He was the one with secrets he couldn't share.

For long seconds she stared, their faces so close all else blurred. "I could have died." Her voice broke. "I've been ignoring it all day. I could have died, Rafe. And I want to live. I want to *live*."

Chapter Sixteen

Natalie was dizzy from the turmoil of her emotions. Sure, gratitude was mixed up in it, but she knew that wasn't the true reason she'd launched herself at Rafe. The true reason was what she'd just confessed.

She wanted to *live*.

She'd put much of her life on hold because of Shyla, either anticipating her next cry for help or trapped by having to deal with the fallout of her sister's actions to the exclusion of her own needs.

Maybe it was time to let at least some of her guilt go.

Rafe hadn't said a word. She held her breath, waiting, watching. Who knew what calculations were going on behind that proud forehead?

His hands on her hips, he pressed her away. Her heart sank. He didn't want her, not like she wanted him. He only felt sorry for her. That was why he'd kissed her back.

Without a word, he took her by the hand and led her out of the room. She had to trot to keep up with his long, sure strides. At the end of the hall, he drew her into what was obviously the master bedroom.

Her heart rebounded out of the depths of her stomach into her throat. He stopped at the foot of the massive king-sized bed with its charcoal cover, took her free hand, and placed both her palms on the bare skin of his chest. Her fingers spread, the crinkly hairs tickling between them. A dull, rapid thudding reverberated behind the wall of muscle.

Still without speaking, he tucked his hands under

the waistband of her shorts—*his* shorts—and paused. He'd obviously discovered she was bare underneath. Sucking in a breath, he slipped them off until they puddled on the floor. She stepped out of them and flicked them away with her toes.

The T-shirt and hoodie she wore were more than adequate to cover her. They were longer than some dresses she owned. Used to own.

She squashed that pathetic thought and lifted her gaze from her contemplation of his chest to his face.

Whatever he saw in hers seemed to please him. The faint lines of concern around his eyes softened and a tiny smile curled the corners of his mouth. "Is this what you want, Natalie?"

"Yes." She barely breathed the syllable. "This."

He shrugged out of his shirt. It joined the shorts on the floor. His shoulders were broad and straight, and his torso tapered to a slim waist. A swimmer's build. The silver and black hair of his chest narrowed into a thin line that disappeared behind the front of his trousers.

Trousers that did little to hide his erection.

She palmed him through the fabric. He hissed and his hips jerked forward into her grip. The overly long sleeve of her sweatshirt fell over her hand, and she pushed it out of the way with irritation. It fell back down again. She released him to cross her arms over her body and grasp the hems of both the hoodie and T-shirt. They were so huge it was no struggle to divest herself of them at the same time. In an instant, she was naked.

Red flushed the harsh bones of his face and his eyes glittered. "May I?" He reached for her glasses. She nodded, and he slipped them off her nose and placed them on top of the high dresser behind him.

Thank god she was near-sighted. As close as Rafe was, she could still see his expression. She didn't want to miss a single moment.

Without touching her, his hands traced her shape, from shoulders to breasts to hips to core. Gooseflesh followed his motions as if he had stroked every inch. She arched her back, her nipples pointed and ready, begging for more.

He obliged. His big hands closed over her breasts, engulfing them, his palms heated brands. She moaned, swaying forward. Electric sparks of desire zipped along her nerves. Dampness bloomed at her centre. This was exactly what she'd wanted...to feel alive in a way she never had before.

Because she'd never been with Rafe before.

He bent over her, his chin brushing the crown of her head. She felt his words as much as heard them. "Undo my pants."

She hurried to obey. Her fingers slid behind the fastening at the waistband and his stomach muscles clenched. With a fumbling flick, she released the button and gripped the zipper tab. Protecting him with one hand inside the fly, she lowered the zip and freed him.

His length was hot and heavy, silky and strong. His fingers squeezed her breasts when she clasped him in both hands, his breath panting hot on her hair, fluttering the strands.

"You feel so good." She rubbed a thumb up the pulsing vein to the crown, unable to take her eyes off him. "You're gorgeous."

"Hah." It wasn't a laugh so much as an exhalation. "I don't know how long I can wait."

"No need on my account." She was ready. *So* ready. She lifted her chin and scraped her teeth on his collarbone. "Condom?"

He froze. "Shit."

"No condom?" She was going to die if he wasn't inside her soon.

"Don't go anywhere."

For a man who prided himself on being prepared, Rafe was a goddamn idiot. He'd known he was attracted to Natalie for weeks now. Why hadn't he bought condoms just in case?

Because he hadn't wanted to jinx it? No. Because he hadn't believed she'd ever allow him to get this close.

If he'd let himself hope and it never happened, it would have killed him.

He left her standing there, flushed, naked, and staring, paced with undignified haste to his ensuite, and scrabbled through the drawers.

It had been more than a year since his last sexual encounter. His partner then had been a doctor doing a three-month locum rotation at the hospital. She had been the perfect candidate—attractive, intelligent, business-like when it came to sex, and with a built-in expiration date.

He unearthed a lone foil packet tucked at the back of a drawer, clutched it, and returned to the bedroom—

—to find Natalie sprawled against the pillows at the head of his bed, legs wide in abandon, fingers stroking herself.

He stumbled to a stop, his knees weak, his stare locked on her beautiful, glistening centre.

"I see you found one. Thank god." Her voice was low, throaty, and relieved. "What are you waiting for?"

He could have watched her forever. His cock disagreed, bobbing hard and demanding against his belly. Quickly he shoved his pants off, ripped open the packet, and rolled on the protection. Her eyes gleamed and she ran her tongue along her lips.

With a lunge that would have done an adolescent boy proud, he launched onto the mattress and crawled up her body. How someone so much shorter than he could be *exactly* the right fit was a mystery he could unravel later.

Searching for control, he kissed her, tasting her sweetness and heat, building the tension past its already unbearable level. She wriggled and moaned beneath him, her fingers digging into his buttocks, urging him to move up.

To move in.

He surrendered to her wordless command. Braced on his elbows, he nudged his cock to her entrance. She opened her legs wider, lifted her hips, and pushed.

Her heat pulsed around the tip of his shaft. Clinging to control, he slid deeper, excruciatingly aware of every clench of her muscles, every gasp of her breath.

She clutched him, her heels hooked in the back of his knees, her arms wrapped around his shoulders. "So good."

He flexed his hips, grinding gently against her. Her head dropped back, and her eyelids fluttered closed. "Yes."

When he withdrew, she moaned. "No."

"Don't worry." He brushed his lips on her forehead. "I'm not going anywhere."

He advanced and retreated, advanced and retreated, setting a rhythm that coiled in his blood, snaked down his spine. She followed his lead, muscles relaxing as she welcomed him in, contracting when he pulled away. Her eyes remained closed, and a frown settled between her brows. He kissed it, hunching his back to reach, and driving himself even deeper.

Her release was a matter of quiet intensity. He held her as she quivered, rocked, whimpered, and then softened beneath him. He held still, his hardness engulfed in her silkiness, until her eyes opened.

With a tenderness that unmanned him, she touched his cheek with trembling fingers. "Rafe."

He swallowed, biting back emotion.

She drew him down until all his weight rested on her. Her lips on his ear sent shivers fluttering over his skin. "Now, Rafe. Take me like you need me."

And he did. He let himself go as he never had with anyone else, slamming home into her encompassing wetness, urged on by her pressing fingers, gripping thighs, encouraging words. Not once did he think about finesse, about technique, about performance.

She offered herself, and he took her, unashamedly, whole-heartedly.

And when he shattered, she held him as he shook, as he shuddered...

As he lost his soul to her.

Natalie's nose pressed into Rafe's armpit. He'd stretched his arm over his head to brace against the headboard, and at the end had collapsed on her as if he'd been shot.

Her lips curled in a Cheshire grin. *She* had done that. Driven him to such distraction he'd lost all control. Inhaling, she sucked in the scent of man, of sweat, of sex.

And with smug wonder, felt desire stir inside her once more. Maybe all she'd needed to regain the lustiness she'd lost after her divorce was a near-death experience.

Whatever the reason, she'd just had the best sex of her life.

With lazy strokes, she trailed her fingers over the bumps of Rafe's spine, feeling the muscles flex and shiver. With a groan he slid to the side. "Be right back."

He rolled to the edge of the mattress and headed to the ensuite, staggering slightly.

Her grin widened.

Water ran for a moment and then he reappeared, bracing his forearms against the door frame and glaring at her. "What the hell have you done to me? My legs feel like spaghetti."

"Me?" She stretched, arching her back and pointing her toes. His gaze swept up and down her, as tactile as a caress. "I didn't do anything."

"Minx." He crawled up from the foot of the bed, stalking her like a lion.

Then crumpled face down next to her. She giggled.

He twisted his neck to reveal one dark eye, the eyebrow above quirked in suspicion. "Did you just laugh at me?" His voice was muffled against the sheets.

"Of course not." She snorted again.

"As soon as I get my strength back, you'll pay for that." His eye closed. "I keep forgetting I'm not as young as I used to be."

She shifted to her side and snuggled next to his torso, lifting a bent knee to rest on his taut ass and laying her cheek on his shoulder blade. "Could have fooled me."

His back rose and fell with his breaths. Her heart, still beating heavily from exertion, thudded in her chest. Her eyes drifted shut, and for a few minutes she did nothing but *be*.

It was wonderful to be alive.

Chapter Seventeen

Natalie had attached herself to Rafe's back like a limpet. In the past, he would have allowed just enough post-coital cuddling to ensure his partner didn't feel rejected. Tonight, he held still so long his spine and hips protested, unwilling to break the bond weaving itself between them.

In the end, it was hunger that chased them from the bed. A gurgling and rumbling resounded in the quiet room and Natalie stirred. "Sorry." Her voice was slow and lethargic, as if she'd been sleeping. "I didn't eat much today."

He raised himself to his elbows and she slid to the mattress. Sitting on his heels, he ignored his aching joints and narrowed his eyes at her. "What do you mean you didn't eat much? I told you to help yourself."

"I had some toast. I just didn't have much of an appetite." She shrugged, her naked breasts lifting and falling. He refused to be distracted, though his cock twitched. Maybe he'd be ready for another round sooner than he thought.

But first, she needed to eat.

"I'll make omelettes." He rose from the bed and strode to the ensuite. "Take your time. Have a shower. See if anything Elizabeth bought you will fit. I'll be downstairs when you're ready."

By the time he returned to the bedroom after his own quick wash, it was empty. Water was running in the main bath down the hall. In the kitchen, he gathered ingredients and set about prepping dinner. Cooking was something he did out of necessity, but tonight he found himself enjoying the process. Cooking for two was a much different experience than his usual solitary meals. Taking care of Natalie was a privilege and joy, not a chore or duty. It carried none of the anxiety he usually felt at being responsible for another's well-being.

An odd feeling filled his chest, and he paused in chopping onions to examine it.

Was that...contentment? More solid than happiness, less temporary than joy?

He couldn't see the mezzanine from the kitchen, but his senses were so attuned to Natalie that she'd barely taken a step out of her room before he knew she was on her way down. Rejecting the urge to stare at her like a thirsty man at a glass of water, he turned the heat up under a low-edged pan and slid the chopped onions and green peppers into it, where they sizzled and popped.

"That smells heavenly." Her voice reached him from the bottom of the stairs, and he finally allowed himself to look up.

His grip on the spatula tightened. She wore black leggings and a blue, loose-fitting top, but now he knew what was underneath the concealing clothes. He couldn't help but picture rosy skin, curvy hips, and lush breasts. He swallowed. "You found something that fits, then?"

"Yes. You must have described me very well. Elizabeth did a great job." She stopped on the other side of the island and waved her hands in a helpless gesture. "I don't know how to thank you. Both of you. I honestly didn't expect this."

"If we forgot anything, or if you need to return anything for another size, please let me know." Did he sound as stuffy to her as he did to his own ears? He couldn't help it. It was either keep a stiff upper lip or fall to his knees and beg her to return to the bedroom.

If he could make it that far without ravaging her.

"I will, but I think I'm covered." She quirked her mouth in a wry grin. "Except for a phone and my car. My cell never did work properly after being dunked in Mexico, so I think I'll have to bite the bullet and get a new one. With any luck, insurance will cover it. But I don't know when I'll be able to get my car keys. And if they've been destroyed, I'll need to figure out how to get another set."

He added diced ham to the softened onions and green peppers, gave it a stir, and then poured the beaten egg mixture over it all. "If I had a second vehicle, I'd let you borrow it."

"You've done enough. Really." She pressed her palms flat on the quartz surface and leaned forward and back, rocking on her heels. "Helen offered to drive me around as needed. I'll arrange that tomorrow."

He realized she was avoiding looking him directly in the eyes. The confidence and affection she'd displayed in his bed had vanished. Sprinkling shredded cheese on the half-cooked eggs, he rounded the corner of the island, stopping a foot away from her. "Is everything okay? With us, I mean? You're not regretting what we did, are you?"

She lifted her chin at that, eyes flashing with familiar fire. "God, no."

The tight knot of tension between his shoulder blades eased. "Then why do you look so...uncomfortable?"

Her back slumped. She sighed and stepped into him, wrapping her arms around his waist. His own arms immediately encircled her shoulders. "I hate needing help. I'm the one who *gives* it. Being on the receiving end makes me twitch."

"I get that. I'm the same way." He curled over her, resting his chin on the crown of her head in what was becoming one of his favourite poses. "Just remember, you don't feel irritated or angry when you help someone, and neither do I when I am helping you."

Her breath huffed out, puffing warmth through the material of his T-shirt. "That's not one-hundred percent true. I do get angry. At Shyla, especially."

She almost whispered the last three words. He could feel the guilt cloaking her and did his best to offer comfort.

"From what I've seen, you have the deepest well of forgiveness and understanding of anyone I've ever known. I've always thought some sins were unforgivable. Yet, you just keep offering your heart to those you love, no matter what they've done."

For a brief moment, he was tempted to tell her about his mother, about his fears for the biography. Maybe together they could figure something out.

And then again, maybe he'd be the first person she couldn't forgive.

He wasn't ready to lose her yet.

An odd tone in Rafe's voice made Natalie wonder if his mention of unforgivable sins had a personal meaning. She lifted her head from the safety of his chest. He was staring into space, a muscle flexing in his jaw, black and silver stubble glinting.

"If Otto or Elizabeth hurt you, wouldn't you forgive them?"

"Of course." He spoke over her head. "But they're my family."

She wanted to ask if he'd forgive *her* something unforgivable, but couldn't. Yes, they'd had sex, but she'd practically begged him to, and as far as she knew it was a one-and-done deal. Nothing had really changed in their relationship, other than the fact she'd seen him naked. Had had him inside her. And wanted him again.

"Shyla's my family. It's not always easy, though." In fact, it seemed to be getting harder and harder. This last betrayal still stung. "Living with anger is draining and debilitating. Forgiveness doesn't mean you agree with someone's actions. It just means you accept them and try to move on."

"Not everyone is as understanding as you are."

His words implied this was a good thing, but an undercurrent of disapproval swirled below the surface. She drew in a breath to explore it further and became aware of a worrisome aroma. "I think the omelette is burning."

"Damn." He rounded the counter with long, quick steps, snapped off the heat and lifted the pan off the stove. Using a spatula, he checked the underside. "I think it's still edible."

She was rather relieved to put the conversation—one that had become more intense than she'd expected—to the side. "It'll be fine. I'm so hungry I could eat shoe leather." Opening the cupboard where she'd discovered the bread this morning, she pulled out a loaf. "I'll make the toast while you dish that out."

In a few moments, they were seated side by side on stools at the island. Her first mouthful was hot and savoury, gooey with cheese. She moaned. "This is much better than shoe leather." She heaped another forkful and shovelled it in.

Rafe ate in a much more dignified fashion, and she was done well before him. Licking her fork, she eyed his plate.

He saw her looking. After a pause he pushed it toward her. "Want to share?"

He was sweet to make the offer, especially since she was pretty sure he wasn't an eat-off-the-same-plate kind of guy. "That's okay. I'll make more toast. You need to restore your strength, too." She gave him a lewd wink.

He had just sipped from his water glass and choked on a mouthful. She grinned. She was also pretty sure he wasn't a spit-take kind of guy, so knowing she could make him laugh was very satisfying. She hopped off the stool and threw two more slices in the toaster. She'd avoid all carbs tomorrow. Today, she deserved the treat.

He crossed his silverware neatly on his plate and folded his arms on the counter. "It's been a long day. You must be exhausted."

"I don't feel that bad, actually." Maybe it was adrenalin. Maybe it was excellent sex. Either way, she was bursting with energy. Slathering peanut butter and raspberry jam on the now crispy slices, she took a bite standing up. "This morning feels like a million miles away."

"I drove by on my way home. Fire trucks were still there, keeping an eye on things."

This news dimmed her optimism, but she replied with bright determination. "That's good. I'm sure I'll get more details soon. Hopefully, I won't have to impose on you for long." She spoke around another mouthful of toast. "Insurance would probably cover a hotel stay. I should look into that, too."

"You are not staying at a hotel."

She blinked at his ferocious growl. "I didn't mean tonight. I'll definitely take you up on that. But I can't stay here long-term."

"Why not?" He shoved back from the counter and carried his plate and glass to the dishwasher and began loading them in. "You'll obviously lose time on the project, having to deal with the aftermath of the fire. We don't want you missing the deadline because you are distracted by personal issues. If you stay here, you can work on the book every available minute."

His words punctured something small and fragile that had ballooned behind her breastbone. He was only being practical and efficient. For someone who had put up plenty of roadblocks at the start of the project, he was now irritatingly focused on the end goal. His offer had nothing to do with wanting her to stay for personal reasons...and she couldn't let him see how much that disappointed her. "I don't know. It will disrupt you, and you don't like that."

"I'll survive." He sounded resigned more than welcoming. "Consider this your home, Natalie. At least for now." He crossed the living room and headed for the stairs. "I've got some work to do in my office. Have a good evening."

She stared after his vanishing form, gape-mouthed with confusion.

Chapter Eighteen

Rafe took refuge in his office for the rest of the evening. Maybe it was cowardly, but he needed time to examine the feelings swarming through his veins like fire ants.

When Natalie had suggested she take a room in a hotel, his knee-jerk need to shout *no* had frightened him. At forty-two-years old, he'd thought he was set in his solitary ways, even *preferred* to be alone. But ever since meeting her, he'd become more and more aware of everything his life lacked.

Having her in his house filled a void he hadn't allowed himself to notice—until she'd crossed his threshold. And now that she'd been in his bed, taken him into her body...he wasn't sure he could give her up.

Even though he knew he'd have to, eventually. He'd known brief moments of happiness in his life but had grown used to the knowledge it wouldn't last. He was sure to make a mistake that would destroy it.

If he was lucky, whatever he did would only hurt himself this time.

Shortly after he shut himself into his study, quiet footsteps passed by the closed door without pause. Soft thuds from the room where his mother's archives were kept gave him reason to believe Natalie had decided to spend time working. He gripped the arms of his chair, determined not to stalk in and demand she leave it be until she'd had a good night's sleep. Maybe he'd used the book as an excuse to keep her near, but he hadn't meant she should start work the same evening she'd lost her home. The sounds only lasted a few minutes, and then there was a pause before a faint click reached him. He poked his head into the hall and noted the door furthest away was now closed.

Apparently, she had gone to bed. It was barely eight o'clock, but she'd been running on fumes for hours. Had to have been. For god's sake, she escaped a burning building only fourteen hours ago. And then he'd ravaged her almost as soon as he'd returned home.

At her behest, but still...

He tiptoed down the hall. At the dark oak panel, he listened intently. Rustling papery sounds and the quiet screech of wood on wood gave him hope she was unpacking her clothes and putting them in drawers. She wouldn't go to all that bother if she was planning on leaving tomorrow, would she?

The sounds stopped and he froze. Was she going to open the door? There was no ensuite in the room so she might be heading to the hall bath.

If he came face to face with her now, would he be able to stifle his overwhelming impulse to invite her to spend the night in his bed?

Rafe was on the other side of the door. Natalie's skin rippled with the extraordinary awareness of his presence, the way it always did when he was near. Her fingers hovered over the handle, her brain warring over what to do. Open it and confront him on his precipitous retreat earlier? Keep it closed and come to grips with the fact he'd only had sex with her out of pity?

Her delay took the decision out of her control. The creak of a floorboard let her know he had abandoned his post. She cracked the door open a sliver in time to see him disappear into his own room. A room she would now forever equate with the hottest sex she'd ever had.

And she meant *ever*.

The nervous energy that had kept her on her feet for hours drained away, leaving her limp and shaky. Shedding her clothes and tossing them haphazardly onto the floor, she dropped her glasses on the nightstand, crawled naked between the sheets, and curled into a ball.

The next thing she knew, light was streaming into the room. Squinting against the brightness, she stretched out a hand to the nightstand in a blind search for her phone, finding only her glasses. She rubbed the heels of her hands into her eyes and then stared down at the unfamiliar blue and grey striped sheets.

Right. No phone. No belongings whatsoever. No *home*.

A small digital clock with bright red numbers told her it was just past seven. She couldn't remember falling asleep. Was it possible to get too much rest? She felt logy and lethargic, unwilling and unable to get out of bed. Flopping face down on the mattress, she let herself wallow, even shed a few more useless tears.

Then she wiped her wet face, flung back the covers, retrieved her glasses, and prepared to face the day.

A glance through the open door of Rafe's bedroom on her way downstairs revealed a neatly made bed and no evidence of its occupant. His absence was confirmed by a survey of the empty garage. Not sure whether to be relieved or disappointed that she hadn't had to chase him off to work like yesterday, she made herself toast and coffee and trudged back upstairs to the archive room. There, she powered up her laptop and settled in to study the files she'd set out last night.

In a couple hours, she'd get a hold of Helen and

accept her offer to go shopping. She needed a phone and a few other essentials that Rafe and Elizabeth had missed. For example, the prescription for her birth control pills. She and Rafe had used a condom, of course, and the chances of having sex again appeared to be getting slimmer by the moment, but that wasn't the point. She needed to get back into her routines as best she could.

For now, she'd start with Eugenia's biography. Because she wanted to, not because anyone expected it.

Rafe wasn't home yet when Natalie returned just after five. She waved goodbye as Helen drove off, made her way inside through the rear as usual, and then unloaded her purchases in her room, grinning with delight at her shiny new phone. She'd confirmed with her insurance company that a replacement device was covered so could appreciate being connected to the world without guilt at the expense. It was amazing how much better she felt simply being able to call, text, and surf whenever she wanted.

Settling against the pillows on her borrowed bed, she called her parents. Though she'd talked to them right after the fire, she knew they would still be anxious about her situation. They repeated their offer to come, but she deflected them, assuring them she was fine. "I'm staying with a friend," she said, "and there's no extra room. You'd have to go to a hotel. It's not worth it." The omission of who the friend was didn't bother her as much as the lie that there was no room. Rafe's house was plenty big enough. But as much as she loved her parents, she wasn't used to being the centre of their concern. Shyla had always held that place. Natalie's role was the predictable, dependable daughter, the one they didn't *have* to worry about.

Of course, they wouldn't have to worry about either of them if Natalie's actions had been different on the long-ago night.

After promising to be in touch when she had more news, she rang off and tapped to her messages app.

When the pimply teen at the store had connected the new phone to her old account, the notifications had flown in fast and furious. She'd only had a chance to skim through them until now and set about replying to each. Of course, they were only random numbers, since her contact details had been lost, but within half an hour she'd managed to coordinate who belonged to what message.

She saved Shyla for last. Her texts were unmistakable, mainly because, unlike the rest, none of them referred to the fire or asked how she was doing. All of them were self-absorbed orders for Natalie to get in touch right away, ranging from abjectly pleading to ferociously demanding.

Sucking in a fortifying breath, she pressed the phone icon, set it to speaker, laid it on her chest, and stared at the ceiling as she waited for her sister to answer.

Half-hoping she wouldn't.

"Hey." Shyla's voice was subdued, the single syllable refreshingly calm and lucid.

"Hey. Sorry I missed your tex—"

"I heard about the fire." A gasping sob echoed from the speaker. "Just today, from Mom and Dad. I'm so sorry."

Thrown off balance by her distress, Natalie needed a moment to form a reply. "Thanks. It was pretty scary."

"I'm such a bitch." Shyla had denigrated herself in the past, but then it had been sarcastic, as if she'd been articulating what she thought Natalie thought. Today's condemnation felt...sincere.

It wouldn't do to agree, of course, no matter what

the truth might be. "It's not your fault. What did you want to talk to me about?"

"I stole your laptop."

"Yes, I noticed." She couldn't keep the dryness from her tone. "And my credit cards."

"I have everything still. I didn't use the cards, and I didn't sell the laptop."

This call was getting weirder and weirder. The plain white ceiling had no answers, no matter how hard she stared, so she asked the obvious question. "Why not?"

Shyla replied with a question of her own. "Why did you come get me in Quesnel? You had to know I'd used the money you gave me for the rehab clinic to buy booze and drugs. Why didn't you just leave me there to rot?"

There was no mistaking it—her anguish was honest. Natalie's heart ached in treacherous sympathy. "You're my sister. I love you."

"How?" The word was a wail. "How can you still love me? I've done nothing but screw you over my whole life."

Again, it was a statement Natalie couldn't contradict, but also couldn't agree with. Not verbally, at least. "You're sick, Shyla. You need help. I know I didn't help you all I could in the past, but I'll never give up on you."

"I'm glad you're okay. I'm sorry. I'm so sorry. If anyone dies, it should be me, not you."

"Don't say that." The implications of Shyla's statement froze the blood in Natalie's veins. "Don't say things like that. Shyla?" Silence. "Shyla?"

Her phone blooped cheerily and she lifted it from her chest, holding it between her face and the ceiling. The connection had been cut.

"Damn it." She draped her arm over her closed eyes and glared at the inside of her eyelids. It wasn't the first time Shyla had made veiled threats about self-harm, but like the rest of the conversation, the statement had been made with a new, different tone.

One that, oddly enough, gave Natalie hope.

Again.

Chapter Nineteen

Rafe paused in the hall just outside Natalie's bedroom door.

He really should quit doing that. It was making him feel like a creep.

He'd heard the voices as soon as he'd entered the living room downstairs. He hadn't meant to eavesdrop, but as he'd climbed to the second floor the words were clearly audible.

He'd only met Shyla the one time, and she hadn't exactly been at her best that day, so he had no idea if the remorse he heard in her tone was sincere. But he knew Natalie pretty well by now, and there was no mistaking her love and compassion.

He didn't know how she did it. How could she be so endlessly forgiving?

He watched her through the opening. She lay stretched out on her bed, eyes covered by one plump arm, the other resting on her stomach. She wore the same T-shirt and leggings as yesterday, her feet encased in thin socks. Not wanting to alarm her, he rapped softly on the door frame before he spoke. "Natalie?"

Her arm flopped to her side, and she lifted into a sitting position, crossing her legs in front of her. "Hi. When did you get home?"

She sounded resigned. He took that as a sign she wasn't accusing him of listening in, but he wanted no misunderstandings between them. "A minute ago. I didn't mean to overhear. I'm sorry." He wanted to smooth away the lines between her eyes. "How are you?"

"Tired of people apologizing for things that aren't their fault." She smiled. "Don't worry about it. I could have shut the door if I wanted privacy."

The fact she was comfortable enough not to shut herself in made his insides ridiculously warm and fuzzy. "Want to talk about it?" He rarely encouraged people to share their feelings, but she was different.

She shook her head. "Nope. How was your day?"

He let her deflect. For now. He could always bring up the subject again if he sensed she needed to vent. "It was good. Thanks for asking."

"I'd like to see you in action sometime." She rolled to her right hip, stood up, and tugged the hem of her T-shirt down, but not before he'd caught a glimpse of the soft, smooth flesh of her abdomen. "I don't really know how you do what you do. It sounds interesting."

"I enjoy it, but there's not much action. A lot of tiny droppers and peering through microscopes and waiting for things to happen." The warm and fuzzy feeling strengthened. His mother and Otto had never had much interest in his career choice, especially after he'd abandoned direct patient care and buried himself in a lab. "If you're serious, though, I could arrange it."

"Great." She continued to fidget with the hem of her shirt, and then planted her hands on her hips and stared him down. Her brown eyes speared him from behind her lenses. "Okay, I've got to know. Was yesterday a one-and-done? I'm a big girl. I can take it. But if I'm going to live here for any length of time, I need to know where I stand."

He should have known she would confront the issue head on. It was rather a relief, as he hadn't been sure how to work his way to the topic that consumed his thoughts.

It sounded like she expected him to shrug her off. If that was what she wanted, he'd live with her decision. But it wasn't what *he* wanted. Not by a long shot. He swallowed. "That's your call. What do you think?"

Her determined expression softened into uncertainty. "I think I pressured you into sex yesterday. If you want to go back to just being friends, I'd understand."

He only realized he'd moved when he felt her shoulders, warm and strong, under his palms. She stared up, eyes wide, mouth parted. "Pressured me? God, I've been holding back from touching you ever since we met. I'm the one that took advantage. You were still in shock. I shouldn't have taken you like I did."

"Oh." She ran her tongue over soft, pink lips.

"Don't you know me well enough by now to realize I'm too selfish to do anything I don't want to do?"

"You're not selfish." Her hands rested on his hips.

His body responded—heating, hardening. He resisted the urge to press himself against her softness and concentrated on what she was saying.

"You are forthright and honest. I thought you might have slept with me because you felt sorry for me. I should have known better."

He groaned and pulled her tight. "Sorry is the last thing I feel for you." She stiffened and he wanted to hit himself. "I mean, I'm sorry about the fire. I'm not sorry it brought us together."

She relaxed again. For several moments, they did nothing but breathe. He became aware of her in a way he'd never experienced with another human being. Her blood coursing through her veins in tune with his. Their heartbeats thudding in tandem. Sparks of vitality arcing from her skin to his fingertips. The hard curve of her skull under his chin, strong yet delicate.

"Just to be clear"—her voice was muffled against his shirt—"this means you'd like to have sex again?"

A primitive voice inside him roared *yes*, the surge of emotion blocking his throat so he could only manage a whisper into her hair. "Anytime. You just have to ask."

A week later, Natalie surfaced from the depths of sleep, stretched, rolled over, and came nose to nose with Rafe. His dark lashes fluttered, and his lids rose, revealing soft, slumbery eyes.

"Morning." His voice rumbled over her like a distant thunderstorm, exciting yet safe.

It wouldn't do to get used to waking up like this, but she couldn't help the fizz of delight that tanged tartly on her tongue like orange juice. "Morning."

Rafe placed a large hand at the small of her back and dragged her close. It was a gesture that was beginning to feel as necessary to her well-being as food and drink. She lifted her knee onto his thigh and cuddled in as a hard, hot length nudged her belly. Rubbing her cheek against the bristly hairs on his chest, she sighed with contentment.

For two people who had lived alone for much of their adult lives, their schedules and personalities had meshed easily. It might have been because they hadn't had time to second guess it—the fire had made it necessary to adapt quickly. She was also on her best behaviour, taking care to curb her natural messy tendencies and not overstepping any of the unspoken boundaries he had set.

Still, it had been one of the most unexpectedly wonderful weeks of her life, despite the low-grade anxiety over Shyla's continuing silence since her last, disturbing phone call.

Her pleasure had a lot to do with the fact Rafe couldn't seem to keep his hands off her. He made it plain he wanted her any time, any place. She'd known he was a focused and intense man. Being the centre of all that attention should have disconcerted her.

Instead, she revelled in it.

Trailing her fingers from his ribs to his groin, she grasped his cock and stroked it. His hips pressed forward, and he groaned. "I have to go to work."

"This won't take long." She slithered down the bed and took him into her mouth.

She was right. It didn't take long.

When he lay spent and panting a few minutes later, she smiled at him with feminine delight. "I'll let you recover while I shower."

He waved a relaxed hand, and she laughed. Wearing nothing but a grin, she headed to the main bath. She might be spending her nights in his bed, but she hadn't brought any of her personal items to his ensuite or closet. That would seem too much like a formal declaration of living together and against the rules of their temporary arrangement.

A temporary arrangement she was beginning to wish could be something more.

Rafe sprawled on the bed, his spine still tingling with the lingering effects of his orgasm, and felt lonely.

For god's sake, Natalie had left him only moments before and was just down the hall. He could hear the water running.

He was pathetic. And worried.

Not a great combination.

He kept waiting for the other shoe to drop. And the fact that that shoe was in his own hand, and that it would be his own doing when it thudded to the ground, only stressed him out more.

It was an immutable rule of life that he would always come second to Otto, and he was reconciled to that. The trouble was, when he stepped out of his older brother's shadow, his mistakes loomed large and threatening—and couldn't be blamed on anyone but himself.

He'd done his best to protect others by locking himself in his lab and keeping his relationships at arm's length. Natalie had picked that lock with shocking ease and slipped inside, showing him just how alone he'd been, making him want a richer, fuller life.

He was very much afraid he wouldn't be able to stuff all his messy feelings back into the box where they belonged when she left.

His phone vibrated. He snatched it up, grimly relieved to have a distraction from his morose thoughts.

Otto. Thank goodness it wasn't a video call. He would have had to turn off the camera to hide the fact he wasn't dressed and ready to head out the door, like he should be at this time. Natalie was playing hell with his schedule—he'd even missed his usual morning swim the last several days—yet he couldn't regret a single moment. "Hello."

"Wanted to catch you before you got into something at work." The faint sounds of traffic filled the pause at the end of Otto's sentence. "Just reminding you about the fundraiser tomorrow night. You'll be there, right?"

Crap. He had forgotten all about the political dinner his brother had coerced him into more than several months ago. Luckily, he had a built-in excuse. "I never bought tickets."

"I thought you might try that dodge, so I put two aside. They're waiting at the constituency office. You can pick them up today." Horns honked in the background. "I don't imagine you'll be able to round up a date in twenty-four hours, so consider the unused ticket a donation to the party. Be a big boy and come out of your dungeon for one night. I'll see you tomorrow. I fly in around noon, but don't worry about picking me up. Ciao." He was gone before Rafe could protest.

Otto's casual assumption he couldn't find a date rankled more than usual. Mind you, there was only one woman he wanted to ask. The thought of spending a dreaded evening glad-handing and making small talk, while also being polite to any woman other than Natalie, was insupportable. If she didn't want to come along, he'd go stag.

Chapter Twenty

The timer on Natalie's phone chimed frantically. She jolted in alarm, shocked out of her deep focus on Chapter Four of Eugenia's biography. The first draft was coming along, but she had a nagging feeling she hadn't yet hit upon the proper tone for the book.

Her work had been interrupted in this way often during the last few days. If she didn't set the timer, it was too easy to forget about the other chores she needed to be doing. Still pondering the words she'd written, she headed downstairs to Rafe's magazine-worthy laundry room to swap out another load of wash.

She'd been allowed into her apartment last Saturday to survey the damages. Rafe had refused to let her go alone, and together they'd sifted through her belongings, Natalie choking back tears. Firefighters had managed to prevent the flames from completely breaching the wall between her bedroom and her neighbour's, but the water and retardant they'd used had caused almost as much destruction as the fire would have.

After a few minutes to mourn her losses anew, she'd squared her shoulders and set to work. They'd separated what could be salvaged from what couldn't and she'd arranged to store all the ruined items, as instructed by her insurance company. The brightest spot of the day was discovering her car keys had survived, so at least she'd have wheels again.

There had been very little to bring to Rafe's for safekeeping. Other than framed photos, books, and indestructible kitchenware, most of what could be rescued was clothing. But her wardrobe had been so adulterated with smoke it was taking several runs through the washing machine to get the stench out.

She was refilling the washer when she heard the garage door open. Her heart lifted.

Rafe was home. It was fast becoming one of the highlights of her day.

Not wanting to appear too pathetically eager to see him, she waited in the laundry room until she heard the interior door open and close and then counted to fifteen before heading to the living room.

He stood beside the black leather couch, head bent as he perused two bookmark-sized pieces of paper. His chin lifted as she approached and though his lips didn't move into a smile, his eyes warmed in his equivalent of an effusive hug.

While she trusted he lusted after her, she suspected any overt sign of affection might break his unwritten but unmistakable rules, and she'd been careful to avoid any displays of affection outside the bedroom.

Screw it. She laid her hand on his forearm and popped up on her toes to press a kiss on his cheek. She was tired of suppressing her own nature. He'd have to lump it.

"I'm glad you're home." She dropped back to her heels. "Glass of wine?"

He cleared his throat and shuffled the papers in his hand. "Sure."

She breezed by and headed for the kitchen. Taking yesterday's goblets from the cupboard—nothing was left overnight on the drain board in Rafe's house—she poured them each a generous helping of Malbec and returned. He hadn't moved from his position, and as she handed him his glass, he stepped around the couch and sank onto the cushion.

She curled up next to him, close enough to touch

but leaving a small gap. "What are those for?" She nodded at the papers he still clenched in his fist.

He scowled at them as if they might bite. "Tickets to a political fundraiser."

She pressed her lips together to hide a grin. His prickliness was amusing when it wasn't directed at her. "And you're just dying to go?"

He narrowed his eyes, his tone desert dry. "No. I hate these things. But I promised Otto I would."

"Who will be there?" She'd helped organize several fundraisers when she'd been Aubrey Windt's manager. Her political interests had been on hold for almost a year now—since the last election—and she felt the stirrings of curiosity.

"Keaton Hawke."

She nodded, recognizing the name of the newly elected leader of the party Otto belonged to. "I've met him once or twice. When I worked with Aubrey."

He stared out the floor-to-ceiling windows that filled the back wall of his house. A muscle in his jaw flexed rapidly. "Would you like to come with me? It's tomorrow night."

Rafe waited, palm damp on his wineglass, for Natalie's response. He felt like a gawky teenager asking the cool girl to the prom. Not that he had ever done that. He hadn't attended his own prom, choosing instead to sit sullen and alone in his room at home.

Maybe someone should have given that kid a swift kick in the ass.

She pursed her lips. "I don't have anything to wear."

Well, at least she hadn't refused outright. "Do you have time to get something tomorrow?"

"I suppose." She sipped her wine thoughtfully, her mouth pressing against the crystal, his cock stirring at the sight.

Damn it. By now he should have stopped reacting so urgently. After a week of having her in his bed, he should be accustomed to her presence, should have slaked the thirst she inspired.

"I'm starting to miss the political scene. I've been involved since before I was old enough to vote, but after the last election I needed a break. Sure. I'd love to go."

"Fine." The relief he felt was all out of proportion. To hide it, he tossed the tickets onto the coffee table as if they were worthless, pointedly looking anywhere but at her.

"If I'm going to take time off to go dress shopping tomorrow, I should get more work done tonight." She drained the last drops of her wine. He couldn't resist sneaking a glance as her slender neck stretched, her silky hair fell onto her shoulders. "It's your turn to cook dinner, right?"

He nodded. She'd insisted that he not treat her like a guest while she was temporarily in his home, and that had included sharing the meal prep duties. Yesterday she'd made chicken and penne with pesto sauce, which he'd devoured while musing he'd had worse restaurant meals. Tonight she'd have to put up with his own, less varied skills. "I'll call you when it's ready."

She placed her empty glass on the island and skipped up the stairs, disappearing into the archive room. He set about preparing dinner with a feeling of contentment that was almost frighteningly welcome.

Rafe tugged at the pristine white cuff of his starchy dress shirt, trying to settle it properly within the sleeve of his black tuxedo, and then fidgeted with the bow tie at his throat. The day had been overcast and gloomy, so despite the fact the sun hadn't yet completely set, the world outside was dark enough to reflect his image in the wide glass windows overlooking his backyard.

He didn't consider himself a vain man, but he felt a rush of satisfaction at what the glass displayed. Natalie wouldn't be embarrassed to be seen with him tonight.

The suit fit him well and accentuated his natural height and build. His swimming regime kept his body taut and strong. Not that he exercised for conceited reasons. His father had died from a stroke when he was only a few years older than Rafe, and he had no intention of suffering the same fate if he could help it.

Not that he'd have sons to mourn him, like his father. But a tiny part of him, one that had grown infinitesimally bigger since Natalie had come into his life, wouldn't give up the hope that maybe, someday...

The click of heels on the hardwood floor signalled her emergence from her bedroom. He smoothed the satin lapels of his tux, made sure his coattail wasn't tucked inelegantly into his waistband, turned to greet her—

—and almost swallowed his tongue.

She floated down the stairs, one hand skimming the rail while the other, also clutching a small, sparkly bag, held her long skirt out of the way.

When she reached the main floor, she sent him a blinding grin that almost finished him off. "I forgot how much fun it was to dress up. Look at my shoes! Aren't they gorgeous?" She pointed one foot, balancing on the other leg with delicate grace.

Obediently, he looked down. He supposed the shoes were pretty enough, with rhinestone encrusted straps and narrow spikes for heels. But they were overshadowed by the incandescent woman wearing them. He let his eyes drift up, soaking in the sight like a man parched by Saharan winds.

She absolutely glowed with a magnetism that attracted every cell in his being.

He wasn't sure what colour the dress was. Grey

was too sober a word. The fabric shimmered and gleamed in the muted light of the living room lamps. Narrow straps arched over her shoulders, and the neckline, though as modest as a political event demanded, dipped low enough to reveal the upper slopes of her breasts. The waist hugged in just below, the skirt falling sleek and smooth to her toes, hinting at the luscious curves underneath. She'd pinned her dark hair up on the sides with glittering clips that complemented her shoes and bag and exposed her ears, from which dangled jewellery that reminded him of the fancy chandeliers in elegant dining rooms. Her neck was bare, and he could see the smattering of freckles on her collarbone, the same freckles he loved to taste when they lay naked together.

"What do you think?" She spun in a slow circle. The back draped low on her spine in soft folds, and the skirt was slit to her knee on one side. "Will I do?"

He ran his tongue over dry teeth in a futile attempt to work up enough moisture to speak. When he finally found his voice, he spoke with hoarse gruffness. "You look beautiful."

She dipped her chin in a shy gesture. "Thanks. I'm glad you had a chance to see me all dolled up, instead of bedraggled from falling into a pool or escaping a burning building." Her eyes twinkled with amused self-deprecation.

The fact she could laugh at herself was a powerful aphrodisiac. He wanted to absorb that confidence and bind it to his very soul. Maybe then he could see his own mistakes and gaffes for something more than tragedies.

For now, he'd have to settle for basking in the radiance reflecting from her vivacious, vibrant essence.

He should probably improve on his terse compliment, but his brain was fogged and blurred with desire. The best he could manage was a gravelly,

"Do you have a wrap? A coat?" The March night still had a December bite. She couldn't go out in it with so much skin showing.

Not that he wanted to hide its silky softness, but hypothermia wasn't sexy.

"Oh! I forgot it in my room." She turned to the stairs and the bumps of her spine and the strong curve of her calves sent a surge of lust straight to his cock.

"Don't move. I'll get it." He strode past. The discomfort of walking would give him a chance to rein in his baser instincts.

Chapter Twenty-One

Natalie wouldn't have been human if she hadn't enjoyed Rafe's poleaxed expression. She knew she looked good—had taken special care to look her absolute best, in fact—and it had been worth it.

Her credit card was screaming from the expense—again—but she swallowed down the anxiety that had taken lodging in her gut. Tonight, she was Cinderella with her prince, and tomorrow could take care of itself.

They arrived at the large restaurant that had been reserved for the event and joined the stream of people entering. Rafe cupped her elbow, his touch firm but not demanding, more a matter of connection than possession. The ember that warmed her belly whenever he was near sparked into a more determined flame.

Though she'd done her best to hide it, she'd been just as flummoxed by his appearance as he had been with hers. His saturnine good looks hadn't yet lost their power to make her stomach flutter on an ordinary day. Seeing him in what had to be an expensive tuxedo, swept back hair and freshly groomed chin highlighting his stark features, had elevated his gorgeousness to an unprecedented level.

A greeter took the tickets he proffered, and they swept into the main room on a tide of other attendees. In the past, she would have immediately searched for Aubrey in the crowd, but her friend and former colleague had cut off all ties with the party last year.

Still, she saw many familiar faces. She'd been

involved in politics since high school and though she'd been on a self-imposed sabbatical, the landscape hadn't changed that dramatically. As they threaded through the room, they paused for short conversations with several people. Rafe stood silent, his posture stiff and uncomfortable as he replied with monosyllabic grunts to any comments directed his way. By the time they reached Otto, he was fairly vibrating with tension.

"Natalie! So good to see you." Otto brushed her cheek with a casual kiss and Rafe's grip on her elbow squeezed tight. "I should have guessed he would bring you. You're the logical choice, given the project you're working on...and handy, too, now you're staying at his house."

His inflection was cheerful and innocent, but a teasing undercurrent had a sting in the tail. "Handy for me, you mean." Defending Rafe from his older brother was becoming a habit. "I pestered him to bring me along. I'm sure he gave me the ticket just to shut me up."

His thumb rubbed her arm in a tiny motion, whether in warning or thanks she couldn't tell. Probably safest to change the subject to something less volatile. "Is Keaton Hawke here yet?"

"No." Otto glanced at the heavy watch on his wrist. "Soon though. Have you met him before?"

The conversation moved into political channels, and she felt some of Rafe's tension ease, his clasp loosening and eventually releasing her. As she and Otto chatted, she couldn't miss the signs that he held aspirations of public office. She felt faint stirrings of excitement. Aubrey's loss in the last election might have been a blessing for her friend, who had admitted shortly after that she'd only gone into public life because of her politically ambitious father, but for Natalie it had been a disappointing blow to see her favoured party knocked out of power.

Otto Talbot had the charisma and intelligence to take him as far as he wanted to go. She thought it might be fun to watch the ride.

Keaton Hawke arrived and, to Rafe's relief, Otto's attention shifted away from Natalie.

He didn't want to punch his brother in the face at a fundraising dinner. But if he had smiled his *take-your-pants-off-for-me-now* smile one more time, Rafe wouldn't have been responsible for his actions.

Despite her sweet but undeserved defense, both tonight and on the evening of his video-call almost two weeks ago, he didn't blame Natalie for being charmed by Otto. His patter might be practiced, but it was sincere. He liked women and wasn't afraid to let them know it. And it wasn't all surface appeal—he was bright, insightful, and loquacious.

Unlike Rafe's own tongue-tied belligerence. He had yet to flatter Natalie with more than his lame *you look beautiful* comment, had been unable to engage with any of the people she'd introduced him to, and had stood mute while she and Otto had discussed provincial politics with astuteness and enjoyment.

It was a wonder she hadn't abandoned him in search of more congenial company.

Hawke, a short but broad-shouldered man with thinning light brown hair and a sleek aura, glad-handed his way around the room before joining their little group. Rafe's face felt frozen into a rictus of a smile. Torturous memories of his teenage years, when his mother had trotted out her family at these sorts of events, stiffened his spine. He'd survived then. He would survive now.

Hawke greeted Otto with a friendly grin and a manly swat on the shoulder as they shook hands, and then turned to Natalie. "Natalie Minton, right? Used to work with Aubrey?"

"Good memory." She extended her hand. "We've only met a couple of times."

Rafe wasn't surprised the leader remembered her. The way she lit up a room just by being in it? Unforgettable.

"I remember your commitment to her campaigns. Shame about the last one." Hawke pressed her hand between both of his. He shifted his piercing gaze. "I don't believe we've met."

Otto did the honours. "My brother, Raphael Talbot."

Luckily, the politician let go of Natalie before Rafe succumbed to his urge to drag her out of his clutches. He shook the other man's hand, aware of the same crackling energy that Otto and Natalie exuded. In the presence of three such vibrant personalities, he felt shadowed, grim, and hollow.

Hawke dismissed him with an absent smile and focused on Otto once again. "What's this I'm hearing about Eugenia?"

The change in topic was so unexpected he almost didn't realize imminent disaster loomed. Then his gut clenched in an icy ball and his skin prickled with dismay. How much did Hawke know? What had he learned?

Otto, still unaware of the land mines Rafe had found filed away in their mother's archives, answered with calm unconcern. "The biography? Yes. We're very excited." He draped his arm over Natalie's mostly bare shoulders. "Natalie is authoring it."

The biography. That's all Hawke had meant. He swallowed down the worst of his fear.

"Are you now? I was just a young buck when she was in Cabinet. She was one of the giants. Gone far too soon." He shook his head in apparently sincere sorrow.

Rafe took that with a grain of salt. In the wild world of politics, members might offer condolences out of one corner of their mouths while undercutting opponents out of the other.

"Really?" Natalie beamed at the older man. "In that case, I'd love to interview you. Going through her files is all well and good but talking to people who knew her at the height of her career will add a personal layer to the biography. I've been drawing up a list. Can I put you on it?"

Before Hawke could reply, Rafe blurted, "But you've started writing already." He only had a few boxes left to review before handing them off to Natalie. He'd thought he was nearing the end of the danger zone. All of a sudden, here was another avenue through which she might discover the scandal he was so desperate to hide.

Three sets of eyes expressing various levels of astonishment turned toward him, as if a statue had spoken.

"It's just a draft." She took the single step necessary to draw near to his side, which had the welcome effect of forcing Otto's arm to drop from her shoulders. "I'm blocking it out, figuring out what will go where, how the chapters will break down. Interviews are a vital step in the research process."

It hadn't dawned on him she'd want to *speak* to his mother's friends and colleagues. He spent so much of his time avoiding people that he'd assumed she'd be happy with the boxes of documents he'd provided.

Hawke fished out a business card from the inside pocket of his suit jacket and handed it to her. "Call my office to set up an appointment. I look forward to chatting about old times."

With the smoothness of an experienced campaigner, he disengaged and moved onto the next group. A woman with a helmet of curly blond hair and thick red lipstick snagged Otto's attention, leaving Rafe and Natalie in a small bubble of temporary calm.

She opened her tiny purse, dropped Hawke's card

inside, and then tilted her head, her gaze searching his face. "Is there something wrong? You've been keyed up tighter than a guitar string most of the night."

He took refuge in half-truths. "I hate these events."

"Yes. But you were starting to relax until I asked Hawke for an interview. I thought by now you were on board with the biography. Do you still have reservations?"

Air huffed out his nostrils. "Reservations, regrets, reluctance. I may have been outvoted on the project, but that doesn't mean I like the idea."

A flicker of emotion tightened the faint lines at the corner of her eyes. "Don't you trust me?"

Oh. Now he'd hurt her feelings. He was such a heel. What was more important—reassuring her or continuing to hide the real reason for his concern?

The decision was easier than he'd expected.

Ignoring the crowd pressing around them, he ran one finger down her cheek to her jaw. "I trust you. I'm just worried about what you might find."

It wasn't the time or place to explore Rafe's oblique admission that his mother's career might not have been squeaky clean, and Natalie let the conversation collapse. Once again, he slowly relaxed.

She hated to upset him—yet knew she would—but she'd have to bring up the subject again, and soon.

Through the rest of the evening—the meal and speeches, the bad jokes and forced banter—she deflected all inquiries into the biography, of which there were many. Since neither she nor Rafe brought it up, Otto must have been the one making sure it was front and centre in everyone's minds.

The drive home was silent. He'd been even quieter than usual all evening, and she had a tender urge to soothe his discomfort with kisses and caresses. But she needed to clear the air between them first. If he was hiding something from her, she had to know.

In the living room, she slipped out of her twinkly shoes and tossed her wrap on a dining room chair. "What did you mean, you're afraid of what I'll find?"

He appeared resigned, not surprised, that she'd returned to the conversation. He loosened the bow tie at his neck and undid the top two buttons of his shirt before resting his hip on the back of the sofa with a sigh. "There are skeletons in every politician's closet. Those in my mother's might have a trickledown effect to other people. People still active today."

"Otto plans to seek the nomination before the next election, doesn't he?" She drifted toward him, hoping proximity might diffuse what was going to be a difficult discussion.

"Yes. I knew you would figure that out." His smile was small but appreciative. The black curl that habitually fell over his forehead had been held ruthlessly in position by hair-product magic tonight. It returned to its usual place when he ran his fingers through the strands with a tired gesture. "As much as I want to protect my mother's reputation, she's gone. But Otto is still here, and he aspires to be more than just a Member of the Legislature."

Her fingers itched to brush the lock back. She refused to be distracted by the strong cords of his neck rising from the white collar of his shirt and the vaguely wounded expression on his face. This was important. If she was going to do her job properly, she had to know details. "Is there something specific you're worried about?"

"No." His reply was swift and sure. Too swift? Too sure?

"I told you once I wasn't writing an exposé. You're worried for nothing."

"Maybe." His hands cupped her hips and drew her closer. She stepped without protest between his knees and leaned into his chest. His voice rumbled under her ear. "Can we forget about it for now?"

"Of course." She licked his neck, and he shivered. There would be plenty of time to talk tomorrow. Desire had been sparkling through her like champagne bubbles all night. "Did you have something else in mind?"

His quick fingers rucked up her dress, his palms sliding to the back of her thighs. She wriggled against the erection growing against her stomach. "I think it's time we christened the dining room table, don't you?" he said.

Chapter Twenty-Two

Rafe should have felt guilty for distracting Natalie with sex. He didn't.

He dreaded precipitating the end of their time together by discussing his mother's crimes. Because the end was already too close. Not just the end of the biography project, either. The end of Natalie's presence in his life.

He was still hoping to keep her unaware of the stain that haunted him—but that hope was fading every moment. And once she knew what he knew—and learned how long he'd been lying to her—it would all be over.

She brought laughter and light to his dreary world and brightened the dark corners of his soul. He'd cling to that ephemeral joy as long as he could.

During the weekend that followed the fundraising dinner, he focused his efforts on his mother's remaining boxes, removing anything even remotely relevant that might kindle Natalie's curiosity. Now she suspected there was something to find, he knew she'd be keen to ramp up her research. He didn't blame her for that—it was what she'd been hired to do.

Maybe he should have shared his guilty knowledge with Otto from the outset. That might have been the only way to deflect his brother from his chosen path. Too late now.

Sunday evening, he replaced the lid on the last box, stretched his aching spine, and then slumped against the hard wooden back of the chair he used in the archive room. He and Natalie had been working side by side for several hours, and his eyes were starting to cross.

"Time for a break?"

She looked up from her laptop, her gaze unfocused.

He loved seeing her so centred on her work. If only it wouldn't lead to their downfall. "It's after six and all I've eaten today was egg on toast. I'm craving pasta and a big salad."

"Sounds great." She rose to her feet, arched her back, and picked up her water bottle. "I'll get things started. Coming?"

"In a minute."

She ruffled his hair on her way by, her touch lingering on his scalp. He would miss *so much* about her when she was gone. Her dedication to the project, the way she sighed in her sleep, her casual touches and absent caresses.

His heart seized and he pounded his fist lightly against his sternum to restart it. As a physician, he knew it wasn't physically possible for a heart to break from misery alone.

It sure the hell felt like it, though.

His gaze fell upon his mother's ancient computer, standing big and bulky next to Natalie's sleek laptop. When he and Otto had cleared out Eugenia's house, they had transferred everything from her office to this room. If he wanted to do a complete wash job on his mother's files, he'd have to go through the floppy discs stored in the small stack of shoe boxes tucked behind the clunky square monitor. With any luck, the computer wouldn't even turn on. If there was no way to open the files on the discs, they would be safe from scrutiny.

For tonight, though, he'd had enough. Maybe he could convince Natalie to go for a swim before dinner. It would stretch out his cramped muscles. He turned off the light and made his way downstairs.

Rafe was hiding something. Natalie knew it. Ever since Friday night he'd been an odd mix of attentive and aloof—one minute acting as if all was normal, the other withdrawing into the cold, silent shell she'd battered against when they'd first met.

He left the house as usual on Monday morning, and for the first time since he'd let slip there might be a secret in Eugenia's past, she was alone.

As had become custom over the past several weeks, Rafe had stacked the last of the "approved" boxes on the second table in the archive room. She'd long ago run out of space under it for the boxes she'd finished, and those had been returned to the closet and far wall.

Instead of diving into the final cartons, she regarded the computer and the floppy discs piled in the shoe boxes next to it with speculation. She knew Rafe's decree to stay away from anything he hadn't reviewed extended to them as well.

She *knew* it did.

If there was scandal in Eugenia's past, she had to discover it. Whether she would push to include it in the manuscript or side with Rafe's apparent need to hide whatever it was would depend on what she found.

Cautiously, as if it were an explosive device—which the information it might reveal had the power to be—she trailed one finger down the side of the tall hard drive tower standing next to the cube-shaped monitor and pressed the power button.

Nothing.

For a moment, she was relieved at the anticlimax. She wouldn't be able to give into temptation if the computer didn't work. Her brand-new laptop didn't have a CD/DVD drive, let alone a slot that would take the hard, square discs common in the nineties.

Then she noticed the unplugged power cord dangling off the back of the table. Knowing she was taking an irreversible step, she inserted it into the outlet below the table and pressed the power button again.

Whirring and clicking filled the room. She fumbled around the monitor, searching for the switch, and discovered it at the back corner. The screen buzzed on to reveal a monochromatic logo.

While the beast lumbered into life, she opened one of the shoe boxes and flipped through the discs. Each was labelled in a neat cursive, but the codes and acronyms were meaningless to her. The dates, however, provided clues, and she chose one that was near the start of Eugenia's term as Minister of Transport. Impatiently, she waited for the operating system to load.

She wondered how difficult it might be to access the files, but thankfully the desktop populated with icons that, while not familiar, were at least recognizable as to their purpose. Carefully sliding the disc into the opening in the front of the tower, she waited for its icon to pop up, and then clicked on it.

A long list of documents, also with incomprehensible names, scrolled onto the screen. With determination, she chose the first one and set to work.

Natalie began to wonder if her suspicions were unwarranted, the longer she spent studying file after file on the grumbling computer. No matter how much reading between the lines she did, nothing tweaked her bullshit sensor. Just as nothing had with any of the thousands of paper documents she'd already reviewed.

Rafe had to be worried for nothing. He'd never hidden his disinterest in politics. Maybe he'd misunderstood whatever he'd found, misread the subtleties of negotiation and favours owed that cranked the political wheel.

Slowly, she became aware the name Dennis Parrish cropped up with noticeable regularity. His wasn't the only one that repeated, of course, but he stood out as he wasn't a government employee and was one of the few private citizens mentioned in conjunction with the several mega transportation projects that Eugenia had shepherded during her time in office.

Switching to her laptop and the sometimes-doubtful benefits of the modern internet, she searched the name. The top results were an IMDB profile for a behind-the-scenes member of the movie industry, a murderer in Philadelphia, and a YouTube video featuring an elderly guitar player.

Adjusting her search terms, she came up with a listing that looked promising. The good news was it mentioned a Dennis Parrish involved in the transportation industry in British Columbia. The bad news was it was an obituary from several years ago.

While the obit made no mention of any political connections, it did provide a list of companies and organizations in which Parrish had held high-ranking positions. One of those sounded vaguely familiar, but where and when she'd seen or heard the name refused to surface.

She took off her glasses and pressed the heels of her hands into her eye sockets. She'd been at this for hours and her vision was blurring. It was time for a break.

Twisting the blinds open—she kept them closed to prevent reflections on her computer screen—she blinked at the bright light streaming in. So far, March had been grey and gloomy as winter refused to give up its grip, and the clear blue sky outside was an unexpected delight. A short walk might be just the ticket to jog her memory.

Knowing the brilliant sunshine could be deceptive, she layered on a sweater, jacket, scarf, and slouchy toque, and made sure she had gloves in her pocket. She hadn't reached the end of the driveway before she was thankful for her preparations.

A couple of blocks away from Rafe's house, the subdivision was being expanded. With her thoughts lingering on construction companies, it seemed natural to set a course in that direction. Mounds of snow edged the sidewalk and blanketed lawns, but in the distance dark piles of dirt rose where foundations were being framed. The punch of nail guns and growl of machinery grew louder as she strode briskly along.

It was less than two weeks since the apartment fire, and she'd been assured it would be another two weeks before she'd receive any update on when she could move back in. Restoration work was underway, and while most of the building's residents had returned home, those apartments nearest the origin of the fire were still out of bounds.

She was in no hurry to leave. And not just because she'd grown to love this house—its space, its amenities, its modern design.

She didn't want to leave Rafe. She hadn't fallen in love with him, like she had his house. Of course she hadn't. What she felt for him was fondness and affection, but not *love*. He was abrasive and taciturn to others, but to her, he was endlessly fascinating, his scratchy personality hiding tender bits he didn't show to anyone else. At least, she thought he didn't. And the sex—well, it was incendiary, and she wasn't ready to give that up yet, either.

She was certain he would grow tired of her presence long before she did his. It wouldn't do to get too attached, especially with the spectre of Shyla lurking in the background.

Her sister hadn't been in touch since the day after

the fire. She had talked to their parents, a fact that relieved Natalie's concerns after Shyla's last call. But the moment she relaxed, let her guard down, she knew her sister would pop up, just like a bad penny.

Bad penny...

With an almost physical jerk, her brain clicked into gear. She halted on the sidewalk, her motion arrested by her outrageous thought, and stared blindly at the plywood skin of an unfinished house.

She'd figured out the scandal Rafe was trying so desperately to hide.

Chapter Twenty-Three

Rafe stayed at the lab after all his colleagues left for the day, intent on finishing one more analysis before heading home to Natalie. The physicians and patients he worked with still deserved his total focus, even if he no longer needed his career to fill his lonely, solitary existence.

Because he wasn't lonely anymore. Was only beginning to realize how lonely he *had* been.

He dreaded the day she would leave with growing despair.

It was his turn to cook, so he picked up butter chicken with naan at an Indian restaurant she had introduced him to. He hadn't realized how regimented and structured he'd been until she'd blazed into his life. That was yet another lock she'd opened in his world.

He carried the food into the house, the scents of curry and jasmine rice reminding him he hadn't eaten lunch that day. Placing the containers in the oven but not turning it on, he folded the paper bag they'd come in with precise motions and tucked it into the appropriate drawer.

It was all busy work to keep him from racing up the stairs to see Natalie, an impulse he'd thought would weaken with familiarity, but only continued to grow.

His steps measured but his heart beating faster in anticipation, he found her exactly where he knew she'd be—the archive room.

Instead of working at her laptop or digging

through a file box, though, she was standing by the window, her face in profile as she looked outside. His lab was in the basement of the hospital, so he'd missed what his weather app declared had been a beautiful day. It was still very pleasant out. Maybe they'd have time for a walk in the evening dusk after dinner.

She turned away from the view. Her low-voltage smile was kilowatts away from her usual effusive greeting. A trickle of unease slithered into his contentment. "Hello. Something going on outside?"

She shook her head. "No."

Her quiet denial did nothing to ease his growing dread. Maybe if he ignored it... "I went to Dana Mandi. Dinner is keeping warm in the oven. Want a glass of wine first?"

She regarded him steadily and sweat sprang out on his palms. This was it. She was leaving him. And he could guess why.

Her next words gave the dreaded confirmation.

"I found out what you've been hiding." Natalie approached, stepping warily as if expecting him to burst into violence, and stopped next to the hard wooden chair he'd brought up weeks ago. "I know what your mother did."

Colour drained from Rafe's face, his harsh features stark and cold under his pale skin. He straightened his already straight spine, and his hands clenched and unclenched at his sides, but he made no sound. His gaze was fierce and unapologetic...and wounded.

Why should *he* be feeling hurt? *She* was the one who had been lied to.

Natalie gripped the smooth, arched wood on the back of Rafe's chair with both hands, taking solace in its support, and asked the question burning in her mind. "How long have you known?" Maybe he'd only discovered the disgrace recently and it hadn't been the reason behind his initial rejection of the biography project. At least then he wouldn't have been lying to her from the very beginning.

His nostrils flared and his lips moved stiffly as he answered. "Otto mentioned his idea for a biography at Christmas. I'd already been going through Mother's archives and agreed it was an excellent idea. I started paying closer attention to what I was reading, made it a goal to go through them more quickly. I figured it out in mid-January."

The fragile hope she cupped like an eggshell in her palm crumbled into powder. "That's why you didn't want me to look at any boxes until you'd gone through them."

"Yes."

"Did you know before you started digging? Were you looking for anything in particular?"

"No." The denial was sharp and pointed, but a dusting of bewilderment revealed deeper feelings.

Of course he hadn't thought there was anything to find. Though she suspected his relationship with his mother hadn't been a simple one, learning she'd been involved in graft and redirection of government funds had to have been a shock.

Sympathy nibbled at the edges of her hurt. It still didn't excuse his actions toward her, however. She focused on the issue at hand. "Once you agreed to the biography, why didn't you tell me?"

"I couldn't."

"Liar." Shyla was a champion at pushing Natalie's buttons, and Rafe was coming a close second. "You certainly could have. You chose not to and hoped I was too stupid to figure it out."

"It wasn't like that." His gaze flicked away from hers to the computer, the boxes, the window. It was the first sign of remorse she'd seen.

"What was it like, then?" She tamped down a rising fury. She rarely lost her temper, but when she did, it was ugly. "You were just going to let me go merrily on my way, attach my name, my reputation, to a biography you *knew* would be missing vital information? And then, when the scandal came out, because scandals always do, even if it took decades, I'd look like a sap, a stooge paid to sweep it under the rug?"

He shifted his weight from his heels to the balls of his feet and back again. "If you couldn't find it, no one could. You're too smart, too instinctively intelligent, to miss the signs. That's why I had to hide things from you."

She hated the warm tug in her belly at his compliments. He couldn't distract her from her righteous anger with placating words. "This is my career you are talking about. How could you?"

"It's not your career, though. Not really. You're a librarian, not an investigative journalist."

She stared, stunned at this cavalier opinion of her profession. "And that makes it okay to work against me, to prevent me from doing the best job I can? I thought you cared for me more than that."

"I didn't *know* you. Not when I made the decision." He scrubbed his hands through his hair, took two steps toward the closet and then spun back to face her. For the first time, she heard frustration in his sober tones. Colour had returned to his complexion and red highlighted his sharp cheekbones. "I was protecting my mother's legacy. And Otto's future. You know he wants to run for office. What chance do you think he'd have if it was discovered his mother took bribes to award billion-dollar contracts and siphoned money out of those same contracts to support her political campaigns?"

"Otto will be judged on his own merits, not on something that happened when he was in elementary school."

He scoffed. "You're not that naive. Even I know

that's not true."

The fact he was right made her even angrier. She swallowed down a hot ball and blinked back tears. She would *not* cry in front of him, no matter how mad he made her. She went on the attack. "Scandals flare up all the time and are doused just as quickly. Don't hide behind that excuse. You should have been honest with me. Then we could have dealt with this together."

"Dealt how? You want to put this in the book, don't you? You've basically said you *have* to. That will make problems, not solve them."

"Maybe it's not what we think it is. The graft and misappropriation of funds is only a conjecture, one I'm making based on your secretiveness and a couple of letters I've read. Unless you have something concrete, something that lays out her crimes point by point, we could be wrong. Now I've lost weeks of research time that could have been spent finding evidence to clear your mother."

"I'm not wrong." He shook his head, the lock of hair falling on his forehead, his tone defeated. "But even if I am, perception is reality. People only hear what they want to hear. If you so much as hint at this in the biography, whether it's true or not, the media will latch onto it. Maybe even do their own investigations. I can't risk that happening."

"You should have told me. Maybe not on day one, but after..." She waved her hands to encompass their recent intimacy.

"I know. But I didn't. I didn't *want* to." The last words burst out of him like the confession of a man with a noose around his neck. He sank onto the table, resting his palms on the surface and slumping forward despondently. "I expect you'll be leaving now. But you might as well have dinner first. I'll stay out of your way until you're gone."

She stared at him, puzzlement skipping to the top of her long list of tangled emotions. "Leave? Stay out of my way?"

He still didn't meet her eyes, an extremely worrisome state of affairs. He was nothing if not direct, in both actions and words. "You won't want to stay with me, now you know I lied. If none of your friends can take you in, I'll pay for a hotel room until your apartment is ready. It's the least I can do."

Rafe kept his eyes on the floor. It had been agony, meeting Natalie's hurt and angry gaze as she confronted him. But it would kill him to watch her walk away.

Two grey-slippered feet came into view. From this angle, he could only see to her knees, clad in blue jeans.

"Are you kicking me out?"

Her tone was curious, maybe even confused. He risked a glance higher and caught a glimpse of her peering at him with her head tilted to one side. He focused on her toes once more. "Of course not. But I assume you won't be comfortable here anymore." He pushed out the rest like squeezing a sliver from an infected finger. "With me."

She stepped forward, one foot on either side of his own, much larger feet. Small fuzzy slipper, large black-socked foot, large black-socked foot, small fuzzy slipper. Soft fingers bracketed his neck, thumbs pressed on the underside of his jaw, encouraging his head to rise. Her sweet summery scent enveloped him and though he lifted his chin, he closed his eyes, not wanting to see the painful truth in her face.

He knew he'd screwed up, that he was the cause of this chasm between them. Yet, he had the horrifying feeling she felt *sorry* for him.

"Rafe." Her compassionate tone did nothing to ease his embarrassment. Soft cool palms swept down his throat, landed on his shoulders, and pushed

Brenda Margriet

gently. "Look at me, you big baby."

That made his eyelids pop open. With his hips resting on the table, they were nose to nose. "Baby?"

She nodded, a gleam of amusement in her warm brown eyes. "If you're not kicking me out, why do you expect me to leave?"

If anyone was confused, it was him. She had to be furious. Why hadn't she stormed out by now? "You must hate me for what I did. I withheld important information, even outright lied to you."

She jerked her chin in a go-on gesture when he paused. What else did she want him to say? It seemed pretty clear to him. He'd made a mistake, and his punishment was losing Natalie. He thought back over the conversation, wondering how he could explain things so she would understand. She would still leave, but at least she'd have the whole truth.

It was then he realized he'd made yet another glaring error.

"I haven't apologized yet." He had been keeping his palms pressed firmly on the table to prevent himself from touching her. Now he lifted her hands off his shoulders and swept his mouth across her knuckles in a barely there caress. "I'm sorry. I'm so sorry I didn't trust you from the start. Sorry I didn't tell you my fears once I did trust you. Can you forgive me?"

Her expression was half-exasperated, half-tender. "Of course I forgive you. You hurt my feelings and I'm still angry with you. Furious, in fact. But that doesn't mean I'll leave you. It just means we had our first fight."

Her kiss was sweet absolution and cool blessing. The snowball of fear lodged in his ribs melted at the edges. Maybe he hadn't ruined everything after all.

Chapter Twenty-Four

Natalie wondered what had happened to Rafe to make him so certain that a few hurt feelings would chase her away. Yes, he'd made a mistake, but it was one she could sympathize with even as she condemned it.

Besides, it would take a lot more than that to scare her away from someone she loved. It had only been a few hours since she'd denied the emotion, but it was ridiculous to do so any longer.

His lips, at first tentative, grew fierce. He drew her hands, still clasped in his, to the base of her spine and her back arched, pressing her breasts against the wall of his chest. She gasped into his mouth as her nipples ripened like cherries.

She loved Rafe. What else could this heady mix of passion and tenderness and frustration and delight be?

He drew away, his dark, hooded gaze doing nothing to hide the spark of shyness in their depths. His mouth opened and closed soundlessly.

A surge of power rippled over her skin. She knew what he wanted to ask. Knew he was leaving it up to her. "Wanna have make-up sex?" She grinned, effervescent in her discovery.

He groaned and his lips descended on hers again, demanding yet pleading, dominant yet yearning.

Despite his advantages—good looks, intelligence, social standing—she was only now coming to realize how fragile he was. Like a tree caught in strong winds that would snap in half before bending and bowing, he

Brenda Margriet

held himself to such a high standard that every little misstep was a cataclysmic reversal.

He needed her, needed her unwavering support and affirmation. She put her soul into the kiss, sent it to search out the cracks in his armor, the fractures in his foundation, and did her best to seal them.

Hooking his heel behind her ankles, he tipped her backward and laid her on the carpet, kneeling beside her. She wriggled and he released her hands, which she immediately set to unbuttoning his shirt. His fingers scrabbled at the waistband of her jeans, unfastening and unzipping.

With moves that were much less elegant that she wished, she shimmied the tight fabric off her legs, her slippers going with it. He shrugged out of his shirt and tossed it aside. The rest of their clothes were discarded in moments, and he stretched his long length over her, hot skin and firm muscles slick against her sensitized flesh.

After that, it was a matter of urgent whispers and muttered pleas, of licking tongues and searching fingers, of liquid heat and naked need. The short carpet was rough against her buttocks until he slid large hands underneath and lifted her, opened her—

—and sent her flying with a desperate thrust.

Hot. Tight. Wet. Rafe was incapable of any more coherent thoughts.

Beneath him, the tendons in the taut column of Natalie's neck stood out sharp and clear, her gorgeous eyes squeezing shut as her inner muscles clenched around him. Her fingertips dug into his hips, her heels pressed his thighs.

He'd never seen anything so compelling as his lover—*this* lover—in the throes of passion.

He withdrew. Not completely, as he couldn't bear to lose all contact. Her grip tightened and she moaned, brow furrowing.

"No." She was fierce and commanding. Her hips surged toward him, seeking to deepen their joining again, but he laid one palm flat on her belly to hold her down. They'd reached this point in a frantic blaze of lust and desire. It was time to slow down.

If he could.

He eased forward into her welcoming warmth. She sighed, muscles relaxing, accepting his advance. Back and forth he moved, in and out, deliberately teasing, drawing every sensation he could to the surface.

Pressure sparked at the base of his spine, sizzled down his cock, and he grit his teeth.

Not yet. Not until she—

She arched her back, heels digging into the carpet, neck bowing. The sound she uttered was primal and savage, exultant and euphoric. When she collapsed limply to the floor, he moved with her, staying buried deep inside. He propped himself on his elbows and brushing away a strand of hair that had tangled in her eyelashes.

He gave her a minute, let her breathing settle, and then flexed his hips gently. Her eyelids fluttered open revealing deliciously dazed dark brown eyes, though her lazy smile sparkled with the intensity he'd missed earlier. He could have stayed like this forever. His cock, however, had different ideas. It shuddered and quivered in her intimate embrace, demanding satisfaction.

"I can feel that." Her murmur was a purr. In a slow, languorous motion, she raised her arms and wrapped them under his, gripping his shoulders from behind. Lifting her head, she sucked on his earlobe and whispered in his ear. "Your turn."

It didn't take long. A few solid thrusts, with Natalie whispering sultry, passionate encouragement, brought him to his peak faster than he'd thought possible. The world exploded in a shower of incandescent sparks behind his closed lids, strength drained from his limbs, and he slumped flat.

Slowly, he became aware of carpet tickling his nose and the soft movement of fingers up and down his spine. With the return of sanity, another realization fluttered to the surface.

He stiffened and shifted onto his elbows. She tightened her hold on him, hiding her face in the curve of his shoulder. "Not yet. I like it when you squash me."

Incapable of forming full sentences yet, he could speak only one word. "Condom." The enormity of what he'd done—or hadn't done, rather—washed over him with icy dismay.

"I know. It's okay."

"What?" Pressing with his palms, he shifted his hips up and back and knelt between her legs. She sprawled lushly on the carpet, her breasts plump and full with beaded nipples, her centre open and exposed, utterly unselfconscious.

"I thought of it. Before." She waggled her fingers and shot him a sly grin. "I didn't want to...interrupt you."

When all he did was continue to stare at her, she jackknifed into a sitting position. "I'm on the pill. If you had health reasons that made it necessary to use a condom, you would have told me before we had sex the first time. As for me"—she poked a finger in his chest—"do you trust me?"

It was a loaded question if he'd ever heard one, recalling their argument. But he had no hesitation in answering. "Yes."

She nodded decisively. "I'm not saying we forgo the condom every time. A pregnancy right now is not in my plans. But this once, I was willing to take the risk."

He had lied to her, both verbally and by omission, since the day they'd met. Yet, she continued to trust him.

How had he been so lucky to find this woman?

Later, after a leisurely shared shower and reheated butter chicken, Natalie curled up next to Rafe on the couch in his den, a small, windowless room under the mezzanine. A flat screen television—playing one of the nature documentaries she'd been amused to learn he enjoyed—took up much of one wall and bookshelves lined two more. She reflected, not for the first time, that it was a huge house for a single man. Three bedrooms upstairs—four if you counted the one he had converted into his office—a games room over the garage, this den, a butler's pantry off the kitchen, the spacious living/kitchen/dining area, and a separate laundry. And, of course, the pool.

It wasn't a cozy home, in her opinion. It needed softening, with throw rugs and family photos and leafy green plants. It needed the sound of laughter and arguments and friendly conversation. It needed chil—

She stopped herself. That took daydreaming a step too far.

For a moment, she mourned her crowded apartment with its hand-me-down furniture, soft and squishy floor pillows, and colourful posters. She'd be back there soon, but it wouldn't be the same.

Just like she would never be the same, now that she had fallen in love with Rafe.

When the documentary ended, he reached for the remote. Before he could select something new, she asked a question she hoped wouldn't destroy the peaceful atmosphere. But it was one she needed answered.

"Why were you so sure I'd leave you?"

His finger froze on the button, arm in midair. He lowered it to his thigh and slid her a glance out of the corner of his eye. "I told you. What I did was inexcusable. I didn't think you'd *want* to stay."

"Don't you know me well enough by now to know it takes a lot to piss me off?" She folded her knees and sat on her heels, perched sideways on the sofa with one arm lying along the back. "You've met Shyla, right?"

He ignored her jesting second question to answer the first. "I've never seen you lose your temper. But I thought this would do it. And I would have deserved it."

"You deserve to be rejected because you made a mistake?"

"A big mistake. It's not like I mixed up your coffee order. I didn't *trust* you, I *hid* things from you."

"Everyone makes mistakes. It's not life or death."

"Sometimes it is." He jerked to his feet. "I'm a doctor. Sometimes it is."

She still hadn't made that visit to his lab they'd talked about. She really needed to do that sooner rather than later. It was easy to forget he held people's futures in his hands every day. "You're right. I guess even doctors make mistakes. And those can be life-threatening."

He moved to the bookshelves and appeared to be enthralled by an abstract sculpture being used as a bookend, running one long, blunt finger over its sinuous curves. At her words, a shudder ran through his tall frame.

Intuition skittered with spider's feet across her scalp. "You don't have to tell me." She watched him carefully for further signs of discomfort. "But maybe you should."

He didn't deny there was something to tell, but still dodged her question. "It happened long ago. It has no relevance today."

"I think it does." She unfolded from the couch and went to stand beside him. He didn't look at her. "You seem to believe making a mistake deserves a terrible punishment. Maybe some do. But not most of them." His fist rested on the shelf, his elbow bent at a right angle. She laid a hand on his raised forearm, feeling the muscles tense as steel under her touch. "What happened, Rafe?"

It wasn't like it was a secret. His mother and stepfather and Otto knew. Several colleagues knew. There'd been a review of the incident, and the report was available to the public, should anyone ask to see it.

Didn't mean he wanted to talk to Natalie about it.

"Rafe." Her fingers on his forearm squeezed. "You can tell me anything. I'm not going to run screaming from the room."

Tugging his wrist, she led him back to the couch and pressed him to sit down. To his astonishment, she cuddled onto his lap, her feet on the cushion with her knees bent, her buttocks on his thighs, and her head tucked under his chin. His arms encircled her automatically, drawing her close.

"I mean it." Her palm splayed warm and calming on his chest, just over his rapidly thudding heart. "You can tell me anything. Or you can choose *not* to tell me. Either way, I'll be right here."

She exhaled peacefully and her body relaxed as if preparing to sleep. He was unutterably comforted by her declaration, but didn't quite trust it. He knew she meant what she said—now. But when she learned what he had done...?

He'd lied to her once. He couldn't risk their relationship—a relationship that was becoming increasingly vital to his well-being—by *not* taking her into his confidence now. She deserved to know the worst about the person she was involved with.

The words choking his throat escaped in a rush. "I killed a patient."

Chapter Twenty-Five

If his arms hadn't been holding her so tightly, he might not have noticed her tiny flinch. But after that first, involuntary reflex, she remained still and silent.

Waiting.

He continued, each word tasting like poison, numbing his lips. "It was my second year of residency. I was doing a rotation in Emergency, with several fourth-year students under my supervision. A young man came in, presenting with asthma-like symptoms. Two hours later, he was dead."

Natalie rubbed her cheek against his chest, her hair catching in the whiskers of his chin. The room was so quiet he could hear his blood rushing through his veins, ebbing and surging with every pump of his heart. He drew in a deep breath and went on.

"I had assigned him to one of the fourth-year students, and then got caught up with other patients. ER is always busy, but that night was insane. We were all struggling to keep up with the intakes. I only remembered him when a crash call went out. His oxygen saturation level was below fifty percent. I tubed him, gave him adrenaline, everything I could think of. He arrested and died about five minutes later.

"I realized what had happened when I reviewed the records later. His oxygen and CO_2 levels had been checked about an hour after he was admitted. Because he was having difficulty breathing, he'd been put on high flow oxygen right away, so those levels showed normal on a second check. But his CO_2 level was double what it should be. This was a flag for urgent action, and the fourth-year missed it."

"That's tragic." Natalie's voice was soft and compassionate. "But how is that your fault? You didn't even see the readings until after."

"I was in charge. The fourth-years were my responsibility. I should have followed up sooner."

"That's not fair." She straightened, nearly bashing his chin in her indignant haste. Her nostrils pinched as she stared at him. "You said it was crazy busy. You had a lot on your plate."

"It might not be fair, but that's the way it is. Ultimately, I was responsible for that man's death. He was twenty-six years old."

She brushed back the irritating curl of hair that always fell messily onto his forehead. "I understand why you might blame yourself, because you're a caring, intense person who hates to be wrong. But did anyone else blame you?"

The image of the man's mother, her face bone-white with shock, tears streaming down her cheeks as she stood next to her son's body, was forever seared on his mind. Not that she'd said anything, but her eyes had bored into his, condemnation burning through her grief.

He wasn't ready to share that with Natalie. "No one official. There was an internal review, but it was more of a fact-finding, let's-learn-to-do-better investigation than for disciplinary purposes."

"Maybe you could have prevented it. But you're not superhuman. I am sure everyone was doing their best under difficult circumstances."

"That's the thing. It wasn't *my* best." He rolled his shoulders, his skin too tight for his flesh. "I didn't supervise the student properly and someone died. It was my mistake."

"Did that night have anything to do with why you chose pathology?"

The shock of her insight snapped through his bones like lightning attracted to a metal pole. He gave a grunting acknowledgment.

For a long moment, she only looked at him, twisted to face him so he could feel the rise and fall of her breathing. After kissing his forehead with startling tenderness, she cuddled against his chest again, took his right hand in both of hers, and simply held on.

As the next several days passed, Natalie pondered Rafe's revelations, though she didn't bring up the subject again. It had taken a long time for his agitation to pass that night, and she didn't want to cause him more pain.

It didn't matter that she disagreed with his assessment. It only mattered what he believed. At least now she understood him better.

It wasn't the only topic they avoided. Eugenia's scandal was another verboten conversation.

His refusal to bring up the issue made it impossible to do so herself, and the longer he was silent, the more uneasy she grew, wondering if he hoped—even believed—she had agreed to exclude it from the biography. Because she hadn't.

Loving Rafe meant loving everything about him. But accepting him didn't mean she had to accept everything he decreed. So she set herself what was beginning to appear an impossible task—clearing Eugenia's name.

Each day she continued her research, and each day the creeping guilt gripping the back of her neck strengthened. When she found proof Eugenia hadn't done what Rafe believed, she was certain he'd forgive her subterfuge.

Except she hadn't found that proof. She'd interviewed Keaton Hawke as well as several other people whose names had arisen during her investigations, keeping her tone extremely circumspect, dancing around the danger zone, afraid even to hint at the unsavoury possibility. No one had read between the lines of her vaguely worded questions or given her any inkling that might refute her suspicions.

She clicked yet another ancient computer file closed, switched off the screen, and leaned back in her chair, swivelling in short, irritated jerks. Another afternoon with nothing to show for it, at least not in the way of clearing Eugenia's name. The only good news was she also hadn't found anything that outright proved the crimes had occurred, either.

It was almost five o'clock and Rafe would be home soon. She rose from her chair, hips and back stiff. Arms above her head, she arched her spine, hearing tiny pops as her vertebrae loosened, and then gathered up her coffee mug, water bottle, and the plate that had held her lunchtime sandwich.

As she passed the master bedroom on her way down to the main floor, she reflected that the only place she felt truly at peace was in Rafe's arms. Between her self-consciousness regarding her duplicity over her research—no matter how necessary she believed it to be—and his taciturnity regarding, well, everything, it had made for an uneasy atmosphere in recent days. But at night, when her skin met his, when his touch enflamed her, when her caresses made him moan—it was then that a sense of rightness and completion filled her.

She hoped passion would be enough to get them through this bump in their relationship.

Because she wasn't giving up. She never gave up on the people she loved.

Rafe exited the staff door and headed toward the parkade reserved for medical personnel across the street from the hospital. His thoughts were already looking ahead to an evening with Natalie. Maybe tonight would be the night things would get back to the way they had been.

He didn't know how to fix what was broken between them. His confession had been intended to clear the air. Instead, it had only made everything murkier and more unsettled.

In the past, he might have already given up. He hated being in the wrong, hated feeling inadequate and undeserving. But Natalie was different. *She* wasn't the one making him feel this way. He was getting in his own head. If he could figure out how to get past this block, he just knew he could make it right again.

"Rafe? Is that you?"

The voice calling from the shadows of the concrete structure was vaguely familiar. He paused and peered into the gloom. A thin figure detached from the darkness, approaching with slow, hesitant, silent steps.

"I don't know if you remember me..." The woman crossed through a slash of daylight slanting in from the open side of the parkade and he got his first real look.

"I do. Hello, Shyla." He waited, watchful, as she neared, coming to a jittery stop a few feet away. "What are you doing here?"

She wore the same parka she had the evening he and Natalie had picked her up in Quesnel, though the rip in the sleeve had been patched rather haphazardly with a strip of duct tape. Its puffiness gave an illusion of bulk but, when it gaped open, he could see how gaunt she was. Her collarbones stood out sharp and angular above the stretched-out neck of her grimy T-shirt, and it belled out at her waist hinting at a hollow stomach. Her hair was pulled back in a ponytail and her face was clean, but purple bags pouched below her eyes and her skin was sallow.

"Waiting for you." She buzzed with restless energy, like a hummingbird in flight. Shifting her weight from foot to foot and picking at the thumbnail of one hand and then the other, her gaze darted from the floor to him to the ceiling.

"How did you know I'd be here?" A car rumbled down the ramp toward them and they squeezed tighter to the wall to let it pass.

Shyla watched it go by and didn't answer until the sound of the engine had faded. "Dad told me you worked at the hospital. I've been hanging around for a couple of days, trying to catch you."

"Why not call Natalie? If you've talked to your parents, you know she's living with me."

"Don't want to talk to her. Want to talk to you." She gnawed at a hangnail, tore off a strip of skin, and spat it out.

"Why me?" If she wanted medical advice, there were several clinics he could recommend. It had been decades since he'd dealt with patients directly, and he wasn't going to resume that practice with a consult in a parkade. If she hoped he'd write her a prescription, she was totally out of luck.

"I've really screwed things up."

"Yes." She was also out of luck if she wanted sympathy. He'd only been witness to Shyla's disruptive influence in Natalie's life during the last few weeks and maybe he should have felt more charitable. Addiction was an illness, not a choice, after all.

But his loyalty lay squarely with Natalie.

"I want to fix it. I have to fix it."

The echo of his own thoughts softened his rigid stance a fraction. "And how are you going to do that?"

"By getting sober and staying that way." She pulled the elastic band out of her hair and used her fingers to comb the strands back into another ponytail. It wasn't any tidier than the original version. "I haven't had a drink or a toke in two days."

That could explain her twitchiness. If she was in the early stages of withdrawal and was as heavy a user as he suspected, there would be plenty of substances still lingering in her system. The worst was yet to come.

"Good for you." He tried to keep his tone open and friendly but given her flinch he didn't think he managed. "You still haven't answered my question. Why are you here?"

She bit her lip, tugged at her earlobe, and continued to avoid looking him in the eye. "I need money."

Well, that wasn't a surprise. "What for? You lied about it the last time you asked Natalie. Don't lie to me now."

"I told you I screwed things up." Her mouth pulled down in a sullen frown, and then, as if remembering she was trying to befriend him, tilted up in a ghastly smile. She took a step closer and laid her hand on his chest. "I wouldn't lie to you. You're too smart for me."

His nostrils flared at the vinegary scent of her breath. He seemed to recall that was a symptom of opioid use. Not that he imagined regular dental care had been at the top of her list in recent years. "If you're trying to flirt with me, knock it off." He stepped back, out of her reach. "What do you want the money for?"

The sullen look was back. "I can't stay where I'm living now. Everyone there is a user. I can get a bed in a shelter, but I need to buy my own food."

"How much?"

Her red-rimmed, bloodshot eyes widened. She probably hadn't expected such an easy conquest. "A couple hundred bucks?"

"Nice try." He couldn't let her go hungry. But he wasn't the soft touch Natalie was, either. "You can have fifty."

"Fifty! That won't get me nothing."

"Fifty will get you a decent breakfast, lunch, and dinner. Meet me here at this time every day and I'll give you another fifty, as long as you stay clean."

"Don't you trust me?"

"No. And don't think I won't know. I'm a doctor, remember." He waited.

Emotions swept in waves across her face—anger, shame, hope, resignation. "You promise? If I stay sober, you'll give me money for food?"

He nodded.

"Okay."

"I don't have it on me, though. I'll need to go to an ATM." He gestured up the ramp. "My car's that way."

Chapter Twenty-Six

The savoury, rich scents of roasting chicken, cumin, and garlic filled the kitchen. Natalie sat on a bar stool at the island, a half-finished glass of wine in one hand and a comfort read open on her e-reader in the other. The cauliflower and chicken bake would be done in less than half an hour. Rafe should have been home by now, but if he was held up much longer it would be easy to keep warm.

Even as she had the thought, the door leading to the garage opened and then closed with a quiet click. She spun the stool and leaned her elbows behind her on the counter. As he entered the living room, the welcoming smile lighting up her face warmed her from the inside.

Boy, she had it bad.

"Hello, Natalie." He draped his coat over the back of the sofa and smoothed it with his hands.

Her smile slipped and she straightened from her relaxed slouch. "What's wrong?" His face was solemn with a wariness that did *not* bode well for the peace of their evening.

He focused on her, holding his position behind the couch. "I spoke with Shyla today."

Her eyebrows shot to her hairline. "You what? When? Why?"

A brief gleam of amusement lightened his dark gaze, and she felt some of her nervous tension ease. "She was waiting for me in the parking garage after work. That's why I'm a bit late. She asked for money."

Of course she had. But that wasn't her main concern. "How did she look? Was she...okay?" Okay being a relative term in regard to Shyla.

"She said she'd been clean for forty-eight hours. She was jittery and thin and not particularly well groomed, but lucid. And polite." He qualified his last statement, his mouth twitching. "Mostly."

Still, this encounter sounded like an improvement over his only other experience with her sister. She sucked in a slow breath through her nose. "What did she want the money for?"

"She said food."

He deserved points for at least trying to hide his skepticism. She offered a half-smile and asked her next question with trepidation. "Did you give her any?"

Instead of answering, he moved from behind the sofa and came to stand in front of her, placing his large palms on her knees, enveloping them in his warm touch. He was so near the sharp scent of antiseptic hospital cleaner clinging to his clothes was detectable amid the aromas escaping the oven.

"You told me, while we were driving to Quesnel, that you'd given Shyla two thousand dollars to reserve a place at a treatment facility." His voice was as deep and dark as the depths of his espresso-coloured eyes.

He hadn't asked a question, but she answered it anyway. "Yes. We both know she didn't do that." She swallowed. Cradling her wineglass in both hands, she rested her arms on her thighs, leaned her forehead on his chest, and closed her eyes. "I was so hoping she would."

"If the two thousand was a down payment, how much did the whole program cost?" His fingertips rippled around her kneecaps with gentle, rhythmic motions, like playing scales on a piano. She wished he would put his arms around her. Maybe his embrace would chase the chill from her skin.

She didn't know where he was going with this but could see no reason not to tell him. "Fifteen."

"Where was she going to get the rest?"

Oh. She didn't answer. *Couldn't* answer. Not that she needed to. He would understand her silence.

"You can't give it to her, Natalie."

"I have to." Despair washed through her and she started to shake. "I have to. It's the only thing I *can* do."

His long-fingered hands gripped her biceps and held her away from the refuge of his chest. She stared at one of the small white buttons that fastened his shirt closed. "How much have you given to her over the years? Your parents? When does it stop?"

Shame dragged like an anchor, but she tipped her chin up and stared through teary eyes. "When she's better." The other alternative, one Shyla herself had hinted at, was unthinkable.

"You can't force her to heal. That's up to her."

"You think I don't know that?" Swamped by a new wave of mortification, she gulped for air and flapped a hand in a "move away" gesture. He gave her space, and she hopped off the stool. Wine sloshed in her glass, and she turned her back on him, slapping it on the counter. A delicate ting rang through the air as the crystal base cracked when it met the quartz surface.

She was going to have to tell him what she had done. Why she had to give Shyla anything she asked for.

Striding away from the island, away from Rafe, she gripped the back of the leather couch and dug her fingertips into the supple material. "It's my fault she's still an addict."

"You know that's not true. You've done everything you could to help her."

"You're wrong." She couldn't look at him. Didn't want to see the condemnation in his face when he learned what she had done. "She came to me several years ago, when I was still married to Ricky." She'd told Rafe about her ex-husband shortly after they'd become intimate. He'd accepted the news with equanimity...unlike his response to this discussion.

"She asked you for money." The censure in his tone was laced with pity.

She hunched her back and replied, bitterness coating her tongue. "And I did what you want me to do now. I refused her. Ricky said we couldn't afford it. He was right, but I didn't want to let Shyla down. He convinced me it was necessary to say no."

She paused and waited for Rafe to say something in support of Ricky's decree. He remained silent. She swallowed and said the words that would shatter his image of her. He thought she was so forgiving, so understanding. Now he would know the truth.

"I was so *glad* to have an excuse. I was tired of Shyla's demands, her neediness. It wasn't even that hard to stand up to her screaming and pleading. I almost enjoyed it." It made her sick to her stomach even after all this time. "Two days later my parents got a phone call. She had overdosed and was in intensive care. It was days before we knew if she'd survive."

Her marriage to Ricky collapsed shortly after that. She'd blamed him, a little unfairly, for the whole disaster and he'd declared himself unwilling to take second place to her sister any longer.

"Now you see why I have to give her the money. What if this is the chance she needs? How could I live with myself if I refused and...something... happens again?" She couldn't even say the word.

"I'm sorry for what you and your family have gone through. Are going through." A movement of air warned he'd approached. Not touching her, but not rejecting her, either. "It wasn't your fault, though. Whatever happens in future will not be your fault, either. At what point does giving in to her demands become enabling, not supportive? After all these years, don't you think she's had enough chances? That it's time for her to live with the consequences of her decisions, no matter what they are?"

She'd known he was a stick-to-the-rules, brook-no-excuses man. But she'd obviously underestimated his implacable nature. Whirling to face him again, she poked him in the chest. "No one beats an addiction on their own. It takes love and guidance and forgiveness. Look what happened when I *didn't* support her."

"Maybe. But it also takes determination and fight and sheer unwavering guts. And when has Shyla ever demonstrated that?"

Rafe stared down at Natalie's flushed face and wished, not for the first time, that he had his brother's eloquence. Otto wouldn't be making such a hash of this conversation.

"If Shyla had cancer, you wouldn't even *question* giving her the money. But because it's substance abuse—" She pushed past him, anger vibrating from the tips of her toes to the crown of her head. He welcomed it. Better she be furious at him than drown under the weight of her obligations to her sister.

"It's not that." He drew in a slow breath, determined to explain himself properly for once. "I know it's a disease, one that deserves understanding. But Shyla's destructive behaviour isn't only hurting herself. It's hurting you, too. You need to shield yourself."

"I'm not the one who needs protection." She paced the length of the sofa, spinning on her heel with the precision of a palace guard when she reversed direction at each end. "I have so much, and she has nothing."

He didn't point out she'd recently lost her home to fire and her career was in flux. He knew what she meant and was fairly certain she'd rip his head off his neck if he split hairs. "You worked for what you have, though. Shouldn't Shyla be expected to do the same for her sobriety? Humans don't value the things that come too easily."

"You think Shyla has it easy?" She stopped in her tracks, her hands flexing at her sides as if imagining his throat between them, incredulity sharpening the pitch of her voice to operatic levels.

He winced. "I just mean that maybe she should be expected to give a show of good faith. Something to prove she's serious this time. And she needs to do that *before* you give her thousands of dollars more."

Her face paled. "I didn't want to give her the money directly. Even then, something inside me didn't believe she was serious." She muttered the words like a guilty secret. "I wanted to give it to the clinic. She accused me of not trusting her. How could I let her know she was right?"

"Natalie." He reached out and touched her tense shoulder.

Her clenched muscles slumped like a deflating air mattress. "I know, I know. I should have stuck to my guns."

A bell chimed. With a startled exclamation, she circled around the island, turned off the oven, and removed a large baking sheet covered in deliciously browned chicken thighs and cauliflower florets. His stomach rumbled at the peppery, mouthwatering scent.

She stood with her hands full and stared vaguely at the counter, as if expecting a trivet to appear out of nowhere. He pulled open a drawer and retrieved one for her. She lowered the tray, removed the mitts she'd used, and then simply stood, as if uncertain what to do next.

Stepping closer, he trailed his hand down her arm and took her fingers. Despite the fact she'd just removed a dish from the oven, they were chill and limp. "I'm sorry if I've upset you. The last thing I wanted was to make you relive something so painful, and I know this is none of my business and you should tell me to go to hell. But I—I care for you." His heart spasmed and fluttered at this pallid admission of his burgeoning feelings. Feelings he kept tucked deep in a corner of his soul to avoid acknowledging them. "And my next question is *really* none of my business, but I have to ask it. Do you have fifteen thousand dollars to spare? You're going to have extra expenses because of the fire, even with insurance coverage. The book will be done soon, and you'll be paid then, but what are your plans after that?"

"I'll find something. You're so warm." She offered her other hand, and he cradled them both, tenderness clogging his throat at her casual gesture, especially after the tenseness of the last several minutes. "I'm getting twenty thousand for the biography. There will be a little left over after setting aside the money for the program."

He couldn't stand by and let her throw away the very food from her mouth into a bottomless pit. The thought of nourishment reminded him of what he hadn't yet told her. "I never answered your question."

Her fingers tensed in his clasp. "What question?"

"If I gave Shyla any money. I did." His thumbs caressed the bumpy line of her knuckles as he explained the fifty dollars and his reasoning behind it. "If she continues to show up sober, then that might be evidence she is serious about succeeding in a treatment program."

Natalie gazed up at him, a spark of hope gaining strength in her shadowed eyes. "I'll pay you back. If this works..." She trailed off, but her expression was fervent, the flame of her usual cheerfulness blazing strong again.

"We can figure that out later." No way in hell would he accept money from her, but there was also no way he was going to flaunt his embarrassingly excellent financial situation while hers was so precarious. He'd cross that Rubicon when he came to it. "I'm starved. Can we eat?"

Chapter Twenty-Seven

The deadline for Natalie to provide the completed manuscript was less than a month away. She'd fallen behind her intended schedule of having the first draft ready at the halfway point, so buckled down during the next few days for the express purpose of finishing it.

That this resolution also gave her an excuse for holing up in her office was an added bonus. She couldn't avoid Rafe completely, and didn't really want to. What she wanted to avoid was the polite stiffness strangling the atmosphere between them ever since their confrontation. He'd implied he didn't blame her for Shyla's overdose, but he hadn't said it outright and she was certain he disapproved. How could he *not* disapprove of the actions that had risked her sister's life? It was only at night, when she would rouse drowsily to find herself cuddling against his warm back, or in the very early morning, when she would wake to his strong arms wrapped around her, that she felt truly at peace.

Until she remembered Shyla wasn't the only burr between them. There was also the betrayal she had perpetrated against him. One he was yet to discover.

Late Monday afternoon, she stood in his office, watching the printer slide out page after page of neatly typed text. Watching the tangible proof of her work and words...the very work and words that could sever any affection Rafe might feel for her.

She'd put the final touches on the draft an hour ago, and had decided it would be best to present it to him in print instead of emailing a document. Her hope was that reading it on paper would give him the distance he'd need to approve what she'd written, to understand why she'd shared what she had.

By which, of course, she meant the scandal.

In the end, she'd had no choice but to disregard his expressed wishes. Every professional instinct she had, as both an historian and political adviser, had revolted at the thought of ignoring the issue. She had hoped laying it all out in black and white might soften its edges. Instead, it had only solidified the evidence, making it clearer than ever that Eugenia had been unethical at best, criminal at worst.

She lifted a sheaf of paper, still faintly warm, out of the printer tray and stacked it neatly with others she'd already removed. The machine continued its smooth, methodical motions, inexorably revealing, line by line, her breach of faith.

Including the truth of Eugenia's disgrace had the potential to destroy her relationship with Rafe. It had created other, more concrete problems, too.

Her contract stated she'd be paid nine thousand dollars—half of the total remaining after the initial two-thousand-dollar advance—once she submitted the first draft, regardless of what happened after that. While the money wouldn't be much more than a band-aid over the sucking chest wound that was her financial woes, it certainly wouldn't hurt.

The only thing was...she couldn't send the draft to Otto until Rafe had told his brother about their mother's wrongdoing. He deserved to be told in person, not have it revealed in grim, uncompromising text as if he were no more important than any other reader.

But Rafe was refusing to tell him. She'd asked him to do so on a daily basis, ever since she'd decided it *had* to be mentioned in the biography. And every day her hopes he would finally see her side of things were dashed.

He was beginning to get a twitch in his eye when she brought up the subject.

She was walking a very fine tightrope. For several days now, Shyla had shown up sober in the hospital parking garage, and he had kept his promise to give her food money. He'd even gone to meet her on Saturday and Sunday, despite not having to go to work either day. While Natalie was terrified of doing anything that might infuriate him and cause him to stop, she couldn't put off giving him the first draft any longer. She could only pray that the start he had helped Shyla get would be enough, should he cut off all ties with them after he'd read the biography.

The distant trill of her phone sounded faintly over the nearer hum of the printer. She hurried down the hall to where she'd left it next to her laptop in her own office. When she saw the ID, she connected the call with hope and dismay warring in her chest.

"Fred. How's it going?"

Her apartment building manager's gruff and gravelly tones rumbled into her ear. "I wanted to update you on the restoration. Looks like you'll be able to get into your place by the end of the week."

Pleasure at the thought of having her home back was tempered by the thought of leaving Rafe. She hated the idea of abandoning him to his solitary existence, but with the way things were between them—and the way things might rapidly deteriorate in the near future—this was good news. Her love didn't blind her to his irascible temperament, and once he read the draft, he'd probably need privacy while he processed it.

"You still there?"

She started out of her gloomy thoughts. "Yes. Sorry. Thanks, that's great. When can I get the new keys?"

"Call me Thursday."

She disconnected and returned to Rafe's office. A couple of pages had slipped off the tray and lay in bright white patches on the dark carpet. She bent to retrieve them, lifted the stack still on the tray, and set to finding whereabouts the loose pieces belonged.

Rafe would be home soon.

And then she wouldn't be able to put it off any longer.

Rafe hated to admit it, but it had been a relief to go back to work on Monday morning. The tension between him and Natalie was so taut the very air twanged with the force of an elastic band stretched to its limit.

He'd immersed himself in the detailed minutia of his work, surfaced briefly for a quick sandwich eaten at his desk, and then re-submerged until just after five o'clock. In the parkade, he waited until five thirty, but Shyla didn't appear. She'd missed their Saturday appointment, too. He hadn't told Natalie, deciding he would do so only if she missed two in a row. Since she'd been waiting for him on Sunday and still showed no signs she was using, he wouldn't mention it today, either. He wasn't sure which sister he was protecting by keeping the information to himself but felt uncomfortably responsible for both.

As he drove home, he wondered if Shyla was clever enough to hide the evidence of her abuse. He liked to think he wasn't that gullible or naive, but since he couldn't exactly ask her for blood or urine samples, there wasn't much he could do other than make careful observations. Surely if she was using his fifty dollars to enable her habits he'd notice *something*.

Pondering Shyla's situation kept his mind off the state of affairs waiting for him at home. But the instant he walked into the living room, his reprieve was over.

Natalie perched on his black leather couch, knees primly together, back straight. A neat stack of paper lay on the low table in front of her.

His gut clenched and his step hitched. She'd finished the biography.

She spoke as if continuing a conversation from seconds ago. "Remember, it's just a first draft. I still want to tweak the language, add a few reference notes. But the main frame is here. The way I think it should be laid out, the quotes I want to use from the interviews. Everything I believe that needs to be included."

Had he imagined it, or had she emphasized *everything* just a touch? He'd made his feelings perfectly clear regarding the less savoury bits of his mother's career, had stood firm against Natalie's determined arguments. No matter what her personal opinion, he couldn't believe she'd jeopardize her fee by going against his wishes. "Have you sent it to Otto?"

"No." She laid a hand on the ream in a tender, protective gesture. "You need to read it first."

That sounded less than reassuring. A chill wriggled down his spine and he rolled his shoulders to alleviate the frisson of disquiet. "Why?"

"Just read it, Rafe." Her gaze was direct but a flicker of uncertainty in their brown depths belied her firm tone. "Keep an open mind and read it."

His alarm grew stronger. She hadn't done what he now suspected. Had she?

She had.

Her treachery struck so deep he couldn't breathe. Black spots suffused his vision, replaced by sparks that strobed dizzily. He sucked in oxygen on a choking gasp, air sliding solid as chunks of ice into his lungs, despite the warmth of the office where he'd gone to read the manuscript in private.

Any appetite he might have had for dinner had vanished when Natalie had pressed the manuscript into his hands. Mouth too dry to speak, he'd simply nodded and climbed the stairs, holding the heavy stack so tightly the paper crackled, tempted to throw it over the mezzanine railing as if doing so would erase every word inked on the white sheets. Instead, he entered his office, closed the door, and laid it gently on the desk before sinking into the high-backed chair behind it.

The first page was innocent enough—a list of potential titles. He placed it face down to the left of the stack and revealed a table of contents. The chapter headings made it simple enough to skip to the section of the book he was most concerned about.

And discovered the whole of his mother's nefarious activities laid out in excruciatingly exact detail on the pages before him.

He laid his forearms on the desk and pressed his palms flat to still their trembling. How was it possible to be icily numb and burn with rage at the same time?

The evidence Natalie had presented didn't come as a shock. In fact, she'd missed some of the more damning testimony—probably because it was locked in the safe hidden at the back of the closet in this room. He'd long ago come to terms that his towering giant of a mother had had feet of clay.

It wasn't even that she'd included it in this draft. He and Otto had the right to make any changes they wished. If Natalie wanted to be paid, she'd do what she was told.

No. It was the fact that she had ignored his request, his heartfelt, passionate request, that made him want to howl with fury and pain.

He'd thought she was different. Had thought he might have finally found the person that would put him first, would cherish his thoughts and opinions above their own.

He should have known better. He should have known not to hope.

And now that hope was shattered like a mirror, sparkling shards scattered at his feet, seven years of bad luck just beginning.

Seven years. Hah. He had enough bad luck to last a lifetime. Or was it bad luck when you brought it on yourself? He was the one who had believed she liked and respected him enough to acquiesce to his needs. More fool he.

Moving gingerly, as if his muscles had atrophied along with his heart, he walked with slow, measured steps out of his office and across the hall. Gripping the railing overlooking the living space below, he worked saliva into his mouth.

Natalie stood in the kitchen, staring up at him, silent and still. She held a knife in one hand and something green and leafy in the other. A cutting board lay on the counter before her and a pot steamed gently on the stove at her back.

"Go." The syllable was barely a whisper. He cleared his throat and tried again. "Go." He tasted blood, as if the word had cut his tongue on its way out of his mouth.

"Rafe..."

He closed his eyes, but that just brought her image closer, so he opened them again.

"Go," He unclenched the railing, fingers curled into claws, and retreated to his office, shutting the door with a click that echoed like a gunshot in his soul.

Chapter Twenty-Eight

Natalie did the only thing she could think of. She called Aubrey. Her friend agreed without hesitation to her request for sanctuary, and she drove to her home on autopilot.

Other than her laptop and phone, she brought two small bags of clothing and personal products with her. She only needed enough to last a couple of days. When she got the keys to her apartment on Thursday, she'd return to Rafe's—at a time when she could trust he'd be at work—and pack up the rest of her things.

Only what she'd bought or brought herself. She never wanted to wear anything he'd given her again. He could donate it all to a thrift store.

Hopefully, he wouldn't change the lock code on his door. If he did, she'd have to abandon everything she left behind. The thought of talking to him—or worse, *seeing* him—made her organs seize.

She parked in front of Aubrey and Phillip's home on Cedar Street with no memory of driving there. Dusk was deepening and soft light gleamed from the two square windows on either side of the bright blue front door. Clinging to any thought that kept her mind off Rafe, she recalled her first horrified sight of Aubrey's impulsive purchase—a worse-than-ramshackle house with a long-neglected hedge and scraggly yard. The now lovingly restored home, with its neatly tended though still winter-bare gardens, was one she'd visited often. Its easy familiarity wasn't enough to dispel the disconnect she'd suffered at Rafe's uncompromising rejection. She had the disturbing sensation her head wasn't attached to her body.

The front door opened, and Phillip strode down the steps. He ducked to peer through the passenger window, his silver hair gleaming with the last rays of the sun. She waggled a hand, opened her own door, and climbed out.

"I don't need any help." She reached into the back seat, lifted out her laptop, and hooked her fingers in the loops of her two bags. "There's not much to bring in."

"That's okay. I'm here now."

He waited on the sidewalk as she rounded the hood. Every movement took conscious effort, as if the air was made of Velcro, and she made no protest as he took the bags from her. She clutched her laptop to her chest as she followed him up the winding brick path and through the front door.

When Aubrey had bought the house, there had been two small front rooms with a narrow hall leading to a cramped kitchen. She had had several walls torn down and it was now a cozy, welcoming living space that encompassed eating, cooking, and sitting areas. Phillip disappeared to the right and she trailed after him, arriving at a guest suite with a private entrance to the main floor bathroom. She had never stayed there—it was mostly used by Aubrey's stepdaughter when she visited from Toronto or Phillip's son on his infrequent trips from Winnipeg.

Aubrey was in the suite, fluffing pillows and straightening the downy comforter. Suddenly, Natalie was exhausted. She put out a hand to brace herself on the door frame, wanting nothing more than to curl up under the puffy duvet and drop into sleep.

Phillip placed her improvised luggage on the floor by the closet. "Dinner is ready when you are. Take your time getting settled." He stepped past with a brief pat on her shoulder that spoke volumes about just how shattered she must look. He wasn't a touchy-feely guy under usual circumstances.

Aubrey lowered onto the bed and patted the mattress. "Come sit before you fall down."

She did as instructed, laying her laptop on her knees and clasping her hands on its smooth black surface. "Thanks for letting me come."

"Of course. You're always welcome here."

The tears burning the back of her nose threatened to erupt. She swallowed them down. The only place she wanted to be welcome was Rafe's and she'd ruined her chances there. She had never dreamed he'd eject her so forcibly and abruptly. She'd thought he'd give her an opportunity to explain.

Though why she'd hoped one more repetition of her reasoning would change his stubborn, block-headed mind she didn't know.

"Do you want to talk about it?"

All she had told Aubrey was that she had to leave Rafe's and couldn't get into her apartment for a few days. "Not really."

"How about something to eat?"

Her stomach was a shuddering mass of roiling nausea. She didn't think she'd be able to keep anything down, but she couldn't sulk in her room like an angsty teenager. "Sure. Just give me a minute to put some things away."

"Of course." Aubrey stood up. "I mean it, Natalie, and so does Phillip. You are welcome here anytime. Stay as long as you need. You don't have to be alone until you're ready." She left the room, her long skirt swishing about her ankles.

Natalie collapsed backward onto the bed, aware she was clutching her laptop like a security blanket. She laid it aside and rubbed the heels of her hands in her eye sockets, forcing back the still brewing tears.

She wasn't sure she'd ever be ready to live a life without Rafe. But she had no choice but to try.

Rafe arrived home on Thursday and made his way directly upstairs. While her possessions had still been in her office and bedroom, he'd held out hope she might reject his rejection, forgive him, and return.

The ghost of her summery scent greeted him as he neared the archive room. For a split second his heart lifted. *She's here!*

But when he looked in, his momentary exultation evaporated. The sunflower mug, slippers, and other items he'd grown accustomed to were gone. He hurried to her bedroom, where nothing seemed changed...until he rolled back the closet door and several empty hangers tolled dolefully. He didn't bother opening any dresser drawers. The evidence was clear.

She was gone. For good.

A large cardboard box rested on the floor next to the door. He wanted to kick it across the room, but instead unfolded the flaps, revealing neatly folded clothing. At first, he didn't understand. Why had she not taken these? Was she coming back to get them?

And then he realized what they were. The clothes he had bought—that Elizabeth had bought—after the fire.

This message was even plainer. She was cutting him out of her life, making a clean break of it. She wanted nothing from him.

Numbness settled over him like a muffling quilt, dulling his senses. Too bad it didn't mask his searing pain.

He went through the motions of changing into casual, at-home clothes and making a sandwich for dinner, though he choked down less than half of it. Now he was clicking sluggishly through the offerings on Netflix, unable to raise enough energy to choose one. Maybe he should go for a swim. Physical exertion might knock him out of his funk. He discarded the idea. It was possible the apathy cloaking him would sink him to the bottom of the pool. Television was a safer bet.

The doorbell rang and he leaped to his feet as if electrocuted.

Natalie.

She'd changed her mind. She'd come back. His life would have lightness and joy again.

He hurried to the front door with eager, rapid steps, ready to throw himself on his knees and beg her forgiveness—only to discover Otto was his unexpected visitor.

"Oh." He stared blankly. "I didn't know you were in town."

"I wondered if you'd seen my texts." Otto entered without waiting for an invite. "Normally I get some sort of reply, even if it is just a virtual grunt."

He had only been checking his phone to see if Natalie's name had appeared. If he'd seen messages from his brother, he couldn't remember them.

"Why are you here?" He followed Otto to the living room, depression once more dragging at his heels.

"I told you. Because you didn't answer my messages. You're a big boy, but you *never* ignore me for that long." He spun slowly on his heels, his gaze sweeping the room, an expression of worried incredulity creasing his features. "What the hell is going on?"

Frowning, Rafe took in the dirty dishes littering the kitchen island, the stale remains of his sandwich on the coffee table, the coat discarded on the back of the sofa instead of in the closet where it belonged. By many standards, just an ordinary, lived-in home.

By his rules, a disaster scene of near epic proportions.

He didn't bother answering, assuming Otto's question was rhetorical. He did, however, gather up the plate and glass from the coffee table, bring them to the kitchen, and start clearing up the debris.

Otto planted himself on Natalie's bar stool. He wanted to order him to choose another and only refrained by dint of pressing his lips together. Needing to move, to *do*, he decided to wash the dishes by hand.

"Something's up." Otto slouched against the low back of the stool and swivelled gently. "And it has to do with Natalie Minton, doesn't it?"

He turned on the hot water, reached under the sink for the dishwashing liquid, and squirted a generous amount under the stream.

"Rafe. Tell me. What happened?"

He watched the bubbles foaming, white and clean and fragile. Ignoring Otto was not an option. His brother would nag and prod until his head exploded.

It was time to come clean. About so many things.

"She's gone." He loaded the sink with glassware, turned off the tap, and searched below the suds for the dishcloth.

"Gone where?"

He didn't know, and that gnawed at him with sharp, guilty teeth. He assumed she was with friends— she *had* friends, after all, not like him—but he didn't *know*. "I'm not sure."

"Why did she leave?"

"I told her to."

"For god's sake, Rafe. This is worse than pulling teeth. Spit it out, will you?"

He rinsed a glass and placed it precisely on the drying mat. The silence was broken only by the faint pop of bubbles and the hum of the refrigerator.

Otto sighed and slid off the seat. Without asking permission, he headed to the cupboard that held the liquor glasses and took out a short, squat tumbler. "I'll just have a drink, then." He knew where to find the Scotch, too. When he'd helped himself to two fingers, he resumed his seat and sipped as if he hadn't a care in the world.

Rafe's teeth clenched and a muscle jumped in his jaw. The tendons of his neck were so tight he imagined he could snap them with a twist of his chin. He'd never been one to share his misery, preferring to hide all emotions, wary of being ridiculed. If he didn't want to talk about Natalie, no one could make him.

Otto twisted the tumbler between his fingers, amber liquid sloshing gently against the sides. "I've read the draft."

Rafe's gaze flew from the dish in his soapy hands to his brother's bland face. "You couldn't have."

"Natalie emailed it to me two days ago."

Chapter Twenty-Nine

He should have anticipated this. Of course she would send it to Otto. She needed to be paid, and Otto was the one who held the funds. Just because Rafe had rejected her didn't mean she would give up. The money was too important to her and Shyla.

"She called me first, warned me what I would read." Otto watched him with piercing attention. "Said she'd tried to get you to tell me but that you wouldn't. Explained why she felt she had to include what she'd found in the book."

Feeling as if his joints had rusted together, he stretched out an arm and placed the dish he'd been washing next to the others on the drying mat. Then he gripped the edge of the sink and rocked on the balls of his feet, anxious energy fizzing and twitching his nerve endings. He had no clue what to say.

Otto didn't seem to require a reply. He continued in a calm tone. "I'm going to demand she delete all mention it if she wants her money. If she doesn't, the contract is null and void as per the terms we laid out, and we won't owe her anything."

It was what he had wanted. Not only someone to understand that the scandal had to remain buried, but for someone to take his side. If he'd told Otto like Natalie had wanted, he would have saved himself months of scheming and conniving. But he'd been trying to spare his brother, hadn't wanted him to learn the ugly truth.

The thing was, hearing Otto agree their mother's secrets had to remain hidden... It was wrong. It was wrong to demand Natalie lie for them, betray her own principles.

And she was more important than his mother's reputation or Otto's potential career.

He'd always believed causing the death of a patient in his care would be the nadir of his existence. Until now. Not trusting Natalie, not listening to her side of things, not supporting her integrity, her beliefs—*that* was the biggest mistake of his life.

He'd learned to live with errors made under the intense pressure of medical training. He didn't think he could learn to live without Natalie.

"You can't do that." Conviction rang in his tone and Otto's eyebrows rose. "Natalie's right. Hiding it would only make it look worse. And she deserves to be paid in full, no matter what."

Otto's pale blue eyes pinned Rafe. "That's not what you told Natalie. You kicked her out because of what she'd written. I thought you'd agree with me, that this was what you wanted."

"I was wrong." He hated being wrong. It put him on the defensive, made him doubt himself. Not this time, though. Admitting his mistake was freeing, liberating. "We have to include it in the book."

Otto shook his head. "We can't. No good would come of it. It all happened so long ago there's no reason to shout it from the rooftops now. And you know what it could do to my chances for the nomination."

"Screw your nomination."

Otto's eyebrows winged higher. "Excuse me?"

"If the party can't see you are a separate entity from our mother, that what she did has nothing to do with you, then screw them. Natalie's right. We have to let it come out. It's the truth, and the truth needs to be shared."

"I suppose there's no way to stop her from releasing the information on her own. We should have put a non-disclosure clause in the contract. I never dreamed we'd need it, though."

"She wouldn't do that." He was as certain of that as he'd been of anything in his life. "She's not a tabloid journalist. She wouldn't take what she knows and sell it to someone else. But she also won't put her name to a project that hides the truth. She has too much integrity, too much respect for herself and her professional reputation."

"So, if we refuse to use her manuscript, refuse to pay her, she'll just walk away? Let someone else do the biography, someone who will accept our demands?"

"Yes."

Otto drained his glass and slapped it down with a flourish. "Here's what I propose. We pay her the half she has owing for the draft, but we make her sign a new contract that includes an NDA and the right to give her draft to another writer. We can edit out the dishonourable bits ourselves before sending it along. Her name would not be associated with the book, and we don't lose as much time as we would if we had to start from scratch. I'm willing to cough up the nine grand to keep us on track.

"What do you say?"

The apartment smelled strongly of fresh paint and floor glue. Natalie dropped the last load of what she'd retrieved from Rafe's in the echoingly empty bedroom and wandered back to the living area. She couldn't help comparing the small space to the airy elegance of his home, though it was pointless doing so. She'd only ever been a temporary resident there and shouldn't have let herself grow accustomed to it. Or to its owner.

The busyness of buying replacement food, furniture, and fixtures had kept her from obsessing over Otto's reaction—or lack thereof—to the biography. He had made no comment when she'd told him about Eugenia's corrupt activities, simply instructed her to send the document immediately so he could review it. Other than a terse thank you email including a generic promise to be in touch, she'd heard nothing since, and that had been two days ago.

He hadn't paid her yet, either.

Her phone rang with the chime indicating someone was requesting access at the apartment building's front door. Her new furniture wasn't being delivered until the next day, and the Silverberries weren't expected until Saturday for a casual housewarming party. Not that they were calling it a house*warming*—Helen having pointed out it might be too on the nose for celebrating the return to a home that had been damaged by fire.

She connected the call. "Hello?"

"It's me," Shyla said. "Can I come up?"

She blinked in shock. Though she desperately wanted to know if Rafe had stuck with his promise to support Shyla, she hadn't been able to bring herself to message either of them. She might have lost what little control she had over her emotions if he had ignored her texts, and it had felt too intrusive to call Shyla directly. She'd done enough to jeopardize her sister's recovery by alienating Rafe. Putting her back up by asking if she was staying sober wouldn't help at all.

"Natalie? Can I come in?"

"Of course. Sorry. Still getting used to this app." The lie came far too easily off her tongue. She unlocked the building entrance, opened her private door, and stuck her head out in the hall. Moments later, Shyla appeared, walking sure and steady, head high.

Oh, thank God. Natalie's eyes brimmed with tears. "You look so *good*." Too impatient to wait, she let the door swing shut and hustled down the hall. "You look *great*."

She wanted to wrap her in a tight hug, but Shyla

had rejected such advances in the past. So it was doubly welcome when her sister gave her a quick, shy, unprompted embrace.

"Thanks. I hope it's okay I came by." She tucked several strands of brunette hair behind her ear. It hung past her shoulders, the ends uneven and thin, but gleamed shiny and clean in the hallway lights.

"Of course it is. You can stop by anytime." She opened the apartment door. "There's nowhere to sit yet, except the floor. My furniture doesn't get delivered until tomorrow."

"That's fine." Shyla shoved her hands into her pockets and went through the small hall to the living area. The sliding glass doors looked south, and the setting sun was hidden by clouds heavy with impending snow. With no lamps or ceiling fixture, the room was dim and gloomy, despite its new coat of paint.

"You really do look great." Natalie couldn't help repeating herself. Shyla's skin, while still ravaged around the eyes and mouth by years of drug and alcohol use, no longer had a greasy, oily, neglected look. "How have things been?" She didn't dare ask anything more pointed, no matter how much she wanted to know about Rafe.

Shyla's answer rang with honesty. "Fucking hard. But I'm hanging in there."

"Good for you." What else was there to say? Topics for small talk were few and far between. In the past, any mention of her own career or friends or future plans had resulted in accusations of flaunting her good fortune. As for well-intended questions meant to draw Shyla out...her sister tended to consider them in the same light as the Spanish Inquisition.

The silence between them was about to reach awkward heights when Shyla blurted out, "Rafe misses you."

Natalie's heart pumped hard once, stopped for a

breath, and then began again in a rapid rhythm that made her lightheaded. "What do you mean?"

"What do you think? I saw him yesterday and today. He looks like a truck ran over him. Twice. When I asked what was wrong, he told me you moved out."

There were many surprising things about all that, not least of which was the fact that Shyla had even noticed Rafe's appearance. She rarely tuned in to other people's emotional states. Natalie, however, couldn't let the first statement go. "He said he missed me?"

Shyla pushed her fists deeper into the pockets of her jeans. She noticed, as if from a great distance, that though they were worn and faded, they were clean. "Not in so many words. But he's a wreck."

"Don't take this the wrong way, but it's not as if you've known him long. How can you tell?"

"He just handed over the money. Didn't ask me any of the usual questions. Like he didn't really care anymore."

She squeezed her eyelids tight for a moment, swamped by relief that Rafe hadn't abandoned Shyla despite her betrayal. "He's still holding up his end of the bargain."

"Yeah. Why wouldn't he?"

If Shyla hadn't realized that the dissolution of Natalie and Rafe's relationship might endanger her recovery, there was no need to spell it out. "Never mind. If he had asked his usual questions, would he have liked the answers?"

Shyla lifted her chin, defiant and proud. "Yes. I'm clean. I know it's barely been a week, but I'm going to do it this time."

"What about White Spruce? Do you still want to go to the rehab program there?"

She nodded vigorously. "I do. I have to. I'm tempted all the time, even at the shelter. I need to get right away from that life, make a true break."

"Is there still space for you?"

"Yes." The look she slid Natalie was shamefaced but not sly. "Mom and Dad put up the deposit. I had them send the money right to the clinic. I should have let you do that in the first place."

The tiny ember of hope that had been flickering faintly for the last week grew a little stronger. Maybe this truly would be the time Shyla made it. "What about the rest?"

Her mouth pressed together. "I didn't ask them for it. They think the two thousand is all that's needed. There's a counsellor at the shelter that says there might be other ways to get the rest, funding and grants and stuff."

Natalie had never heard of such opportunities and hoped this counsellor could be trusted.

Because she was very much afraid the Talbots weren't going to allow her to finish their mother's biography.

Goodbye, eighteen thousand dollars.

Chapter Thirty

Rafe stewed over Otto's suggestion all Friday. His brother had agreed to wait until Monday before making the offer, and he was hoping he could come up with an alternative before then. So far, all he'd come up with was paying Natalie what she was owed out of his own pocket. He wouldn't tell her, of course, or she wouldn't take it. But giving her the means to walk away with her head held high would be worth every penny.

He wasn't sure why he wasn't happy with Otto's plan. On the surface, it seemed a fair compromise. Natalie would be compensated for the work she'd done and wouldn't have to suffer the indignity of revising the manuscript. But asking her to sign the non-disclosure agreement stank of cover up and secrecy.

Probably because it was.

As he waited for Shyla at the entrance to the parking garage—he'd left work a little earlier than usual, unable to focus—he continued to mull it over.

Natalie had been adamant that the truth should be told, not just to protect her integrity as an historian but because the public record should be set straight. She believed no one should be lauded for greatness when that reputation had been built on lies and deceit.

He knew she would rather wash her hands of the whole affair than take money that reeked of bribery. But he also knew she needed the cash, wanted it more for Shyla than herself.

He hated to think she might be desperate enough

to compromise her beliefs. Hated to admit he'd been the one to drive her into such a position.

Hated to realize how much he loved her, now it was too late. Because the most important conclusion he'd come to after his conversation with Otto was that he loved Natalie. He was ready to toss his brother and his mother into the political wilderness in order to make her happy, to make her proud of him.

He'd never felt that way before. It had to be love.

It was *awful*.

Shyla came into view at the far corner of the parkade. He straightened out of his slouched position against the concrete wall and watched her approach. He'd given her the allowance, as she now referred to the money, the last couple of days without paying her close attention, too caught up in his misery. Today he would ensure she was keeping up her side of the deal.

"Hey." She shuffled to a stop beside him. "How's it going?"

"Well enough." He studied her, not bothering to hide his scrutiny. "You?"

"Good. Still off the junk." She traced one index finger over her left breast in the shape of an X. "Cross my heart and hope to die."

The jitters were gone, and she smelled of soap and mint, though she was still excruciatingly thin. "Here you go." He handed her two twenties and a ten.

She stared at the money, but didn't reach for it, her nostrils flaring.

"What's wrong?"

"I don't know." She sounded bewildered. "I don't want to take it."

"Do you have a choice? Any other way to feed yourself?"

"No."

He stretched out his arm again. "Then take it." Natalie might never forgive him for being such an asshole, but he could do this much for her.

Shyla took the bills gingerly, with none of the eagerness and lack of self-consciousness she had exhibited even as recently as the day before. "Why are you doing this?"

"Because I promised your sister. And because you're staying clean." The last thing he wanted was for her to develop a conscience and refuse to accept his money. She was his only connection with Natalie, and he couldn't lose that. "If you think it's charity, it's not. You're doing a job by staying sober. Consider this your pay cheque."

She folded the bills and tucked them in the front pocket of her jeans. "I saw Natalie yesterday."

Yes! This had been his hope, that if he continued meeting Shyla, she might feed him snippets of information, enough to ease his worry, his guilt. "How is she?"

"Miserable."

He rocked on the balls of his feet as if readying for a fight. "Why? What's wrong?"

"What do you think?" She stared in disbelief. "She misses you, you idiot."

It wasn't the insult that set him back on his heels. "No, she doesn't."

Shyla quirked a wry smile. "Yes, she does. I don't understand it either. You're a cranky bastard most of the time. But when I told her I was still meeting you, she got a look in her eye. And even though we talked about other things, she kept circling back to you."

Was it possible she didn't hate him? She'd forgiven Shyla over and over again for seemingly unforgivable actions. Could Natalie possibly extend that same compassion to him?

"Happy Homecoming!" Helen carolled before the door was fully open. She wore a dollar-store tiara on her short grey hair and carried another in her hand.

She promptly placed the second on Natalie's head. "You must be so pleased to be back."

The cheerful faces of the other Silverberries—Nathan, Terrance, Penta, Stephanie, Aubrey, and Lynn—beamed at her over Helen's shoulder. They carried balloon bouquets and cellophane-wrapped flowers and various other parcels and packages.

She stepped back, amused and touched by their exuberance, and they trooped in with noisy confusion. "I thought this was just going to be a casual thing."

Nathan kissed her cheek. "You should know better by now. And here's a little something that might be more useful than a crown." He handed her a grocery store gift card.

Terrance flourished two bottles of wine with silver bows fluttering at their necks. "The Silverberries do nothing by halves, darling. I don't suppose you've restocked with crystal, which is what this wine deserves, but needs must. Where are your glasses?"

Emotions choking her into silence, she pointed at a cupboard.

Her quiet apartment filled with chatter and laughter as her friends made themselves at home. Penta offered a handmade quilt, Aubrey a stack of luxuriously fluffy bath towels, and Stephanie a compact but fully equipped toolbox.

Lynn handed her a folded piece of purple construction paper decorated with a toddler's rendition of a house and tree. "Oscar made you a card, and Benjamin sends his best wishes."

"Thank you." Natalie hugged her, impeded by her hard, rounded belly. "How are you feeling?"

"Exhausted. Excited. Ready for this to be over." Lynn arched her spine and pressed her fists into her lower back. "My hips feel like they're going to fall apart."

"Not much longer now." It was little consolation, but all she could offer.

"Thank god."

Stephanie poked her head out of the tiny galley kitchen and pointed a demanding finger at Lynn. "Go sit down. Natalie, do you have a vase for these?" She brandished the bouquet like a sword.

In her hurried restocking of her home, frivolities such as vases had taken second place. She filled her water bottle from the tap and handed it to Stephanie, and then joined everyone in the living room.

The flowers, balloons, and conversation couldn't help but make her smile, though the muscles felt rusty from disuse. She still hadn't heard from Otto—or Rafe. Not that she expected the latter to call, no matter what Shyla had said. As much as she wanted to believe her sister was right that he missed her, she couldn't afford to put too much faith in it.

It would hurt too much when it came to nothing.

Over the clamour, she heard a knock at her door. No one had buzzed her to get into the building since the Silverberries had arrived. Was it a neighbour, complaining about the noise already?

She pulled open the door...to discover Rafe standing in the hall.

Rafe drank in his first sight of Natalie in days. He'd spent hours trying to fix her in his mind but had forgotten how the tips of her eyebrows tilted up, the way her hair swung against her cheek, the exact curve of her waist as it flared to her hips.

She stood square in the doorway, planted like a sentry. "How did you get in the building?" Her tone was mild enough but not exactly welcoming.

"Someone was leaving as I arrived." He'd been wondering what to do if she wouldn't let him in when he buzzed, so his timing had been fortuitous. He wasn't so sure now. Having her reject him face to face would be agonizing.

A burst of laughter reached his ears, and he realized she wasn't alone. In fact, it sounded like she was having a party. So much for believing she was pining away in solitary gloom, as he had been. He shouldn't have let Shyla's impressions give him hope. Natalie had had a life before they'd met, and she would have one after him.

"You're busy." He shuffled backward several steps. "I'll go."

"Wait." She crossed the threshold, pulling the door after her but not quite closing it. "Why did you come? Was it about the biography?"

"Damn the biography to hell!"

Her eyes widened, but she didn't flinch.

He drew in a deep breath. "Sorry. I'm sick to death of the biography. I came to see *you*."

The hall light flared on her lenses, making it difficult to read her eyes. After a pause that felt like eons, she reversed through the door, holding it open. He didn't move.

"Well?" She gestured to the interior of the apartment. "Are you coming in or not?"

Chapter Thirty-One

Natalie's heart beat fast and light, a hummingbird trapped in her chest. Rafe remained where he was, blank-faced, his posture stiff. She couldn't believe he had come to her. It was as if an injured wolf had shown up on her doorstep, wary and cautious and dangerous yet desperate for comfort.

Shadows hooded his eyes, deepened the hollows of his cheeks, stained the whiskers on his chin. For several moments, she thought he would flee.

When he did accept her challenge, her knees weakened and she had to press herself against the wall to remain upright. He paused where the hall branched into the living room. She sidled past.

Conversation stopped mid-sentence, and seven pairs of eyes swung between her and Rafe, expressions ranging from interest to suspicion.

"You all remember Rafe." She narrowed a warning glare, daring her friends to say anything other than polite platitudes. Aubrey was the only one who knew what had happened earlier that week—though even she didn't know the whole story—but Natalie had the sneaking suspicion she'd hinted at the drama to the rest of the group. "We need to talk for a minute. I'll be right back."

She gripped his wrist and dragged him to her bedroom. His bones were strong and firm under her fingers, his skin warmer than hers. Once inside, she released him and shut the door. Her palm tingled from the contact, and she curled her fingers, not wanting to lose the sensation.

He stood at the end of her queen bed, barely an arm's length away. The room was just big enough to hold the bed, a nightstand, and a narrow dresser. She'd chosen a duvet cover splashed with enormous sunflowers and bright yellow sheets, and thanked the heavens she'd tidied up this morning in anticipation of the Silverberries visit.

Through the barrier at her back, she heard the murmur of conversation resume. Outside the window, a horn blared angrily, fading as it travelled through the intersection.

He remained silent. It seemed as if she'd have to be the one to jump start the conversation.

"Are you going to answer my question?" She crossed her arms behind her and leaned against the door. It was a little uncomfortable but would prevent her from touching him like she longed to do. "Why did you come?"

He didn't answer. She waited, doing her best to be patient. Rushing Rafe had never worked in her favour.

"I shouldn't have sent you away." He bit out the words and she wondered who exactly he was angry with—himself for giving the order or her for cornering him into making it.

"I shouldn't have gone." *That* surprised him. Not that he gave any overt indication, but she knew him well enough to read the tiniest of his twitches. "I knew you were going to be angry. I should have waited you out. Given you space but staying close enough we could talk when you were ready. Are you ready now?"

His nod was a sharp, short jerk. "I think so."

Another silence brewed between them. She'd taken the first step. The next move was up to him.

He lowered to the bed, his long legs folding abruptly. "Otto is threatening not to pay unless you sign an NDA and give us the rights to what you've done so far."

Her stomach dropped, leaving a queasy hollow

inside her belly. "I suspected something like that." Knees weak, she perched on the nearest corner of the mattress, ensuring there was a good two feet between them.

"I think he's wrong."

She tilted her head and squinted. He was silhouetted against the window, and it was still bright enough outside to make it hard to see his face. "You do?" She tried to keep the doubt from her voice, but didn't think she succeeded.

"You're right." The admission didn't sound as if it was easy to make, his voice tight and grim. "Hiding what we know, now that we know it, would be a mistake in the long run. I told Otto that."

"You did?" He was launching one surprising admission after another, and she was having trouble keeping up. She cleared her throat. "I mean, thanks. For sticking by me."

"I know I've been an ass about the whole thing. It's just, my mother never accepted second-best. That's why Otto was the favourite son. He could do no wrong, and she would have done anything to see him succeed. And that would definitely include hiding her sins. Less for herself than to prevent them from coming to roost on his shoulders."

"Maybe she should have thought of that before she sinned." Natalie didn't bother to hide her sarcasm.

Instead of defending his mother again, he shrugged fatalistically. "Maybe. I was just doing what I thought she'd want."

She supposed it didn't matter how old you were. You always wanted your parents' love and approval. "I can understand that. I hope you can understand where I was coming from, too."

"I do. At least I think so." He shifted and the mattress dipped. She braced herself on one arm to avoid falling toward him. "I know we can never go back to what we had. But I'd like it if we could still see each other. Once in a while."

"You want to be friends? Only friends?"

His chin dipped shyly. "If you're open to the idea."

"I don't think I am."

He reared back, his face draining of colour. "Of course. I just thought...never mind. I'll go." He bolted to his feet, but the smallness of the room meant he had to squeeze by her knees to get to the door.

She reached out and grabbed his waistband. "I don't want to be your friend, Rafe. I want to be more."

Rafe didn't think his heart could take much more stress. It had stopped and started half a dozen times during his conversation with Natalie. If he'd been hooked up to a monitor, the irregular pattern would have looked like he was having a myocardial infarction.

Natalie's position sitting on the bed put her head dangerously close to his cock. She tugged and his hips arched toward her before he could stiffen his spine.

"What?" He croaked like a raven, harsh and grating.

"I want more than your friendship, Rafe." She stood and hooked her free hand into the waistband on his other hip.

The crown of her head reached his chin—barely—and he fought the impulse to wrap his arms around her and curl over her in an attempt to absorb her into his very being. She was everything he needed—light, warmth, nourishment.

"I kicked you out of my house." As much as he longed to believe her well of forgiveness was deep enough even for someone as wretched as him, he couldn't believe she'd be able to look past what he'd done. He'd basically tossed her out into the street, with nowhere to go, no one to look out for her.

"You were pissed off. I don't blame you—for being

angry or for what you did."

His ears buzzed with the drone of a thousand flies. He shook his head to chase the sensation away, and the annoying lock of hair fell over his forehead. He ignored it. "How can you not?"

"I put my opinions and needs ahead of yours. I didn't understand exactly how much it bothered you, how conflicted you were. You're a painfully honest man, Rafe. I know that. You'd decided keeping the truth buried was the best course of action, but I should have realized how difficult that was for you. And then to see it all laid out in my draft"—she leaned forward, slid her arms to his back, and laid her cheek on his chest—"no wonder you lashed out."

He gave in. He clutched her with such ferocity she let out a startled *oomph*. He didn't apologize. He was holding her again. She was finally where she belonged.

Nudging her temple with his chin, he urged her to lift her face. Her glasses had slipped, revealing a red mark on the bridge of her nose. Behind the lenses, her eyes were bright with wonder and hope and something tender he wasn't sure he could name. Her lips trembled open, and he didn't wait for further invitation.

He wasn't sure he had the right to lay claim to her, not yet, and intended to make his kiss gentle, hesitant, pleading. But the instant his mouth touched hers, she moaned deep in her throat and plastered herself against him.

His beast, the one he'd kept chained in the dungeon for far too long, took over.

He devoured her, his tongue fierce and demanding. His hands roamed from the silky strands of her hair to her slender neck to the delicious heft of her ass. In between kisses, he told her breathlessly how much he had missed her, how sorry he was, made promises never to send her away again. The words were disjointed and frantic, but he couldn't be rational. Too much emotion flooded him, overpowering, uplifting, enlightening.

The bedroom door burst open, startling him out of his erotic haze. Natalie pivoted in his arms, and they faced the intruder.

Terrance stood clutching the handle, white-faced, quivering. "Lynn's gone into labour."

Chapter Thirty-Two

A deep, guttural moan rolled down the hall, followed by startled, twittering babble.

Natalie bolted from Rafe's suddenly slack hold and raced down the hall, bouncing off the walls as she tried to regain her equilibrium. His touch still burned on her skin, on her lips, his words still echoed in her ears...but all was erased at the sight of Lynn.

She sprawled on the floor near the small sofa, legs in a butterfly fold—soles together, knees out. Despite the chill of the early April day, she'd worn a loose, flowing dress, joking earlier that she carried her own furnace with her. She curled protectively over her protruding belly, face contorted.

Natalie fell to her knees beside Penta, who held one of Lynn's hands. On her other side, Helen rubbed her back, a helpless expression on her usually cheerful face. "Has someone called Benjamin? Or an ambulance?"

"On it." Aubrey waved a hand and moved toward the patio doors, her phone pressed to her ear.

"It's going to be okay." She patted Lynn's knee and shot a desperate glance at Penta. "What happened? She was fine a minute ago."

"Her water broke. The contractions started almost immediately." A mother of four, she looked pale but determined.

"Sorry about your couch." Lynn panted and leaned back as the contraction eased. "I'll replace it."

Natalie became aware of a fecund, fertile smell and saw the large damp patch on what had been a pristine cushion. "Don't worry about it. You just hang on until the ambulance gets here."

"I don't know what's happening. It wasn't like this with Oscar." Her voice was high and panicky. Penta winced and discreetly changed hands, shaking out the one Lynn had been squeezing. "Here comes another one." Her face flooded with fiery colour.

Natalie craned her neck, looked past the hovering Silverberries, and focused on Rafe. "What do we do? You're a doctor. Is there anything we can do?"

So much had happened in the last few minutes that Rafe didn't feel connected to his feet. He watched the tableau before him as if it were happening on a muted screen.

Until Natalie pinned him with a dark, frantic look and pleaded for advice.

He snapped back into his body with a ferociousness that made his head spin. Scent, colour, and sound came rushing back. Aubrey's voice reached him with diamond-sharp clarity. "911 wants to know if we can get her to hospital ourselves."

Lynn growled in a savage, wordless protest.

"Right. I'll tell them that's a no." Aubrey returned to her phone.

"Rafe. Please." Natalie's hand rubbed Lynn's thigh in an automatic motion. "What should we do?"

He'd spent too long hiding in his laboratory. His medical instincts were rusty. He should have leaped into action, immediately responded to Lynn's need. Instead, he was gawking like a spectator.

His fingers trembled and his heart fibrillated at the thought of taking responsibility for another life. *Two* lives. But he had no choice. Doing nothing wasn't an option.

"I haven't attended a birth in twenty years. More." He wound his way through the small group and crouched beside Helen. Lynn's hand lay at her side, limp in the lull between contractions. He lifted it, his fingers automatically searching for the pulse point in her wrist. Rapid but strong.

Lynn's legs shot out and her fingers gripped his with superhuman strength, crushing the bones of his knuckles. "Uuuuunnnngggggghhhhhh!"

Oh, god. Faint but terrifying memories of all the things that could go wrong in a rapid birth flashed through his brain. *Precipitous labour.* That was the proper term. Much good that knowledge did him now.

The contractions were coming almost on top of each other. Sweat dripped from Lynn's temples and darkened the neck and armpits of her dress.

"The ambulance is on its way." Aubrey spoke somewhere over his head.

He'd done several rotations in obstetrics and searched frantically to recall the long-lost lessons. The memory of dim lighting, soothing music, and calm encouragement surfaced. While there wasn't much he could do about the first two, the last he should be able to handle.

Mind you, he'd never had a great bedside manner. It wasn't in his nature to candy-coat things. But he had to defuse the panicked atmosphere somehow.

"Did you hear that, Lynn? The ambulance is on its way. Now we're going to do what we can to make you comfortable, okay?" He spoke as soothingly as he knew how. "How about you lie on your back?"

"No!" Her shout rang off the walls. "Don't move me! I have to stay this way. I can feel...I can feel..." She broke off in a sob.

"All right, that's fine." He withdrew the suggestion hastily. "Maybe we should find out just have much work you've done already. Do you mind if I examine you?"

"Do whatever you want. I don't care." Her head thrashed from side to side. "The baby's coming. I know it is. I want to be in hospital! I want Benjamin!"

While Penta, Helen, and Natalie did their best to calm her and the other Silverberries huddled at the far side of the room trying to be invisible, Rafe washed his hands at the kitchen sink. Despite the need to hurry, he scrubbed thoroughly between his fingers, under his nails, up to his elbows. He used the time to review what he could remember of potential complications. To Lynn—hemorrhaging from the uterus, tearing of the vaginal tissues, lacerations of the perineum. To the baby—increased risk of infection due to a non-sterile environment, potential inhalation of amniotic fluid. What else?

He couldn't do this. Too much could go wrong. He didn't have the experience. He would make a fatal mistake. He couldn't bear it if he was responsible for another tragedy.

A shriek from the other room cut through his spiralling thoughts. "I need to push!"

He *had* to do it. He was a doctor for Christ's sake. He had a sacred duty.

Back at Lynn's side, he placed one hand on her quivering knee. "I'm going to examine you now, okay, Lynn? It won't hurt. I just want to see where we are."

"What do you mean by goddamn we?" Lynn spoke through gritted teeth. "I don't see you pushing a baby out of a teeny tiny hole."

Natalie choked and he met her eyes. Amusement briefly obscured her alarm, and it steadied him.

Someone had placed a towel under Lynn's hips...a blindingly white, pristine towel. It was speckled with a few tiny flecks of blood and discoloured with fluid, but nothing unexpected.

Lynn jackknifed her legs, hunching over her tight, swollen belly. "Don't push," he ordered. "Not yet. Breathe through the contraction. Someone coach her!"

"Lynn, look at me, sweetie. You've got this." Penta

crooned the words, encouraging her to huff and pant as she struggled through the instinct to eject the baby from her body. Between her legs, a damp thatch of dark hair appeared. He touched it briefly, relieved to feel a strong pulse pounding under his fingers.

"Your baby is crowning." He hoped Lynn couldn't hear the nerves in his voice. "On the next contraction, go for it with all you've got."

Natalie had heard birth described as a miracle but hadn't really understood until this moment.

To see a brand new, fully functioning—and perfectly healthy, thank god—human being come into the world with such violent suddenness had been shocking and disturbing and absolutely, completely, totally *amazing*.

The paramedics and Benjamin arrived on each other's heels. Lynn had been too far along to move, and Natalie's apartment had become a makeshift delivery suite. Rafe and the first responders had melded into a team, Benjamin had taken over from Penta as coach, and in shockingly few minutes, a dark-haired boy made his appearance.

Natalie would have to sort through her jumbled impressions later, but she knew several would be forever preserved in her memory—

- Rafe's calm but firm guidance, despite the fear lurking at the back of his eyes that she was certain only she could see.

Lynn's wonder and awe at the first sight of her baby as the slick, shrieking bundle was laid on her chest.

Benjamin, shaking and tearful, kissing the top of his wife's head, his arms wrapped around her and their new son as if he'd never let go.

The whole experience had taken less than forty-five minutes. Natalie couldn't get over it. How was it possible there had been no baby...and then moments later, there he was?

The paramedics checked Lynn and the infant and declared them in wonderful condition despite the dramatic entry. They insisted on bringing them to the hospital for observation, which Benjamin wholeheartedly endorsed. He remained glued to Lynn's side, his expression fluctuating from bemusement to joy, and by the time the gurney was trundled out the narrow hall, he hadn't yet recovered his usual healthy colour.

Exuberant and relieved, the Silverberries shared celebratory hugs but decided continuing the party just seemed...anticlimactic. They said their goodbyes with promises to make it up to Natalie later and drifted down the hall, rehashing with astonishment the event they'd shared.

She was rather glad they'd left. She was as wilted as a week-old lily, her muscles slack, her brain foggy. Some quiet time was just what she needed.

Shutting the door, she sagged against it and closed her eyes. Through the wall at her left, where the bathroom was, the sound of water running stopped. A door clicked open and soft footsteps approached.

"How are you doing?"

Her smile bloomed even before her eyes opened. "I'm wiped. I can't imagine what you feel like."

Rafe's face lit with a grin the likes of which she had never seen before. A shadow, one she hadn't realized had always been present until the cloud lifted, was vanquished. "I'm fine. Lynn did all the work."

"She was amazing. I think she could move mountains if she wanted to." She pushed off the door and stumbled into his arms. They encircled her automatically and she sighed. "I am so freaking proud of you."

"Why? I didn't do anything." He sounded honestly astounded.

"You were there for her. For us. You stepped up, big time." She'd seen the horror on his face when she'd first asked him what to do, known his reaction was coming from a place of low self-confidence, not cowardliness. For a man like Rafe, one who was so terrified of doing anything *wrong*, to get past that and accept responsibility in an emergency... Well, she had no words for what she was feeling right now.

Other than love. Pure, unadulterated, life-affirming love.

Chapter Thirty-Three

Natalie was proud of him.

Rafe couldn't remember the last time someone had told him that. He wasn't sure anyone had *ever* said it.

He repeated his denial. Not that he was fishing for more validation. He just couldn't quite believe he'd heard her correctly. "Really, I didn't do anything. It all happened so fast."

"You did more than you think. Just having you there helped Lynn, I know it." She gave his ribs a squeeze, her breasts squashing against his chest. His cock stirred.

Exhilaration and pride transformed in a heartbeat to sexual arousal. Birth was a life-giving battle, and primal instincts bubbled in his veins. The need to mate, to pass on his genes, to ensure the survival of his bloodlines, roared into life.

He clasped his fingers on her jaw and lifted her head. He didn't know what exactly she saw in his face, but her brown eyes sparked, brows lifting. When he crashed his mouth against hers, she met his attacking caress with a fervour that matched, flame for flame, stroke for stroke.

He kissed her until he was forced to draw breath and then trailed his lips down her neck, bending her over his forearm so he could reach the delicious freckles on her collarbone. Her nails pricked his scalp as she gripped fiercely.

"Does this mean you forgive me?" Her voice trembled in his ear.

He nipped her lobe. She made a delightful squeak, so he did it again. "For what?"

"For writing the biography the way I did."

For a moment, he couldn't remember why he'd been so upset with her. What his mother had done was decades ago. Natalie was here, right now, in his arms.

"I thought I said that." She was wearing a short-sleeved blouse with tiny buttons down the front and slim black pants. Far too many clothes for what he intended. He unfastened the top three buttons and then gripped the hem of her shirt. "Put your arms up."

She did as instructed, but being Natalie didn't let it deter her from her conversation. "No, you didn't say so, not in so many words."

"Neither did you." He slid his palms along her hips, under the stretchy fabric of her pants, and bent down, taking the fabric with him. She braced herself with one hand on his shoulder and one hand on his head, lifting her feet obediently so he could toss the clothing aside to join her blouse on the floor.

"You're right. I didn't." She clung to his hands, preventing any further disrobing. She wore only a thin, pale blue bra and white panties with tiny flowers in a darker shade of blue. "I forgive you, Rafe. For sending me away."

He'd never been good with words, but this was obviously important for her to hear. He lowered his head, rubbed his nose against hers, and stared seriously into her eyes. "I forgive you for not doing what I told you to do."

She stiffened. "Excuse me?

He tried to backtrack. "For not doing what I asked?"

Too late. She pushed him away, brown eyes going black with anger. "I didn't ask to be forgiven for *not doing what I was told*." The sarcastic air quotes around her last words blazed like neon.

"That's not what I meant."

"It's what you said." She glared at him, arms crossed under her breasts, half-naked and totally irate. "I know I upset you by including the scandal in the manuscript, but I didn't do it to rebel against your orders. I did it because it was the right thing to do."

"I know." He scrambled to explain. "It's just, I've always come second. Otto was the first born, the first son. He was a better student, better athlete, better everything. When I read what you'd written, I felt like I was coming in second again. This time to what *you* wanted, what *you* thought was best, regardless of how I felt."

Her tense expression softened. She worried her lip, head cocked as she contemplated what he'd said. "Okay then. That I understand. So, forgive me for that."

He frowned. "I don't know what you mean."

She closed the distance between them, laid one soft hand on his forearm. He hadn't even realized he'd crossed his arms in a mirror image of her stance until then. "Forgive me for making you feel lesser. For making you feel unimportant. Because that is the last thing I want to do."

"Okay. I forgive you for that, then." He didn't quite see the difference, but if agreeing with her meant she would let him kiss her again, he'd say whatever she wanted.

"Maybe we can avoid misunderstanding like this in future if I confess one more thing." Her fingers trailed up his biceps and she interlaced them at the back of his neck.

"What's that?" He was exhausted, drained, and perplexed. He didn't think he could take any more surprises.

"I love you, Rafe."

Natalie waited, her heart alternating between

thrashing in her throat and rolling like a rock in her belly.

She hadn't intended to tell Rafe she loved him. Not today, and certainly not without working up to it gently. But she'd realized that hiding her true feelings might only make things more difficult. His deeply rooted belief that he would never come first in someone's life had to be eradicated, and this was the best way she could think to do so.

He remained speechless, his hands clamped on her hips as if she was his anchor, his foundation. His breath whooshed out in a sudden sigh, fluttering the hair at her temples. It was followed by a dragging inhale. "You love me?"

It killed her to see him so shell-shocked, so staggered. Had no one ever told him so before?

"I love you, Rafe," she repeated with firm conviction. "I want to laugh with you and fight with you and make a life with you. I promise never to put you second again."

"I need to sit down." He didn't move, but swayed alarmingly, listing forward like a fir torn from the ground by high winds.

Tucking herself under his shoulder, she led him toward the couch. Someone had removed the stained cushion and put it outside on her tiny deck. She pressed him to sit on the remaining padding and perched on the arm.

"Are you okay?" Maybe her first instincts had been right, and she shouldn't have told him yet. Maybe she shouldn't have told him *ever*. His reaction was scaring her. "You look like you've seen a ghost."

A hint of colour returned to his harsh cheekbones. "You love me." It was a statement of fact, not a question, and he addressed it to the floor, not her.

"Yes." It was too late to recant now. She eyed him warily, not sure whether he was going to explode or collapse.

He hooked his arm around her waist, scooped her into his lap, and buried his face in her neck. His moves were so sudden she couldn't help a small shriek and grabbed his shoulders. He trembled so violently the whole couch was shaking. "Rafe? What's wrong?"

"Nothing." His voice was muffled against her skin, his lips tickling her throat. "Absolutely nothing. Because I love you, too."

Saying the words created a chemical reaction inside Rafe that made him feel as if his skin was glowing. He'd never experienced such joy, such relief, such... He couldn't think of another word to describe it.

Natalie's arms curled around his shoulders, her hands cradling his head, pressing it to her breast. The last of the shudders faded, his body relaxing, his mind at peace.

Her voice was soft and tender, vibrating under his ear. "Are you happy about that? You sound a little..."

"Happy's not the right word." He pressed his lips to her collarbone, certain he was going to screw this up, but also certain she wouldn't reject him for any clumsiness. "Terrified. Exhilarated. Uncertain and uplifted."

"I know exactly what you mean."

He wanted to take her to bed. He wanted to stay exactly where they were.

He wanted so much, but the one thing he hadn't known he wanted had been given to him freely, without strings.

Natalie loved him.

Chapter Thirty-Four

Not quite two weeks later, Rafe found Natalie where he knew she'd be—in her office in his house.

She didn't notice him in the doorway and frowned at her laptop, the screen filled with neat black text. Muttering and grimacing, she used the touchpad to highlight a few words, deleted them, and then tapped briskly on the keyboard.

He knew she had hoped to put the finishing touches on the final manuscript today, but it didn't look like she was done with it. He wasn't worried. Whatever she was doing was going to be exactly right.

She'd given him nothing but a wry look when he'd handed over the documents he'd squirrelled away in his safe. Not one word of blame or condemnation passed her lips. He still couldn't believe he'd found a woman who understood him so well.

He wasn't the only one she'd managed to convince, either. Even Otto had succumbed to her stubbornness. During an awkward, tense meeting, she had expressed her unequivocal opinion that hiding the scandal would cause him more trouble in the long run. Including it now meant he could handle the fallout well before his own political run. He'd finally agreed to the wisdom in this and had actually offered her the job as his campaign manager, should he ever need one.

She hadn't said yes, but she hadn't said no, either. Rafe figured his days of ignoring politics were done. It wouldn't be the same as when he was a child, though. He trusted Natalie would never let the game jeopardize what they had between them.

He knocked on the door jamb. Her concentration lifted from her laptop and the smile she gave him just about blew off the top of his head. Would he ever get used to the warmth and affection she so freely offered?

"How's it going?" He stepped behind her chair and stooped to cross his arms over her chest and rest his chin on her head. He couldn't hunch like this for long, but he needed to touch her.

"I'm having trouble with the last bit." Her reflection in the screen scowled. "I hate writing conclusions."

"You'll figure it out."

Her hands come up to grip his wrists, her fingers warm and soft. "At some point I'm just going to have to let it go."

"Speaking of letting go..." He straightened, spun her chair, and crouched on one knee in front of her. "I brought Shyla to the White Spruce Treatment Centre today."

She stared. "You what?"

"They had a space come available sooner than expected. She asked me to take her."

Her mouth pinched and a flicker of hurt flared in her eyes. "She asked you? What about me?"

He laid a palm on her knee and rubbed it consolingly. "She wanted to show you she can handle things on her own, that you don't have to be responsible for her anymore." She'd also said she felt guilty enough, using Natalie's money, since the other avenues she'd hoped for hadn't materialized. But he'd promised not to mention that reason.

"Right. Good for her." He could see the struggle she had to accept her sister's decision battling on her face. Looking after Shyla had been a part of her life for so long, he could understand why it was difficult for her to accept she was no longer needed.

"I'm proud of you." Natalie had given him this gift

after the birth of Lynn's baby. Now he wanted to give it back. "I know this is hard. You care for her so much."

"I do." She brushed back the lock of hair from his forehead. He really should get it cut, but she seemed to like touching it. And he wanted to give her everything she ever wanted.

"Come on." He rose to his feet, taking her hand and tugging her to follow. "Let's go for a swim."

Wearing a light robe tied loosely at her waist, Natalie stood at the edge of the pool. She'd used it more in the days since she'd returned to her apartment than in the weeks she'd lived with Rafe after the fire.

She waited while he tested the waters, making sure the PH levels were correct. His movements were precise and practiced, his expression absorbed, and she thought she might burst from the love that bloomed ever brighter each minute.

They hadn't talked about her moving into his house, even though she was spending most of her days and nights there. He'd taken a big enough leap admitting he loved her. She was willing to give him enough time to grow comfortable with that before making any plans for the future.

She had no doubts that she'd be giving notice at her apartment soon, though. He grumbled and complained whenever she announced it was time to leave. It was humbling and thrilling to know she'd captivated this dour, sober man so much he didn't want her out of his sight. But the invitation would have to come from him.

"Okay, we're good." He stood beside her, wearing a towel around his hips, which she knew from experience could be remove with a single swift tug. She'd refused his frequently repeated suggestion she swim in the nude as he preferred to do. It was a silly thing—he'd seen her sprawled in sexual abandon too many times to count, but she had been too shy to swim naked even so.

She fiddled with the knot of her belt, second-guessing her impulse. Before she could talk herself out of it, she shrugged off the robe.

He hissed in a breath.

She squared her shoulders, which lifted her naked breasts, and cocked a knee, determined not to hide an inch of her body. "I thought it was time to join you in your hedonistic habits."

His towel did little to hide his reaction to her. "I may have made a mistake." His teasing tone relieved her immediate embarrassment. "I might not be capable of swimming with you like this."

It wasn't that long ago that he wouldn't have been capable of making such a playful comment. She threaded her fingers through the dusting of black and silver hairs on his chest and batted her eyelashes. "We'll have to see, won't we?"

And pushed him.

It wouldn't have knocked him into the water if he hadn't wanted to go. What she hadn't anticipated was that he'd snatch her wrist and drag her with him.

Together they fell into the clear blue. Though the water was heated, it felt cooler than the air, and chills raced over her flesh. Her nipples pebbled and the sensation between her legs was unexpectedly arousing.

They'd been standing near the deeper end. He had no trouble finding his feet, the water lapping at his shoulders. She was forced to dogpaddle inelegantly to keep her head above water.

He gripped her hips and tugged her against his chest. Her legs automatically wrapped around his waist, and she realized he'd shed his towel somewhere along the line. His cock was a hot, heavy bar at her centre. She wriggled, settling herself so it jutted between their stomachs. Trusting him to support her, she leaned back in the water, arms spread out, breasts bobbing.

Slowly, he spun in a circle. With her ears below the surface, she could only discern the hum of the pump, the swoosh of the tiny waves he created. She closed her eyes and savoured the sensual caress of the water, the heat between her thighs, the muscles of his ass flexing under her heels.

His hands left her hips, slid up her ribs, and cupped her breasts. With gentle motions, he rubbed his palms on her already sensitive nipples. She clamped her legs tighter.

His touch was demanding yet tender, enflaming yet soothing. He made love with sweet determination, sending her soaring, never letting her sink.

His cock slid inside, and she moaned, drowning in sensations. He brought her to her peak with controlled intensity and then followed her, shuddering and shaking in her arms.

They ended with her back pressed against the tile wall, her shoulders scraping against the rough non-slip edge around the pool. She didn't mention her discomfort—it was a vague irritant easily overlooked in the delight of being squashed against his chest.

"I love you." He'd only said it twice since the first time. She didn't mind. It made each a moment to be treasured.

"I love you." She'd said it more often, but he needed to hear it more than she did. Not that he'd admit such a weakness—if it was one—but she knew it was the truth.

She knew him better than he knew himself. Just as he knew her, to the marrow of her bones.

Forgiveness, healing, acceptance...check.

Love, affection, trust...check.

Happily ever after...check.

Thanks for reading
Strictly by the Book.

Reviews and ratings are a great way to help other readers discover new authors. Just a line or two is all that's needed—or simply click the number of stars you think it deserves. I encourage you to post your honest opinion at the retailer where you purchased your copy, on GoodReads and BookBub. Thank you so much!

Visit my website to discover more titles in the Silverberry Seduction Seasoned Romance Series.

I'd love to stay in touch. Subscribe to my newsletter and you'll immediately receive *Margin of Risk,* a companion short story in the Silverberry Seduction world. You'll also be able to tag along with my dog-walking adventures, find out what I'm reading when I should be working, and other randomness...along with all my writing news, of course! Find the sign-up form at www.brendamargriet.com.

Natalie's Cauliflower and Chicken Bake

1 tablespoon ground cumin
1 tablespoon ground coriander (or seeds, crushed)
2 teaspoons paprika
½ teaspoon cayenne

1 large head of cauliflower, cut into florets
1 large onion, sliced
3 tbsp. olive oil
Salt and pepper to taste

6 chicken thighs (bone in or boneless)
Salt
2 tablespoons olive oil
1 garlic cloves, minced

Flatbread
Yogurt or tzatziki

Preheat oven to 425F.

Mix first four seasoning ingredients together.

Place cauliflower and onion in a large bowl. Drizzle with first measurement of olive oil. Sprinkle with salt and pepper and half (a generous tablespoon) of the spice. Mix well.

Place chicken in a large bowl. Sprinkle with more salt. Add remaining spice mixture, second measurement of olive oil, and minced garlic.

Spread cauliflower and onion on large baking sheet. Nestle chicken among cauliflower. Bake until chicken is done and cauliflower tender, about 35 to 45 minutes (longer time required for bone in chicken).

Serve with flatbread and yogurt or tzatziki.

ABOUT THE AUTHOR

Brenda Margriet writes savvy, slow burn, contemporary romances with ordinarily amazing characters. In her own ordinarily amazing life, she had a successful career in radio and television production before deciding to pilfer from her retirement plan to support her writing compulsion.

Readers have called her stories "poignant," "explicit and steamy," "interesting, intriguing and entertaining," and "unlike any romance you've read before" (she assumes the latter was meant in a good way).

Join Brenda on social media—she is most active on Facebook and Instagram. And you can always discover more about her and her books on her website, brendamargriet.com.

ALSO BY BRENDA MARGRIET

SILVERBERRY SEDUCTION SEASONED
ROMANCE
Secrets Under the Covers
Loving Between the Lines
Turn the Next Page
Strictly by the Book
Too Good for Words
The Complete Silverberry Seduction Series
(e-book only)

TIMELESS SEASONED ROMANCE
After Words
Richly Deserved

THE BENDIXON SISTERS SERIES
Allegro Court
Gateway Crescent
Crossroads Corner
Taking His Measure: The Complete Bendixon Sisters
Series (e-book only)

STANDALONE READS
Mountain Fire
Reserved for You
No Life But This
When Time Falls Still
The Promise of Frost

Read excerpts and find buy links at
www.brendamargriet.com

www.ingramcontent.com/pod-product-compliance
Lightning Source LLC
Chambersburg PA
CBHW030806020726
47499CB00006B/1790